Betrayed by Blood

Leslie Asbill Prichard

A One Nosey Broad Novel

ISBN: 979-8-9889480-6-3 (paperback)
ISBN: 979-8-9889480-7-0 (eBooks)

Cover design by: Leslie Prichard/One Nosey Broad
Library of Congress Control Number: 2024921554
Printed in the United States of America

This book contains mature subject matter.

This book is dedicated to my dear family and friends, who have given me more support than I thought possible. And to my readers for your encouragement and for buying my books.

And to my mom and dad….always for you!

Prologue

Sensational stories are the lifeblood of media outlets. Scoops, exclusives, gotchas…it's what sells, garners clicks and provokes engagement. The more scandalous, the better…Rachel Rose was scandalous.

"We're interrupting our regularly scheduled program to bring you a sad report. Law enforcement has confirmed that a private plane traveling to Las Vegas, Nevada, crashed in the infamous Nevada Triangle early this morning. Rachel Rose, daughter of Senator Rose, was a passenger on that plane. There were no survivors." The local KRTV morning anchor delivered the news with misty eyes.

～

"We have learned that Rachel Rose, the daughter of Senator Rose, who was involved in a lengthy criminal trial against her father, has perished in a plane crash in the Nevada Triangle. We will bring you more news as this story develops." The Today show host reported with little emotion.

～

"A private plane crashed in the Nevada Triangle a few hours ago. Rachel Rose, the daughter of Senator Rose of California, has died in that crash. You may recall that last year, Rachel Rose accused her father of involvement in a drug trafficking ring. The senator was acquitted of all charges. It was recently reported that Rachel Rose had been suffering from mental health issues and that the allegations were part of a delusional episode. Our condolences go out to the Rose family." The CBS news anchor reported in a sympathetic voice.

Special Agent Tolliver monitored multiple television screens in his office as the media spun out of control with the reports of the plane crash and the death of Rachel Rose. Social media was exploding. And as with all headline-grabbing tragedies, the world temporarily tuned in, listening intently to the heartbreaking details. In a week, the next titillating story will replace this one, and the world will move on. At least that's what the FBI PR rep stutteringly conveyed in an emergency meeting this morning.

Tolliver desperately wanted to believe that would be the case, but after thirty years in the FBI, he knew better. Plus, he'd never heard of such a foolish idea of staging the death of a witness in a fiery plane crash. He'd been more than vocal about his doubts, but they'd been swept under the rug, as usual. He'd been given "do not refuse" instructions telling him the California Witness Relocation and Assistance Program, CalWRAP, was in charge of the operation and to assist where he could.

Over the years, he'd provided assistance to the U.S. Marshal's WITSEC program in placing high-risk witnesses in protection, but this was his first coordination with the state office, typically because it was federal witnesses needing protection, not state witnesses, this was unusual. But then, his entire involvement in this case was unusual, with local law enforcement calling in the FBI in a massive attempt to avoid any appearance of a conflict due to the senator's involvement and the DEA lurking in the shadows. The federal prosecutors had punted the case, bouncing it back to the state district attorney, and then right smack into his lap. The hot potato nobody wanted had exploded on him. That was eighteen months ago, before the investigation, before the charges, before the failed trial, before the persistent heartburn.

The more he dwelled on that fact, the more this case burrowed under his skin. It had been his responsibility to put the case together, protect Rachel Rose, and keep the good name of the FBI from being besmirched. It was a balancing act that was more difficult than it looked because nothing about Rachel Rose or this case was standard operating procedure, and he wasn't naïve enough to think the dangerous people hunting her would ever move on. People like the cartel and Senator Rose had long memories, and the truth was, she needed protection. Not the cockamamie staged death concocted by CalWRAP. In his mind, it served to generate more questions, drew more focused eyes, and produced fewer answers.

Agent Tolliver finished typing his final report and hit print, two copies, one for the interoffice circulation, and one for the file, which he hoped would get lost in the depths of the monstrous agency filing cabinet. He concluded his last exhausted thoughts on the case by writing, "Per the Director, the CalWRAP office, in conjunction with the Department of Justice, have extended protection to Rachel Rose due to her father's position as senator and a rumor he may be the next presidential candidate. Jurisdiction remains with the state instead of the federal program as the court case was intentionally prosecuted within state jurisdiction to shield federal responsibility. If the cartel should succeed in eliminating Ms. Rose, it could create a political firestorm between the U.S. and Colombia, and Mexico has made noise of interceding should that occur."

Snatching the report off the tray as it reeled through the printer, he read it over one last time, rubbing his eyes, trying to erase the weariness already setting in, even though it was the mere beginning of the workday. Without looking, he knew his eyes were bloodshot. Every morning for the past year, red, bleary eyes stared back at him. Sleep had evaded him since this case began. He could count on one hand the number of cases that stole his sleep over the years, mostly gruesome cases that ate away at his soul when pouring through crime scenes and stepping around pools of blood. Why this case was under his skin hadn't been sorted out in his mind. All he wished now was to be done with Rachel Rose and for her to walk up the steps of the transport van while he watched the door slam shut behind her before being whisked away across the country to her new life. Then he would sleep again.

Viewing the exterior security camera, he watched Marshal Mayer pace from one end of the transport van to the other while waiting to take over the Rose case, practically wearing a hole in the concrete with each step. Marshal Mayer was the sole person Rachel listened to, a calming force. The same could not be said of him and Rachel. Tolliver had butted heads with her daily for the past eighteen months, even though he considered himself affable and easy to get along with, but not in this case. He was exhausted. His recollection of her relentless rejection of the majority of his practical suggestions caused bile to rise in his throat. Headstrong and defiant, she'd stood by her story and was beyond infuriated that the FBI couldn't find the evidence needed to send her father to prison. He learned to dodge her calls, which became pointless because she'd show up at his office, typically cornering him while she ran through her list of his deficiencies. Tossing the word *failure* at him repeatedly. That failure haunted him, mostly because silently he agreed with her.

The unsubtle reminders by Rachel of his incompetence had prompted him to mark off days on his motivational calendar containing inspirational sayings splayed across each month, given to him by his wife, hoping it would mellow his days. It hadn't. The countdown to retirement was underway as he slashed each day as it rolled past. That small ritual buoyed his spirits more than the quotes of optimism. Eight hundred twenty-one days stood between him and permanent relaxation and a decrease in his daily heartburn if he took early retirement like his wife suggested daily. This case and Rachel Rose had accelerated his hair turning gray and made his jaw unconsciously clench at the sight or sound of her name. That's probably why his head pounded daily for the past year.

Despite the FBI's best efforts, not one agent had uncovered a tight connection between the senator and the cartel. Regardless, the case had moved forward based on circumstantial evidence and Rachel's testimony, upon the insistence of someone with a paygrade higher than his and in spite of the reluctance of the district attorney to prosecute the case. Collectively, they'd all hoped the sketchy evidence would be enough to convict the senator, but all the legal brains involved had underestimated the power of Senator Jay Rose.

Tolliver stretched his mouth to release the tension creeping across his jaw and resumed typing to add one last piece of information. "It's uncertain whether the allegations were part of a delusional episode suffered by Ms. Rose. Psychiatric testing and monitoring are incorporated into the protection agreement. However, there was physical evidence making a loose connection between the two alleged suspects, which partially negated the mental instability theory."

He continued, "Ms. Rose understands and has agreed to all terms. Today, Ms. Rose appears to be more stable, without hysterical or aggressive behavior as periodically exhibited throughout the last six months of the trial. Transport set. Marshal Mayer is her assigned handler. Alias for Ms. Rose is Jennifer Howard. Name change protocols are in place should Rachel Rose's location be discovered. The Marshal's office will notify this office of any breach of identity. Marshal Mayer verified and delivered all documents and accounts to Ms. Rose yesterday when she signed the program agreement. Ms. Rose's trust funds reverted to her family trust upon death. She understands the ramifications of her decision." Agent Tolliver couldn't wait to pass the torch to the marshal.

A month later, Agent Tolliver submitted a second report. "The Marshal's office has reported that the identity of Rachel Rose (Jennifer Howard) is compromised. Witness relocated to Stillwater, Oklahoma. The new alias is Megan Ford."

Thirty days later, Agent Tolliver submitted a third report. "The Marshal's office has reported that the identity of Rachel Rose (Megan Ford) is compromised. Witness relocated to Phoenix, Arizona. The new alias is Susan Phillips."

Agent Tolliver never submitted the fourth report of a credible threat and compromised identity. It all unraveled too quickly for neatly typed reports.

Chapter 1

Starting Over
(eight months later)

The violent pounding on the door at 3:00 a.m. sent shockwaves through Rachel's body. She dove to the floor instinctively, wedging herself between the wall and the bed, trying to click her mind into action. She'd been sleeping soundly for the first time in weeks, having finally settled into her new home in Arizona and the third identity over the past eight months since she'd entered the witness protection program.

Had they found her?

"Open the door, Ms. Rose. This is Marshal Gagne, with the California Marshal's office."

The booming voice echoing through the house cemented her to the floor. No way was she moving from her spot. It could be anyone at the door, she smartly told herself, and she'd never heard of Marshal Gagne. Her handler was Marshal Mayer.

Peering over the edge of the bed, she saw her phone sitting on the nightstand, plugged into the charger. Damn.

A flash of light swept past the window. She watched it pass slowly across the room and back again, making her crouch lower. She held her breath to hear more clearly and stay out of sight of whoever was stepping on the gravel in the flowerbed under the window. Even though she couldn't see them, the crunching was distinctive. Someone was mere feet away from her on the other side of the bedroom wall.

"Ms. Rose, you need to get packed. We're moving you," the man shouted at the window.

"Go away," she screamed back. Pulling herself up, she scrambled across the bed to grab her phone, then darted to the bathroom, slamming the door and locking it behind her. She frantically pushed Marshal Mayer's contact button on her favorites.

"Pick up, pick up, pick up," she whispered.

Breathing shallow breaths, listening to the succession of rings with no answer and no voicemail, she hung up and dialed again. *Maybe it didn't connect right?* She assured herself. The ringing began again, still no answer. Immediately hitting redial as the threat of tears burned behind her eyes, prompted by the continual buzzing on the line vibrating in her ear before abruptly disconnecting.

Why won't he answer? He never ignores my calls.

The banging on the front door resumed. "You're being relocated. Get packed!" the marshal shouted.

Shuddering at the brusque command, she shouted back, "It's 3:00 a.m." Trying to steady the panic gripping her throat, certain it was a killer coming for her. "How do I know you're a marshal?"

"Come to the door and I'll show you my badge."

The calmer voice didn't fool Rachel. Sinking to the floor, her back pressed against the bathroom cabinet, she considered her options while trying to slow her adrenaline and pull her senses together. Wide awake now, her heart thumped out of her chest, providing evidence that every cell was at full alert. She sighed and closed her eyes, accepting there was no choice but to comply and open the front door. It was clear the marshal wasn't leaving if she didn't.

What was equally troubling as the screaming marshal was the thought of moving again. This would be the fourth time in eight months. In the last move, a team of brawny agents, discreetly disguised as movers, helped her carefully pack, then professionally and calmly loaded the furniture into a truck and expertly slid her car on the trailer and transported her to her new destination. Nobody sent her heart racing in the middle of the night.

Maybe they confirmed an imminent threat?

Rachel grasped the edge of the vanity cabinet and pulled herself up. The reflection in the mirror, gawking back, showed a harried face one would expect at 3:00 in the morning. Shimmying her sleep shirt up, she grabbed her bra, threw it on, then pulled her sweatshirt on over it. Her pajama shorts were much too short to answer the door in, so she stripped them off, tossed them on the floor, and grabbed the leggings carefully folded on the shelf for her morning run, then tucked her phone in the pocket on her thigh.

Frowning at the mirror, she hurriedly scratched the brush through her now mousy brown hair, a beautiful blonde only a few months ago. The "light as sunlight" color she was blessed to be born with that her friends envied was no longer staring back at her. A reflection that still made her recoil each time she confronted it. Even if she could manage to restore her regular color, it would never be the same. That was an undeniable fact, having known too many friends who experimented with hair color only to lose their natural hue forever.

The pounding on the front door resumed. Rachel clenched her teeth. Cursing under her breath, slamming her bedroom door, she vacated the safety of her room and stomped to face the rude man beating her door down in the wee hours of this already irritating day.

Peeking through the peephole, she watched the agent pace back and forth. "Show me your badge. I've never seen you before or heard your name."

He slammed his badge against the viewer. "Satisfied? Start packing now! Take only your personal belongings. You'll have new furniture, a new car, and a new life in another state by morning. It would thrill most people to have the government provide a life for them, a safe one at that," he grumbled before plodding away.

Rachel pulled herself from the door and scuttled to the window in the living room, drawing the curtain back, peeling the faux wooden blinds apart enough to examine the marshal. He stood near the street, next to an SUV towing a small U-Haul. A second man stood next to him, leaning against the car, flicking ashes from a cigarette.

Marshal Gagne opened the car door, grabbed some boxes and carted them to the front porch, tossing them there.

Closing her eyes in defeat, she exhaled, knowing if she wanted to stay in the protection program, it was time to pack. She'd agreed to their terms after all, not that she had much of a choice. She wanted to live, and if this was the only means, then she would do what the marshal said. Leaving the window, she walked back to the door and yanked it open, finding the unkept, middle-aged man who needed a shave standing on her porch.

"Where's Marshal Mayer?" Rachel snapped.

"He's been reassigned."

Their eyes met for the first time. A surge of reality that this hostile man was now her handler made Rachel swallow hard. "I want him back on my case. He never yelled at me or scared the wits out of me in the middle of the night." Rachel set her hip and crossed her arms.

In fact, it was quite the opposite. Agent Mayer was a man who spoke calmly and with comforting authority, walking her through detail after detail of what to expect at each step of the plan, and what to do if it went awry. And what to do was to call him first, then 911, if she ever felt her life was in danger. He'd never tired of her anxious questions, not even when she repeated them three times over. Instead, he'd soothed her with reminders of taking a deep breath, which in the anxious early hours of the morning, thinking someone was outside wanting to kill you, was hard to do.

Answering her perpetual and frantic calls and offering meaningful tips to keep her mental health positive. Tips like planting flowers in the backyard. A new recipe to try. A movie that was inspiring and avoided violence while she adjusted to her new life. Even tossing out a suggestion that she take up crochet to calm her nerves, which she'd given half a shot, but the meager potholder she managed to string together in haphazard rows ended up with more gaps than a cohesive, tight plan. Much like her life, with the gaps unraveling faster than she could stitch. Sadly, the gaps threatened her safety. Tonight, she'd followed Marshal Mayer's instructions to the letter, and he had ignored her.

"Too bad. He's gone, and you've got me to deal with

now, so get a move on."

"I don't want to keep moving, Marshal Gagne. This isn't what I signed up for," she told him flatly.

"Do you want to stay alive? If you do, you'll move when we tell you, but this should be the last." He took a step back, trying to avert eye contact, refusing to be taken captive by Rachel's famous violet-rimmed eyes analyzing his every move.

Rachel assessed the man bellowing commands on her front porch. His weak assurances and empty eyes exposed the lie in his words. It all fell on her like an icy wind, blowing right past her and leaving her shuddering with no confidence that anything he would spew was the truth. A chill prickled across her forearm, searing in her mind a disturbing first impression of her new handler. Nothing about him inspired confidence that she could turn to him for support or that he would protect her.

Rachel trudged across the porch, grasping the boxes, pulling them inside. "Aren't you going to help me pack?" she called after the agent, who was retreating to the car.

Tossing a smirk back at her, apparently enjoying watching her go it alone, he grumbled, "Nope, that's your job, and hurry up. We need to blow and go before they track you down." He slung a roll of packing tape in the general direction of the porch.

Rachel scrambled for it as it bounced across the concrete steps. "The least you can do is load the boxes from the garage," she huffed. Tucking the tape under her arm, she wrestled the last of the boxes, dragging them through the doorway, kicking the door shut behind her.

Blowing out a shallow breath, she opened the flat boxes to construct them, pulling the tape sharply across the bottom to secure it before gathering items to fill it with. Stuffing blankets, clothes, and towels around the fragile items since there were no packing materials. Cursing every tedious moment as she picked at the edges of the tape to reattach it on the roller before sealing another box.

Stifling a frustrated scream threatening to escape, she scanned her belongings strewn about the house. Stepping over the smattering of boxes, it was easy to calculate, most of her belongings were going to be left behind. Strategically cherry-picking what held the most value was her mission now. Fortunately, the most important box she owned sat unpacked in the garage. Covertly tucked inside were a couple of sweet mementos of her former life, deceptively hidden away from the agents. Keepsakes she was determined to save, knowing the coming years wouldn't bring memories she cared to cling to.

She'd been resistant to unpacking the remaining boxes containing newly acquired knick-knacks and winter clothes after the moves from Kansas City to Stillwater, and then to Phoenix. All the result of an anonymous, yet unexplained, credible threat. What was the point of unpacking a box simply to pack it again in a matter of weeks? This was the fourth new city in eight months. It's highly unusual, they keep saying. So the boxes remained packed and stacked in the garage. Sometimes, procrastination was a friend.

Now she was being sent to who-knew-where, minus Marshal Mayer to help her through it all.

Rachel closed her eyes, forcing away the surge of loneliness welling against her, not understanding how she was going to manage without the first person since beginning protective custody who didn't set her fight-or-flight instinct in hyper-drive.

There had been days over the past eight months when she surprised herself by divulging parts of her broken heart to Marshal Mayer, the pieces shattered by her own father. Even though it wasn't the marshal's job, the understanding man pierced a tiny hole in her protective wall, letting a pinpoint of light shine through. It couldn't be called trust in full appreciation of the word, but it had come close. Predictably, in the end he'd proven to be a disappointment, abandoning her without a word of explanation or even a goodbye. A stark reminder that her life insisted on reinforcing all the reasons she could never trust another human.

How had she allowed herself to let down her walls?

Replaying in her mind her recent litany of complaints to Marshal Mayer, she blamed herself for his departure. Her endless grilling of detail after detail. Relentless accusations that the agency was incompetent. Early morning calls to him, when she could tell he'd been deep in sleep, simply to hear another person's voice and not feel so alone.

It had to be her fault. She had driven him away.

And now what? Who would keep her from driving herself mad? Marshal Gagne? An odd stranger with his burgeoning potbelly that he tried to hide by squaring his shoulders and sucking in deeply. A blunt and cold man, who banged on her front door in the middle of the night with an attitude and expecting her to jump at his command. There was no scenario Rachel could imagine that would have her breaking open her heart to Marshal Gagne, who was outside reclining against what looked like an old, run-down car, while she frantically tried to pack. Something life had not prepared her for.

Shaking the sorrow from her thoughts, she refocused on the empty boxes needing to be filled. Moving quickly, knowing the night was passing too rapidly for regretful trips down memory lane, she made her way to the kitchen, tossing pots and pans haphazardly into a box along with anything not breakable, throwing the two cup towels she owned on top to squeeze in the last items.

She hadn't moved this many times in her entire life, much less in a matter of months. There was the move to and from college and grad school, but that didn't count because there wasn't much effort involved in transporting the meager school-girl dreams and belongings into a dorm room, plus her mom had supervised the movers and the packing, both ways. When she moved back to California after grad school, to the condominium her parents gave her as a graduation gift, decorating wizards had performed their magic before she arrived. She recalled the relentless phone calls from her mother, who wanted to discuss every detail.

"Rachel, I had the most brilliant idea for that little area under the staircase. It's really wasted space. I'm thinking we could turn that into some bookcases that would follow the line of the triangular shape. It would be adorable. Or we could make it into a mini wine room. What do you think, honey?"

Rachel had been curt that day, running from one class to the next, trying to meet graduation deadlines and prep for finals. She'd regretted her tone then and still to this day. "Mom, I really can't deal with this. I have no idea, and frankly, I don't care right now. I have too much on my plate. Can you please handle it?"

And, to her mother's credit, she did handle it and did so with flair. The bookcase under the stairs, with the lovely bench seating and the dainty vintage wall sconces, was Rachel's most treasured space. Her mom had also chosen the décor, ordered the designer duvet cover and sheets, selected the custom furniture, contracted the painters, and decided on the wall colors, which all exuded elegance, then supervised the entire move. It hadn't occurred to Rachel at the time that it took skill and effort to achieve.

Rachel's helter-skelter packing method would appall her meticulously organized mother. The only caution Rachel took was to place her coffee maker, cups, and coffee carefully in a box and etch the word kitchen across the side with a knife. Searching her meagerly stocked drawers, all she came up with was an out of ink pen, so knife scratches on the box would have to do. At least she'd be able to find it when she arrived at the new house. One important trick she'd learned in the last move by watching the considerate agents painstakingly label her boxes.

Rachel huffed out her frustration.

Her anger carried her through each room of the house as she gathered her most important possessions. The fury drove her into a packing frenzy, resulting in the job being completed in record time. Grabbing the first box, securely taped and ready to load, she awkwardly carried it out of the house. Feeling its overpacked weight on her lower back, it slipped from her hands, tumbling across the grass and landing a few feet shy of the U-Haul.

"Well, that's one way to do it," Marshal Gagne said.

Rachel wanted to slap the smirk off his face. "And what exactly is your purpose here? Or his?" Rachel pointed to Marshal Gagne's partner, who hadn't uttered a word all night. Rachel gazed at the pile of cigarette butts at his feet.

Ignoring Rachel's comments, Marshal Gagne extracted his plump body off the car hood and stepped toward the trailer. Relief washed over Rachel, believing the agent was going to provide the muscle to carry the boxes from the house and load them on the truck. Instead, he emerged from the trailer with a dolly, rolled it down the ramp, and headed toward the garage.

"Enter the security code. I'll help with the boxes you said were in the garage," he told Rachel as he passed.

Rachel fumed as she stalked across the lawn and typed in the code, then watched the agent carelessly shove boxes onto the dolly.

"This is Agent Aragon. He's your transport driver," Marshal Gagne told her with a forced grin, pointing to his partner as he strolled past her with the loaded dolly, dropping the boxes on her perfectly manicured lawn, several yards from the trailer.

"Aren't you going to load those?" Rachel crossed her arms, glaring at the lazy agent.

"I'll roll them, you load them," he bit back.

Rachel marched to the back of the trailer, narrowing her eyes, drilling a disapproving glare into the marshal, internally cursing the marshal's office for sending such a crude handler into her life. Awkwardly lifting one box, blaming herself for the weight, she stumbled up the ramp and placed it in the small trailer.

"Where the hell am I being relocated to?" Rachel stopped to catch her breath after loading the fourth box.

"Houston. Let's go!" Marshal Aragon answered.

"Do you see these boxes? And I have more in the house. If you'd like to help, then we can go, but not a minute before." Rachel snapped at the marshal, who looked more like an ex-con recently released from prison. Both men were nothing like the pristine, fit marshals in snappy clothes she'd met thus far in the world of the protection program. These guys had no crisp shirts and pressed slacks. They resembled goons she'd imagined worked for the mafia in some crowded East Coast city. Turning on her heel, dragging the dolly behind her, she stomped her way back up the walkway to the house to retrieve her remaining belongings.

Marshal Aragon didn't flinch, staying plastered to the side of the SUV, flicking another ash from another cigarette he'd lit from the stub of the last one. Watching her cart box after box from the house to the trailer.

A tiny spark of electricity niggled its way down Rachel's spine as she fought the uncomfortable urge to resist Marshal Gagne's demands. Something about this move was unsettling her mind and accelerating her distrust, prompted by the abrupt interactions thus far.

"Where is the van with the recliner seats, like the other moves?" Rachel stopped, hands on her hips as she confronted the men.

"You'll be fine in the Forerunner. It may look a bit weathered, but it's roadworthy," Marshal Gagne snapped back.

Rachel stared at the rust spots lining the bottom edge of the running board, imagining the interior probably contained tiny tears in the upholstery. "Why would the agency send this?" Rachel glared at Marshal Gagne.

Marshal Gagne shrugged, providing no answer.

"You're a world of help." Rachel rolled her eyes at the uncooperative man and retreated to the house.

With the last box delivered to the curb, Rachel bent over,

hands on her knees, to catch her breath. It was nearly dawn. Sunlight would soon flood the canyon, and light meant she was more visible to the lowlifes hunting her. Her lower back was pulsing with pain, and her right knee weakened as a sharp bolt of fire stabbed through it. She was spent and done with packing and loading.

"You two are going to have to load the rest of these boxes or I'm going back inside and going to bed. Then I'll call the FBI and the Marshal's office and file a formal complaint."

Marshal Gagne jerked his head toward the other man, knowing he'd pressed Rachel far enough. Marshal Aragon pushed himself off the car, grabbed a stack of boxes, shoved them on the dolly, rolled the boxes up, disappeared inside, then reappeared and jumped off the truck bumper. After making quick work of the tasks at hand, with a snarl across his face and an unlit cigarette dangling from his lip, he gave a side-glance to Rachel, who was still trying to gain her composure. He slammed the roll-down door and smashed the bolts in place without uttering a word. Then lit a cigarette, sucked in a long draw, flicked a stream of ashes onto the street and walked back to the SUV.

Sweat dripped down her cheek as she covertly watched the strange and silent man, dreading the fact that she would soon be seated behind him while he drove her across the country.

Ignoring her mood, Marshal Gagne shoved a shiny smartphone into her hand. "Take this. It's your new phone. Give me your old one."

Struggling to stand upright, racked by the lack of sleep and physical exhaustion, Rachel reluctantly pulled the old phone from the pocket of her leggings and handed it over as commanded. In doing so, erasing her sole lifeline for the past eight months. Now, her only safety net was an aggressive man, making the hairs on the back of her neck stand up.

She gripped the new slender phone, and pushed the power button, watching carefully as two preloaded numbers popped to life: Marshal Gagne and an unknown contact labeled "Account Info." Marshal Mayer's number had been eliminated, and along with it, her only sounding board, and pathetically, her only friend.

"I thought agency policy is no smartphones, so I can't be tracked?" They had drilled it into her head when she signed the papers, agreeing to the program.

"We've got new location jamming technology embedded. Don't question our methods. You're safe," the marshal mumbled. "Here's your new identity. You're no longer Rachel Rose, daughter of Senator Jay Rose, or Susan Phillips or any other name. You're now Jeannie Smith, and you live in Texas. Your driver's license and bank card are in there. Memorize your birthdate and forget your other identity."

"Thanks. I know the drill," Rachel forced, accepting the manila envelope the agent shoved at her. Peeling the flap back, peering inside. She spied the new ID bearing her photo and her new identity. And just like that, in an instant, Jeannie Smith was born, and Rachel Rose was dead…again.

With a final walk-through of the house, she locked the door behind her and hoisted her last bag with her most personal items over her shoulder. She trudged to the open car door where Marshal Aragon stood in the blackness of the waning morning. His dark eyes bore through her, sending an uneasy feeling screaming through her brain. She paused before climbing in, turning around to ask Marshal Gagne one more question about the credible threat received, but no answer came. The marshal had vanished.

Strapping her seatbelt across her shoulder, a brimming fury pulsed through her as Marshal Aragon fired up the engine, accelerating abruptly, snapping her hard against the seat. A rude start to the journey that would take them through what was left of the night and extend through the next day. Seventeen hours straight on the road, she calculated from Google Maps. The countdown of time to another new life began.

Chapter 2

The Long Drive

The rhythmic clink – clink – clink of the highway under Rachel's feet played a monotone song as the unfamiliar neighborhoods disappeared one-by-one and the world awakened with the sun peeking over the horizon and washing the Arizona cactus in golden light.

Scooting along, the clinking on the black road morphed to a perpetual humming once the highway opened up, taking them east as civilization was swallowed up behind them replaced by vast desert lands of brown with dots of green sagebrush sprinkled all around like a Doug West painting.

Trying to pass the time and avoid the glancing looks of Marshal Aragon in the rearview mirror, she repeated her new name over and over in her mind, hoping to make it reflexive, but it sat dead on her tongue when she whispered it to herself. When they reached New Mexico, the silence was unbearable and the view unchanged.

"I can help drive. We can take shifts," Rachel offered.

"I'm the transport. I'll drive," he said, shooting her a look of disapproval in the mirror.

The obviously annoyed agent had outdone Marshal

Gagne in presenting a lackluster first impression. After watching him warily through suspicious eyes for several more hours, the boredom won out and sleep overtook Rachel. Once her eyes closed, she remained comatose for six solid hours, something she hadn't planned on, but gratefully it made the drive shorter and ended the forced interactions with the stranger at the helm of her transport. Besides, the only conversation the agent was capable of was curt instructions, which had grown tiresome.

"We're getting gas. You have ten minutes to take care of business and get a snack if you need one," he told her at their three brief stops.

"Can I get you some coffee? A candy bar? A personality makeover?" she'd bantered.

The stoic marshal never replied. Instead, at each stop he silently stood holding the gas pump nozzle, eyes fixated on the dollar indicator turning from one number to the next.

Back in the car, her skin crawled when the thick-mustached man spit sunflower seed after sunflower seed onto the floorboard. She wanted to spring from the car and kiss the ground when they finally rolled through the maze of concrete highways in Houston as the sun was sinking into the horizon.

The agent must have felt the same. He bolted from the car at their final destination, slid the trailer door open, chucked the boxes onto the curb, mumbled details about the house, then handed her the keys and garage remote to the new house on Meadow Lane and sped off without another word. Taking the dolly with him and leaving Rachel to battle the boxes as the darkness of the night grew.

With no choice, she lugged each box up the long sidewalk and up the front steps, keeping her head on a swivel, snapping around at every noise, trying to survey her unfamiliar surroundings. Battling nerves jumping about inside her stomach as her mind raced through scenarios of her impending death, she openly cursed the marshals who abandoned her, forcing her to fend for herself from the looming credible threat.

Electric fear intermittently shocked her nerves, turning them into raw conduits of imagined terror lurking in the still of the night. Rachel sighed, exhausted and angry, as she rolled the last box, end over end, up the three gray concrete porch stairs and through the threshold with one last shove, sending it tumbling onto the tile floor only inches inside the door. The echo through the empty house driving home the fact that she was alone.

She collapsed on the entryway floor, grabbing the edge of the door and pushing it shut, and with the last bit of energy, she reached up over her head to turn the deadbolt. Rubbing her sore hands, battling away thoughts of rude agents and how she got here, a familiar ache nudged at her. It was relentless. It was one of missing the coastline of California and the clean breeze that sweeps in off the ocean, absent humidity.

Her thoughts dropped her to bygone days, pushing her to the place of longing to sit ocean-side and watch the waves roll in, exhibiting Mother Nature's power with wave after wave slamming the sand beneath it. Yearning for those simple days when the sun washed over her as she melted into the beach without a care. Her longings and loss cascaded, casting fear through her that her life would never be carefree and simple again.

The cruel truth of this relocation was that it boiled down to the exchange of one sweat-inducing location for another.

Arizona exchanged for Texas, but the rest of her existence remained the same. Unlike the desert of Arizona, where the summer had been hotter than the surface of the sun with no water in sight, only cactus, Texas did have a beach. It was the only saving grace she could muster to appease her negativity. But from what she could tell from her brief introduction to Houston, it was also as hot as the surface of the sun.

The gulf a stone's throw away was the sole comforting thought getting her through the night. It offered the possibility of some refuge from the heat and her new world. But the Texas coast and the California coast were not the same. That she knew for certain. And even though Houston was further from California, there was no distance that could make her feel safe. Plus, California was her home…or was. The flood of memories rising to the surface with each move only multiplied what she felt…she was homesick and lonely.

With only her boxes occupying the space, she paused to refocus and survey the bare room. The emptiness made the vaulted ceilings feel higher than they were. It was a blank slate, white walls, beige builder-grade carpet, nothing to write home about, even if she had anyone to write to. Instructions in the envelope from Marshal Gagne said her furniture would be delivered on day one. The only problem for Rachel was she was unsure if today was day one or tomorrow would be day one, since this day was nearly over, and the hours were blurred. Her reality forced its way into her heart as she struggled to stand and begin an inspection of her forced domicile.

Walking through the empty house, set in stone that she had nothing left that slightly resembled the life she'd known. She wasn't even Rachel Rose any longer; she was now Jeannie Smith with an empty house, and a smattering of boxes holding her meager and meaningless belongings. Sadly, it was all that remained in her life, that, and the people who wanted her dead. Neither appealed to her. Both were her unfortunate actuality. She had to accept it, whether she liked it or not. And she did not.

Chapter 3
Rose of Boston

Rachel never expected to become an expert at unpacking boxes or decorating houses, having done so now four times in the past eight months. She envied her mother who could look at a room and within minutes conjure up the perfect color scheme, designate fabrics with varied textures, and locate elegantly crafted furniture that accented the architectural style to create a soothing palette and fully communicate the mood of the room. None of that was anything Rachel could construct in her mind, much less execute. Making a home beautiful was not in her wheelhouse, with the artistic gene failing to make its journey through the bloodline from mother to daughter.

Until being trapped in this new life, all her moves had been effortless. Never lifting a finger for any of her moves had not served her well. A brutal awareness of that fact slammed down on her. Reluctantly admitting that perhaps she'd taken it all for granted and simply expected her mother to manage her life. Today, that expectation disappeared as she glared at the boxes that needed to be unpacked. And where was she going to sleep? She pulled her cell phone out and pushed the agent's contact button with as much force as possible.

"Marshal Gagne." A grumpy voice answered.

"It's R..Je..Jeannie." She stuttered as she vocalized her new name for the first time out loud. "I need to know when the furniture will be delivered. Your note makes no sense. Day one? When is day one?"

"Day one will be tomorrow. The delivery guys should be there at the crack of dawn."

"Where am I supposed to sleep tonight? Do you have a hotel room for me?"

"No, sorry. Tonight, you'll have to rough it. It's nearly midnight. It won't be long until morning."

"What? I'm supposed to sleep on the floor?"

"You packed your blanket and pillow, didn't you? You'll be fine. The main thing is you're safe. Nobody knows where you are. Remember that. We've done the job we are supposed to do."

"I've never been treated like this, Marshal Gagne," Rachel raised her voice, waiting for a response. All she heard was silence. "Marshal Gagne?" The screen blinked. Rachel glanced at it, only seeing the words, "call ended."

"Aaggh," Rachel shouted, finally releasing frustration that had been boiling since being startled awake at 3:00 a.m., the syllables bouncing around the bare room, amplifying her anger. Tossing her phone across the carpet, she gathered her emotions and focused on finding her comforter and pillow. Her body signaling it was past the point of functioning.

The past eight months in the witness protection program had crystallized how pampered she'd been throughout her life. Leaving little doubt she'd lived a life of luxury, something she never denied but also never acknowledged. Luxury had been meticulously extracted from her existence as she reluctantly trudged through her new world. Having her world shift off its axis was more than disorienting. It was heart-rending. And regrettably, those days of being taken care of were long gone.

Standing over the boxes in the living room holding scissors she'd found in the scratched-labeled box containing her kitchen items, she patted herself on the back for marking the box, even ineptly. She'd broken two nails trying to pry off the tape to reach the scissors, but when she opened the coveted coffeemaker box, they'd been there, sitting on top, another essential item for her survival. She watched the light gleam off the metal, then whipped the scissors open and, with one long slice of a single blade, expertly severed the clear tape precisely down the crease where the two folds of cardboard almost met. A tap on the last piece of tape with the sharp edge freed the last chunk of the box. The flaps popped open.

Crossing her arms, she examined the contents, which she'd memorized. The open box held the hand-knitted quilt her grandmother sent to her when she, Rachel Marie Rose, was born. A grandmother she didn't meet until age five. Her father's mother, the matriarch of the Rose family. Known to her as grand-ma-maaa of the Roooses of Boooston. Her grandmother had drawn out the "Os" when they met, leaving an unforgettable impression on her young, moldable mind. For the rest of that week, she'd walked through the house, working hard to round her lips and produce the same hollow sound of an "O" in order to imitate her grand-ma-maa's curious pronunciation of the family surname. Her father had laughed at her efforts, scooping her up and kissing her on the forehead before sending her on her way to continue practicing being a Rose.

The Rose family, with their embedded wealth and command of politics. A true royal family, if such a thing existed in America. Their property and influence spread across Boston, to the beaches of Martha's Vineyard, down to Washington D.C., and expanded across the nation to the coast of California, where the family had now been for decades. Growing with each generation as the sons, grandsons, nephews, and cousins multiplied and intensified the permeation of their political reach. Propagating the seed of the Rose family was a responsibility the men bore. Protecting the reputation of the Rose name rested squarely on the shoulders of the women, who were capable and clever and more respectable than the Rose men. It was advantageous being a Rose man and leaving a wake of destruction in your path, and a disadvantage of being a Rose woman who cleaned up after them and put reputations back together. And in spite of both, even though her name was now Jeannie Smith, the Rose blood would always course through her veins. She was still part of the Rose clan, whether they liked it or not. And she knew they did not.

Rachel's memories of her domineering grandmother's face had long since faded, though she did recall the family pride emblazoned in every word her grandmother spoke and every step she took when speaking of the family back in Boooston. The flowery smell of *Estee Lauder* powder her matriarchal grandmother smothered herself with lingered somewhere in the recesses of her senses, bringing ambivalent emotions to the surface. Only one extended visit with the woman and the impact remained branded on her heart. And one conversation that Rachel never understood at the time still haunted her dreams.

"How old are you, my dear?"

"I'm five." Rachel hazily recalled spreading her fingers wide as she held up her hand to confirm that she'd reached the ripe old age of all fingers on one hand.

"Well, you are old enough to understand that it is going to be your job to protect the Rose name. That means you must do better than your father, who's been quite the disappointment."

"What's a disappointment?" She'd innocently asked.

"It means that your father doesn't have the gumption to do the hard things in life to keep this family on top. Sometimes you must break the rules."

"I'll get a time-out if I break the rules."

"No, my dear. You will be a success."

"No, I don't want to break the rules," she'd shrieked, which brought her father running into the room, snatching Rachel from her grandmother's lap.

"What's going on here?" Rachel fuzzily remembered her father screaming.

"I'm teaching Rachel something you have never learned, to be tough." Her grandmother had countered.

"She's five years old. You finally come visit us to meet her, a child you've never had time for in the past five years, and you want to give her grandmotherly advice? It's no wonder the rest of the Rose family turned their backs on you after Father died."

"They turned their backs on me because your father left nothing in his will for his good-for-nothing brothers, your worthless uncles."

Rachel wasn't certain if she truly recalled that day, the arguing and raised voices between the two as her grandmother scolded her father, or if the memory had been cemented from her father's retelling throughout her childhood. Whatever the source, it sat firmly in her soul.

"You are my only child, Jay Rose, and the legacy of this family falls on your shoulders, but I don't believe you're up to the job. Neither did your father, for that matter."

Rachel's father had held her tightly while they sniped at each other, recalling how they'd roared and how she wanted to run away. During her early childhood, she'd never seen her parents argue, so watching her grandmother and father lock horns imprinted the first distaste of the Rose family in her young mind.

"You need to leave. And you need to leave my daughter alone. If there's one thing I will succeed in, it is keeping my child away from your clutches. And stop staring at me with your soulless eyes. Rachel, go find Mabel and run play. You don't need to be in the middle of this."

Grand-ma-maaa was an indomitable presence that was certain. In recent years, Rachel had witnessed her father's eyes turn from that old merry glint to the darkened black orbs that he wore now. The slide from the joyful man she adored to the malevolent side of himself occurred in bits over the years as her father aged. Losing the spark for life she witnessed as a child, a black flame that burned with corruption stepping into its place.

The critical matriarch died shortly after returning to Boston that summer. With her late grandmother's death, it sealed grand-ma-maaa not continuing to bear witness to whether the familial aspirations would ascend to the heights she imagined or fall to the wayside through some unknown fatalistic intervention. Rachel assumed the once proud grandmother was thrashing wildly in her grave at her granddaughter's betrayal of the family.

"Well, grand-ma-maaa, I guess I'm not quite what you

had envisioned," she spoke to the quilt.

"You are a Rose. A Boooston Rose." The sharp voice of her grand-ma-maaa pierced Rachel's thoughts.

"Correction, grand-ma-maaa, I was a Rose, a Boooston Rose, now I'm a Smith. A nondescript, unknown, run-of-the-mill Smith of Texaasss," she quipped with a fake southern drawl during her one-sided conversation with a dead woman.

Rachel smoothed the wool plugs of the child-size quilt, knowing it provided a necessary, yet painful reminder of what and who she was. Carefully pulling the corners back, she pushed through the first layer of the fabric, searching even deeper inside for a more striking reminder of her heritage. Gingerly removing the silver frame that encased the perfectly posed photo of her parents, herself, and her brother, Scott. Faces fixed with deceitful smiles. The photo was the only detectable link to her former life. It seemed only a year and a half ago she barely had time to remove the dust from the frame or pick up the quilt off the bedroom floor. Now, their importance loomed over her and jumbled her senses.

The federal agents had forbidden all photos, requiring the signature of an official document under threat of perjury, claiming she had no evidence of her prior life that could point a finger to her true identity. The photo albums she'd carefully constructed throughout the years had been confiscated as evidence and either stored away or destroyed. Nobody would tell her which. She'd managed to stash the single photo and kept it hidden away from the nosy men. Every time she pulled the contraband from the box, it sent a slight thrill up her spine.

"You must remove all traces of your former life if you want to live." Agent Tolliver had lectured her sternly the day they erased Rachel Rose and handed her a new identity.

"Isn't that a little extreme?" she'd posed to the agent. "Can't I keep a couple from my childhood? Nobody will see them. I'll lock them away."

She protested mildly at first over the requirement, then became defiant and protested boldly, then tired of the battle with the stoic men, acquiesced and signed the waiver, attesting she had no photos or evidence of her prior life. It had been a lie. Lying was second nature for the Roses of Boooston, though she'd always been the honest one, but it had been critical to her emotional survival. Her conscience felt no pain from her lie.

She pushed the photo back inside the safe spot, deep inside the beige wool, and re-taped the box. Her former life would remain safe and undetectable there, as she would remain safe in her new life. The cost had been to give up everything: her family, her friends, her job, basically…her life. In exchange, her body would continue to breathe and walk around and exist in its present state as Jeannie Smith. Rachel Rose was dead as far as the public and her father knew. It had been confirmed to the world by the media.

Who wouldn't believe the media?

The image of her fake, fiery death in a plane crash after the trial haunted her. The federal agents fed the video to the gossip outlets, which prompted a frantic inquiry by the news stations, and the spiral spun, further fueling the frenzy that already existed post-trial of California's beloved Senator Jay Rose. Her once adored father, appropriately exonerated of all charges by an unbiased jury of his peers. Also reported by the media.

The headlines stung when she read them after being

whisked off to safety. Sealing her fate as unstable and delivering the false narrative, *"Troubled Daughter's Troubles Are Over," "Senator Stunned by Delusional Daughter's Death,"* and other derogatory headlines painting her the mad villain.

"It's a sad day for the Rose family," the senator's spokesperson assured the media while he made the talk show rounds over the first forty-eight-hour news cycle. "Rachel was suffering from a mental breakdown of sorts, and unfortunately, the senator was a target of her delusions. In spite of the help the family sought, Rachel declined over the past few years, beginning after her breakup with Roger Williams."

The diversion game began.

Apologies were spread all around, even to the federal agents for the waste of time and taxpayer money their ill daughter had caused. The senator gallantly made an empty gesture to reimburse the legal fees incurred by the government. The government refused, naturally.

Sympathy for the poor senator from California poured in faster than his handlers could exploit the moment. His ratings shot up ten points or more by the time the fake funeral was over. A funeral she tortured herself with by watching it on television, telling herself it was necessary to ensure her family believed she was dead. She knew the truth, though; she wanted to know if they cared about her at all. It should have broken her heart watching her mother grieve, but her family had abandoned her months earlier, so she couldn't muster any fake pain for them when her mother stood next to the empty casket, dutifully dabbing her eyes with a tissue.

Once the senator's spokesperson finished his media blitz, the morning shows produced "close" college friends who admitted there was something "off" about Rachel Rose, as far back as college. Rachel seethed as she tried to remember if she'd ever met any of those so-called "friends."

College had been a breeze, even at Harvard. Most professors underestimated her when she was Rachel, with her long blonde hair, assuming she was ignorant, or that "daddy" had purchased her entrance into the prestigious school. It was far from the truth. Rachel had earned her way there on her own merit. Her positive attitude toward studying was the catalyst for her academic success. A remnant of occupying her time alone in her bedroom as a teen when she and Scott were to make themselves scarce year after year when important political business and campaigns were being discussed.

Her true academic gift was in history, not that it had many practical applications in the real world. A fact she soon learned during her senior year interviews. That realization prompted her to continue to grad school. Her father had pushed her to tackle law school, but she'd opted for her master's instead. A decision she'd arrived at because academia was of particular interest to her, and she yearned to become a college professor.

"You're going to law school," her father had insisted when the battle began.

"I have no interest in going to law school. I want to be a professor, a history professor," she'd countered.

"This discussion is over," he said, before telling her to go home and check out law schools.

Rachel had known then how to maneuver her father, so she appealed to his more practical side. "But, Dad, think of the benefit I could be to your career. If I'm a professor, I can immerse myself in the world of college students, young voters, teaching them history, influencing their minds and thoughts and politics. It's a demographic with which you have a lackluster performance."

It was an artful explanation to her closed-minded father that she could be his touchstone, and the information could further his political agenda through a more common position.

"You might have a point; it could be a benefit. You would be an incredible lawyer; you do realize that, don't you? You're certainly persuasive."

Those conversations with her father were brutal, taking her over a month to persuade him, and having to make promises to work for him for one year after graduation before applying for professor positions. She knew the argument was hers when he smiled and squeezed her shoulder.

"Okay, let me know where to send the tuition check and for how much."

"Thank you, Daddy." She could see his satisfied smile at her standing her ground. He'd raised her to be a strong woman, believing she would be his sidekick in the political arena.

It had taken all her time and energy in college and grad school to maintain the grade point average expected from a senator's daughter, shirking her social life to ensure making the Dean's list. So, she was certain that none of those professing on TV to be her "friends" in death were her "friends" in life at all. Perhaps they considered her to be "off" because she wouldn't participate in their weekend rituals of drinking and sex. She saw no purpose in it and had lived her whole life under media scrutiny and threats by her father not to sully his name with irresponsible antics. *Ironic.*

Rachel shook her head, ridding herself of the tortuous

memories which served her no purpose now, and refocused on her current dilemma. She pulled the closest box towards her, trying to recall which box held the items she searched desperately for so she could collapse on the floor and rest. Few boxes had labels; all were stuffed with an unorganized mish-mash of items. Tiredness settled in her joints, plopping down onto a stiff box to catch her breath. She sat overwhelmed by her surroundings. A slight burn edged its way behind her eyes.

What had she done? How was this her life?

She'd lost the man she loved, which was his fault, not hers. And over the past eighteen months since she turned state's evidence against her father, she had withdrawn from the Ph.D. program she'd finally convinced her father to back after graduating with her master's and agreeing to work on his campaign before pursuing it. Then, she'd tossed all her dreams away, shunned her family, and tilted further away from any balance that once existed. What she knew for certain at this moment, sitting on a dusty cardboard box, staring at emptiness, was that this was not life. This was what regret looked like.

Chapter 4
Unpacking it All

Wiping her tears and mustering the last speck of energy she could find, Rachel forced herself to move to the next box to stop her spiraling thoughts. Inhaling a calming yoga breath, hoping to find her center, she refocused on the task at hand and stopped questioning the point of unpacking and pretending anything of value was left in her life.

Before the trial, she believed in the legal system, naively thinking there were good guys and bad guys with recognizable differences. In the aftermath, staring at the faces of the players, they all looked the same. Trying to discern who was honest and who believed the media drivel about her rumored mental imbalance drained her optimism down to her toes. And even though the FBI kept their end of the bargain to provide protection, they had added one non-negotiable condition: her participation in a full psychiatric evaluation. That was eight months ago, and she felt the same today as she had the first day of her evaluation…like she'd fallen into a crevasse and was grasping in the dark for a rope to pull herself back up.

There were days when a force surged inside her, making her want to shout in the streets that she was not Jeannie Smith but Rachel Rose and not crazy. She imagined running up to strangers and grabbing them by the collar, screaming in their faces, "Do you know who I am?"

Logically, she realized that would be crazy and dangerous, and even if she hadn't accepted it, her new identity was a secret that had to be buried forever. There was no choice but to forget herself, her life, and erase years of her existence because if anyone discovered her identity, she'd be dead within hours. That's what the marshals repeatedly told her. And despite her mental wrangling, it had sunk in.

Biting the inside of her lip, staring at the box, dread washed through her. "You are Jeannie Smith," she announced to the bare room in her empty house, hoping to convince her empty self.

The real question she tried to answer in the wee hours of the morning when sleep was elusive over the past years of her life was whether doing the right thing was worth it. It was hard to decide who she was angrier at, herself for not being stronger and loyal to the family. Her father, for being the dishonest, evil man he was born to be. Or Roger, for the pain that crept upon her at the most inopportune time and wrecked her heart, ripping it wide open again and again.

Roger, another disappointment.

When she let her guard down and conjured images of his handsome face, the trickle of memories would flood her mind. Particularly the memory of the first time they met, the first time his soft lips met hers on the Santa Monica boardwalk. A sweet gift after moving back home after grad school. That first moment was frozen in her mind, no matter how she'd tried to erase it. Loneliness had crept upon her that night, so she'd gone out looking to surround herself with chatter. And there he was, dropped from heaven at the right spot and at the perfect moment.

Each had been planning to dine alone to avoid their real world and escape for an hour. Roger had stepped on her toes when he backed into her, trying to dodge a platinum blonde woman dripping with diamonds barreling out of the restaurant, oblivious to the rest of the world.

"I'm so sorry." Roger had apologized to Rachel with overemphasized remorse.

"It's fine," she'd managed, clearly irritated until he flashed that wide smile, and his eyes lit up with his energy.

"Please let me buy you dinner. I'm Roger Williams, by the way."

"I'm Rachel, and that's not necessary. My toes will survive."

Even now, Rachel could recall how her face had flushed, staring into his golden eyes. She'd given her best effort to appear aloof, but relented because the truth was, from the minute he'd stepped on her toes, she had desperately wanted to know more about the fair-haired boy named Roger Williams.

"I insist." He'd taken her hand and guided her to the restaurant.

"So, Roger Williams, what is it you do other than stepping on toes?" Rachel had teased.

"I'm an attorney. It's basically a family business. My father and grandfather are both lawyers and judges. My grandfather's retired, but I work at the Williams, Williams, and Williams law firm."

"Wow, that's quite a mouthful." Rachel had snickered.

"Yes, one day it will be Roger Williams, Attorney at Law,

but for now, I need the influence and connections to impress important people. My father and grandfather are respected in the legal world, which I am extended by association."

"I have heard of your father. He's a hardline Republican judge, right?" Rachel asked him.

"Oh, yes. He and my grandfather are movers and shakers in the party and drag me along for the ride."

"You're going to love meeting my father." It had slipped from her mouth without a thought. Their first date and she was already thinking about him meeting her family.

His family's reputation was well known, and Roger, while modest about their influence, upon hearing his last name she knew he was preceded in greatness by his father, grandfather, and great-grandfather, all having sat on the bench as respected judges, a commendable task in the liberal legal atmosphere of California. They were Republican players who threw their influence around to counteract that of the Rose family.

Her father nearly went through the roof when she finally introduced the two men. The hardline Democrat versus the conservative Republican; polar opposites in their lifestyles, their beliefs, even their looks. Roger, with his soft features and smooth skin, curly brown hair, and magical eyes; "handsome as the devil," his grandmother used to tease. On the other side, her father with his hard, sharp features, thick black hair and piercing dark eyes to match.

Roger had slid a sly smile across his face at her blunder. "Who's your father?"

"Jay Rose. Senator Jay Rose."

They'd both laughed at their dilemma, knowing the drama around the corner if their relationship lasted past their first dinner. Which it did, past dinner, to the next day, which turned to weeks and then months, until finally they told their families, and the fireworks began.

It was a relief to Rachel when the two men seemingly reached a truce on the night Rachel and Roger were engaged. As a gesture, her father planned an elaborate engagement party. A grand celebration where the two families would gather and falsely pretend to find some goodness in each other until everyone returned to their own turf to criticize and gossip about the other's shortcomings. What should have been exciting was overshadowed with dread at navigating the familial political discourse when both families were to meet for the first time at the impending party.

"It's going to be a disaster." She recalled crying to Roger night after night as they planned the engagement party.

"It's going to be fine. Trust me. I invited the press to attend." Roger had wrapped his arms around her and kissed her softly up and down the side of her cheek, his subtle way to urge her to relax.

"That's a terrible idea. The blowout will be aired all over the networks when they go at each other."

"You're forgetting, my darling; the media are the ultimate gatekeepers of good behavior. Both sides will want to outshine the other to have their praises sung across social media and cable news."

"You are so clever. I'm so lucky to have you on my side, my nearly husband." The memory of what followed that conversation was sweet bliss.

But regardless of the perfect mitigating plans, the party and the nuptials never came to be when that sweet bliss was killed with poison called betrayal. Roger had let her down, like everyone else who was important in her life. And even though he'd defiantly stood by her in the end on television, in public, and squaring off with the media after her presumed death, it was too little, too late. At least he had been respectful and not flown to New York to make an appearance on the morning shows like her so-called "friends," who no doubt accepted the network's wining and dining. Roger interviewed remotely from Santa Monica, defending her reputation.

"The former fiancée disagrees with recent media reports labeling the senator's daughter as troubled. In fact, he describes her as one of the most grounded women he had ever known," the morning show personality announced at seven-twenty a.m. the day after her untimely death.

When Roger had appeared, deep, dark circles under his eyes made her heart want to believe he was the only one who truly cared. How he continued to profess love after what he'd done was surprising. Some days, the unforgettable moments were forceful and remained with her for hours. But then the leveling memory erased any romantic notions she still harbored. The great leveler was the memory of him in bed with that "woman." Rachel shivered a little as the images tumbled through her mind, flashing over and over.

It doesn't matter now. I'll never see him again. I'll never see any of them again. Whatever they had once been to each other, it was over now. It had shown her how easily their relationship could be destroyed, and her first clue that it had never been strong enough to survive until death do us part. The cold, hard fact was that Roger was gone from her life…and so was she.

Chapter 5
Don't Sleep

Shoving away her thoughts, Rachel stood, stretched her back, and crossed her arms in front of her, taking inventory of the unpacked boxes and trying to flush the memories of Roger. It saddened her to realize her life was now reduced to a dozen carefully packed boxes. But her tears didn't follow her sadness at this particular moment. Instead, a cold prickle crept up her spine, followed by a deep chill, and a burning desire to run as fast as she could.

Scanning the room again, her weariness from the past twenty-four hours gutted her. Noticing the slatted wood blinds were slightly open, the glow of streetlights flickering between the cracks, surmising if she could see out, a stranger could see in. *They could be watching.*

Her pulse quickened. She dropped onto the floor, only feeling safe below the windows and out of sight. The quiet of the empty house swallowing her, pulling the air from her lungs, making her chest heave in a desperate effort to fill them. Droplets of sweat popped on her forehead as she crouched lower. Barely a quiver when it started, the shakiness edged its way through her body as she knew it would.

It always came and assaulted her in the same way after

each move. Rocking her, squeezing her, uprooting the safeguards she kept in place, forcing her to bury pieces of herself in the boxes and keep them securely strapped inside, then rolling back the tape only to pull them out and examine them and remember. Once the thoughts were set free, they climbed and scratched at her heart and mind. Forcing her to face them, battle them, and understand them. She didn't want to understand; she wanted to sprint away and disappear. *Keep the memories away,* she lectured herself sternly. *Go to your tranquil place, seek serenity,* recalling the psychiatrist's words.

Slowly exhaling to settle her mind and trap her thoughts, she forced herself to put the methods to work, imagining the beach, the ocean, the warm sun, as the doctor suggested. But nothing worked when the shaking began and the battle against herself ensued. Moving lower, ducking into an army crawl, on a mission to retrieve her purse and the bottle of pills tucked inside that the psychiatrist had prescribed. Pills she rejected because they made her slow and detached, becoming a person so unrecognizable that in the daylight it scared her more than the shaking; the nighttime brought a different perspective about the pills, wanting only to make the dreams stop.

This episode was coming on strong, too strong. No doubt fueled by the unsettling trip down memory lane. Her trembling hands finally groped the bottle, forcing frozen hands to coax the lid off despite losing control of her stiff fingers. Once the lid was off, Rachel stared at the pills in disgust. The shaking grew stronger. *I can do this without pills.* Her stubborn mind screamed through her. The bottle slipped from her unsteady grip, scattering the pills across the carpet.

A primal growl rebounded in her ears. She looked around

for the source of the noise. *An animal, perhaps?* She groggily imagined before realizing the sound was coming from her own throat. Fear moved across her chest, the panic freezing in her veins, anchoring her body and slowing her movement.

Someone is watching!

If only she could reach the lights and turn them off, it would conceal her, keep her out of sight of the eyes she knew must be bearing down on her. And if she could find the sharp scissors she had in her hands only a moment earlier, she would be safe.

Unwilling to open her eyes, she groped at carpet fibers with awkward fingers, raking across the floor inch by inch. An urge to flee to safety burning hot across her thighs, waiting for a response from her limbs to sweep her to safety. But a body paralyzed with fear can't respond. It can only freeze. With eyes now open, she focused and fixated on the front door, possessed with thoughts *they* were coming for her. They'd found her, the agent had told her. What if they followed her to Houston? What if they stood outside the door right now? What if this were the last moment she would take a breath on this earth? What if now was the time for it all to end? Her racing mind hurled question after question at her, forcing her to believe this was the end.

Uncontrolled, her muscles clenched with the spasms, and her jaw clamped tightly as the fear grew and overtook her. The shaking had grown too intense to physically find the scissors. She abandoned her futile search. Pulling her knees to her chest and closing her eyes tightly again.

This can't be her life. How had she become this person? Cowering on the floor like a child when only a year ago she stood her ground against her father, the most threatening man she'd met in her thirty-two years of life. And now, nobody would recognize her, a tearful mess, lying silently on the plush virgin carpet of the new four-bedroom home given to her courtesy of the government.

She told her story. They provided her with a new identity, a new car, a new house, but nobody…nobody could give her new memories. Those she would carry with her, tortured by her knowledge of the dangerous people she once loved. She was alone, hailed by few and hated by many for her virtue.

The shaking continued to rock her body. Sweat drenched her t-shirt. The dampness cooled her skin, contributing to the chill and intensifying the shaking. The night would be long, and the quaking would take her to the morning unless she was fortunate enough to pass out and rest. If sleep could be called rest. It too was dangerous, and the sharp side of the two-edged sword she dodged in the night, more so than the daytime, when memories could be tricked away with mundane activities. There was no ability to control the dreams when she slept, nor any escape.

Rachel fought to keep alert, her eyes heavy, not wanting to lose control. Not wanting to think of the memories that relentlessly taunt her when she sleeps. Knowing tonight would be no different from a hundred other nights, and certainly there would be more in her future. Anticipating what was coming, she forced herself to recount the dreams that were always the same in an attempt to own them, better them, show she wasn't afraid. Beginning with the ominous glare from the man in the defendant's chair, his Armani suit perfectly starched as usual. His silver hair always professionally styled, his square jaw set, but in control and pronouncing his authority. His dark vacant eyes, endless holes that glared at his only daughter, his flesh and blood, as she testified of all she knew.

As the dream progressed, a smile would finally slip onto his deceitful face, aimed at her, but it wouldn't be the smile she remembered from her childhood, it would be the public faux smile he wore when the judge affirmed the not-guilty verdict and announced, "Senator Rose, you are free to go." The smile that finally made her believe the Rose blood meant nothing to him, and he would do whatever it took to protect his name and his deceitful life.

The subconscious torture would continue to relive the day in the courtroom when she fought to hold herself steady and endure the condemning stares from the face of her father. The defiance she demanded of herself to portray, attempting to send him a message, one that said she wasn't afraid. She wasn't sure if her act had been successful, the quaking in her hands perhaps giving away her true thoughts; she hoped he hadn't noticed. In dreams and in life, it was clear her father meant business then and now. It wasn't the usual business of senators; it was the business of politically correct bribery, money, and murder. Unless there was truth in his words, and she'd been wrong about everything, and her father was innocent.

What if she is crazy, as the media reported? I can't be. I can't be crazy. It happened. Didn't it?

Exhausted by her own internal battle, sleep finally overtook her and stole Rachel from her soul, leaving Jeannie Smith in her place.

Chapter 6
Realization

Jeannie woke with a jolt as her father was speaking to her in a dream. He hadn't spoken to her in more than eighteen months, and now, in the haze of the dream, he stood stoically, looming over her, ready to assail her with his words. Fortunately, the morning light streaming in through the edge of the blinds saved her by cutting the delusion short, leaving her struggling for relief that rarely came to her fatigued mind.

A dull knock on the door penetrated her foggy consciousness, reminding her of who she was and her current predicament. Legs aching and stiff, she uncurled herself and pulled up on the packed boxes, clambering to stand.

Smoothing her hair and straightening her crumpled shirt, she moved towards the knock. The grogginess masking her attention to potential danger. Her tongue thick, prying her jaw open, she rolled her stiff neck.

It must be the furniture delivery. She finally pieced together in her haze.

With slowed thoughts, she reached for the knob, withdrawing her hand with a grimace as if the brass were laced with electricity. The imaginary jolt forcing her brain to click into gear, reminding herself of the real possibility a killer could be on the other side.

Do killers knock?

She peered through the peephole of her reinforced "bulletproof" front door. Agent Aragon had mumbled that helpful detail to her when he chucked her boxes on the curb and abandoned her. Checking the door a second time, she decided she was right. It appeared to be a delivery person on the porch, actually two. Jeannie sighed, annoyed that she had to consider her fate and demise every time there was a knock at the door.

Standing on tiptoes with her eye as close to the viewer as possible, Jeannie sized up the men carefully to make sure they didn't look familiar. Not that she could remember anymore who was familiar and who wasn't. There'd been so many people shuttling through her life during the trial and since her exile, all the faces morphed into each other, making none of the players distinctive any longer. All that remained were the identifiers: special agents, prosecutors, defense lawyers, doctors, and reporters. Whether they were good guys or bad guys was the unanswered question. Lately, everyone felt like a bad guy, even the ones who claimed to be good guys, especially them. Names had long ago escaped her recollection; unable to be matched to any of the fading faces.

The first man standing on the other side of the front door this morning was blonde, tan, and young, twenty-one-ish, chewing gum in rhythm to last night's music, presumably still playing in his feeble mind. The other, an older, darker man, Hispanic perhaps, with his hat pulled low, his gray mustache looming large through the peephole every time he turned his head and looked at the door and then away again. His face skewed by the angle of the viewer as he stood off to the right of the stoop. No expression apparent.

The young blonde one, impatient now from no response, began ringing the doorbell three times in succession. Jeannie cringed at the sharp tone as it announced itself loudly and echoed through the mostly empty house. Unable to bear the chime of the bell in her pounding head, she carelessly swung the door open.

"I heard you already," she snapped at the surprised young man when she instantly appeared at his command. His bright blue eyes meeting hers, she remembered herself and her distinctive eyes, glancing away quickly.

"Sorry, lady!"

Was he sorry? Jeannie didn't believe it.

Running her fingers through her hair, conscious of her frumpy appearance with the term lady being hurled at her, she suddenly felt old and irritated, but more irritated than old. She wanted to sleep longer considering the restless night she spent on the floor hiding from memories.

"We've got some furniture for Jeannie Smith. That you?" the cocky young man said with a heavy Texas drawl.

"Yes!" Jeannie let the door fall open as wide as possible, turning her back on the men and leaving them to their duty.

"We've got a couch, a bed, a hutch, a desk, a TV, a couple of dressers, a few lamps, a bookcase, and some tables and chairs. Where do you want 'em, lady?"

Jeannie wheeled around at the "lady" remark again and the smacking of gum in between words. Her inherited temper revealing itself. At her relatively youngish age, she felt she shouldn't be drawing the label of "lady." Her entire life should be well organized by now. A two-carat diamond on her finger, married with a couple of children, enjoying playgrounds, and checking out overpriced preschools, and other public marks of parenthood. Not that her parents had engaged in such roles, but she knew it was the norm, and she would give her soul to have normal at this moment.

"Figure it out, slick," she spewed back to the harmless kid, immediately regretting her tone and sarcasm. The poor kid had done nothing wrong, but she didn't apologize. Her mood was too far gone.

"Come on, Joey, let's get unloaded," the older, quiet man instructed, trying to diffuse the escalating situation. Years of life had taught him when to leave an angry woman alone, and this was the time.

"What's her problem, man?" Joey remarked not-so-quietly to the other man as they retreated to the furniture truck.

Joey, nice name.

Jeannie knew it wasn't the kid's fault. She was the one searching for a brawl; the dreams sparking her fight mode. The kid was the first available person to be slammed by the brunt of her frustration. She took a deep breath and rubbed her temples, trying to ease the thumping accelerating uncontrollably. She glanced around, noticing the spot where she'd collapsed the night before, eyeing the scattered pills. Rushing to the bottle, scooping the pills discreetly and tucking the bottle in her purse before the men returned. The space in her skull between her temples filling with tension reminded her she needed coffee.

After unpacking the coffee maker, coffee, and cups, she assembled it all for her daily ritual. It was the one constant she could depend on and the most consequential appliance in her life this morning; it was an insignificant victory, but Jeannie welcomed it.

The men brought the furniture in piece by piece, the older man now directing and doing the speaking. "This is a nice place you have here." His smile was gentle, and he spoke to Jeannie in a respectful tone.

Jeannie relaxed and soon became more cooperative, coerced by the man's kindness. "Thank you. Can I offer you some coffee?" Her debutante training was hard to brush aside, even with the foul mood that was set in her bones.

"No thank you, but it's kind of you to ask."

The man's eyes fell on her briefly, non-intrusively. But she was still careful not to meet his gaze eye-to-eye. The brown contacts that hid her recognizable violet-rimmed sapphire eyes for the past eight months were stowed away in her purse instead of masking who she was. Agreeing to wear them only after reluctantly relenting to the agents, who insisted on the drastic steps to conceal her true identity. It was an argument that ensued and continued for more than a week, reminiscent of Custer's last stand, until the agent tossed her a copy of *Time* magazine brandishing her striking eyes on the cover for public consumption. It seemed no argument could counter hard evidence. She was surprised Marshal Gagne hadn't insisted she put them in before the trek across three states last night.

An hour and a half later, all the furniture was in the house, assembled and set up. The efficiency of the delivery was impressive. Most likely, they wanted to escape her sparkling personality, as she had bitten at them sporadically in the beginning. When the caffeine finally kicked in, she forced a smile and thanked them, generously slipping a twenty-dollar bill into the older man's rough hands, trying to make up for her rudeness without actually having to apologize.

"Sorry we woke you when we got here, ma'am," the blonde kid said as he shut the door hard behind him.

Jeannie decided ma'am was no less derogatory, but at least less offensive and obviously the young twerp's attempt at politeness. Still, it was a reminder of her age and her passing life and unfulfilled plans.

Moving forward to start the day, the hunt for the box containing her bathroom items was finally successful. She heaved it up off the carpet and carried it to her new ensuite to unpack it. A hot shower was the priority in order to wash away the seventeen-hour car ride and a meltdown at midnight, but mostly to reassemble herself and reset the day. And a targeted attempt to restore an ounce of civility in her brain and be more adept at being in public and around people.

Staying cooped up in this house would only make her mood nosedive as the day moved along. Getting out of the house moved to the top of the list for the day. And even though she wasn't an expert at moving, putting herself back together day after day was something she'd sharpened her skills in over the past eight months. Fall apart, battle her mood, put herself back together, and behave as a normal adult, each time gaining a sliver of new strength, at least she hoped that's what it was doing and not simply altering tiny pieces of herself into the new fake person. She'd once loved herself, but now the daily struggle was searching aimlessly in the stratosphere for the remnants of the shattered pieces. Maybe they could never be gathered and reassembled.

Being taught at a young age that manners were important, impermeably ingrained in her the need to be polite and socially gracious, that was the fabric she was woven from. Lately, the training from her childhood had gone by the wayside, as anger and irritation followed her through the hours of the days and nights. But when people are trying to kill you, it's hard to relax and smile at the world and say "pardon" and snicker at meaningless jokes. Everyone had to be analyzed and examined as if they wore the last face she would see before her final breath left her body.

Jeannie steeled herself as she ripped the box open with fury to find the towels and necessities. *Would it ever get better?* She didn't like this new person she'd become, Jeannie Smith, bitch deluxe. Rachel Rose would never recognize or approve of this person. Maybe a hot shower would cleanse her, she smirked to herself.

The water warmed quickly from the shiny new brass faucet, rolling the knob to inch the temperature slightly hotter, looking forward to the slow burn when she stepped into the forceful spray. It was better than her morning coffee, snapping all her senses and sensations to full attention. She couldn't afford to be without her acuity. That was another reason she refused to take the psychiatrist's meds. The agents had ensured her that her defenses would adjust as time passed and she became used to her new identity and her new life, but Jeannie doubted that, too.

Many times, she and Marshal Mayer discussed coping techniques. The most memorable conversation was during the initial transport to her first hideout. At least that had been a pleasant journey, unlike this last one with Marshal Aragon.

"How long do you think the cartel and my father will hold a grudge?" She had asked Marshal Mayer.

"Hopefully, they believe you are dead, and they aren't

looking for you." He had tried to comfort her.

"I'm not sure I like those odds, and I'm certain they have a long memory, and I may never be safe. It's not like I pointed the finger at the cartel or that a connection was found."

"You disrupted their operations; you might as well have named them. Look, you will get used to this new life. I promise. And we didn't find any proof of the connection, and nobody went to jail, and the feds have dropped any further investigation, so hopefully they will back off." Marshal Mayer had been honest with her. Something Rachel appreciated.

"If they lost money, I doubt they will let it go." She had quivered at the thought of the endless grudge.

"It's not worth worrying about. You're safe at the moment. We'll work hard to keep it that way. Besides, it could be fun. Not many people get to recreate themselves. You can be anyone you want." He'd tried to lighten the conversation.

The steam hung on the mirrors as she quieted the water and her memories and stepped onto the towel she tossed on the floor. Increasing her mental shopping list to add bathmats, intentionally leaving behind the last set, acknowledging her poor choice in selecting the long shag fiber that looked rather charming in the store, but ended every shower with her picking fuzz off the bottom of her wet feet. What did she know of bathmats? Again, her mom's territory, not hers. But this time, she'd choose more wisely.

The foggy mirror stared back at her. Time slowed as she patiently waited for it to clear, knowing she had nowhere to go. The reflection still surprised her. Getting used to the short reddish-brown hair would take time. The exact color was a mystery to her. She popped the contacts in place, transforming the rare hue to a common brown. Even her eyebrows were dark, erasing all the remnants of her prior blonde life. She would transform the lashes on her own.

Fortunately, her skin tone was even and a deep honey color, not the usual paleness that many naturally blonde women possess. The darker complexion was most likely inherited from her father's side, she mused, recalling the photos of his youth, leaning against a large car, his arm hooked in his mother's. Slick dark hair parted on the side, combed down smooth with hair oil. The transition to gray had been so subtle that Jeannie hadn't even noticed. It wasn't until she and Roger sat watching him speak on television one night and Roger joked with her.

"You know, you do favor your father," he had told her, patting her thigh. "But he's getting gray, maybe from the stress of being insincere."

She couldn't disagree. It was the first night she'd noticed the mark of her father's advancing years.

Staring at her reflection in the bathroom mirror and noticing her father's features on her own face brought oscillating feelings. Even with the emerging similarity, nobody would recognize her. How could they? She didn't even recognize herself. She watched the reflection, seeing eyes welling with small puddles, threatening to spill onto the counter. The realization was the same each morning; she was gone, and this new person was too foreign to embrace. The memories of conversations with Marshal Mayer returned and flooded through her, wishing she could speak with him now. The last real questions she had asked him were still unanswered.

"How can I ever fall in love again?"

"When you find the right person, and you trust him

implicitly, then perhaps you'll tell him the truth, but only if it doesn't jeopardize your safety. The prudent thing to do is simply embrace your new identity and new life and not overthink it." He'd tried to convince her.

"So, I'm supposed to lie about my past. Tell them a made-up version of myself. How can you build a relationship on a lie?"

"Staying safe has to be the number one priority. Passing time will make it all easier to live with. The main thing is you will be alive."

Her brain had taken in what Marshal Mayer had said, but it still fumbled for the answers to all those questions, conjuring none. A lump formed in her throat. She swallowed hard to push it away. It was a looming question that grew with her other life questions, like how she would recognize who to trust? Maybe she should accept the fact that her destiny was to be lonely, no love, absent marriage and children, a life of seclusion.

The teardrops bounced off the marble counter when they quietly slipped from her eyes. Maybe they hadn't killed her, but what kind of life was she really living? Moving was exhausting. And looking over her shoulder every second of each day drained the rest of her energy. Plus, remembering and forgetting who she was supposed to be was more than confusing. The hard facts were, she was tired.

She'd been told in therapy that acceptance of her place in life now would calm the thoughts. But how do you accept shattered dreams that would never be put back together? How do you accept death of yourself? Accept being Jeannie Smith, a stranger assigned to you? It was taking her emotions a bit to catch up to logic.

An optimistic person would recognize the opportunity for a second chance at life, the ability to create a new personality. Be more daring, not so uptight and proper. Deciding who this new person is could be fun, as Marshal Mayer suggested, she tried to convince herself. Maybe she would choose to be a wild, slutty bitch who frequented bars and picked up random men. Maybe throw caution to the wind and become a biker chick and run with the Hell's Angels. She imagined there were a few of them hiding their identities and living false lives, kindred spirits, perhaps.

Her mind raced through the possibilities of who and what she could be, but as her thoughts slowed, she settled back to knowing she had nobody to confide in and nobody to share a new self with. Besides, she was chatty when she drank and would most likely innocently spill the entire story to some poor slob who would then run to get his fifteen minutes of fame when he revealed that Rachel Rose was alive and well and living in Nowheresville, USA. It was a blessing she wasn't the optimistic type, at least not anymore.

With reality back at her side, she stopped staring at herself in the mirror and tightened the towel wrapped around her surprisingly fit body, which was remarkable since she hadn't been to a gym in months. Tucking the end of the towel in the folds, she made her way to the living room in search of her meager wardrobe stuffed in boxes.

There were no more designer labels, no more expansive closets filled with more clothes than one woman could wear, or shoes and purses to match every ensemble carefully chosen and coordinated with the help of a personal stylist. Now she had two pairs of shoes, blue jeans, yoga pants, and sweats, all non-label, all intentional to not draw attention to herself. Today she opted for off-brand yoga pants. No more Lululemon for her. They'd been left behind in move number two.

In an effort to stop her thoughts from racing through the perils of her life, she knew it was time to shift gears. Unpack boxes, settle in, and take a run later to scope out the neighbors, whom she couldn't meet or get to know. Inexplicably, she wanted to see their faces, only to provide herself with an artificial connection to the outside world. Knowing life would never be the same with no goals to meet, no deadlines, nothing to look forward to that she could think of. Not like her normal life, which was packed with deadlines, dates, events, and life plans that swirled around her and kept her in the thick of society with sips of champagne at the country club and air kisses from old friends. It was gone, and all that remained the same was an unanswered question: *Why had she traded her life for honesty?* Especially when her sacrifice hadn't made a difference.

Her father, the esteemed senator from California, had somehow orchestrated an acquittal. And while she unpacked and stood in fear every day, he was relaxing poolside at the plush ten thousand square foot mansion. Being served his eggs, bacon, and toast by some busty assistant he hired at three times minimum wage because he is "soooo compassionate and always there for the common people." She nauseatingly recalled his campaign brochures. Sipping his imported Colombian coffee and reading one of six papers, probably one of the last holdouts still reading black and white print instead of getting his news online.

In her scenario of her father's morning, it also included her mother and brother standing dutifully by his side, enjoying their perks for loyalty, no doubt.

She could picture Mabel, their cook, in the kitchen routinely whipping up her favorite recipes, the ones Mabel had happily prepared for her ever since she was a little girl. Even in college and grad school, Mabel would bake double-fudge cookies and overnight them to her. Standing through the years as her champion and protector, while Rachel tried to stay out of the way of the activity that permeated the hectic household she'd grown up in. Mabel was always there with a smile to take her hand and lead her away. She could count on Mabel, finding comfort in the hours spent in the kitchen when her parents were out at functions, slowly creating the corrupt person her father had become.

"Don't you worry, Rachel baby, come into the kitchen with Mabel. We'll have some fun. Your parents need to work."

"Can we make cookies?"

Mabel's answer was the same each time. "Of course we can make cookies, and you can lick the bowl and eat some cookie dough. Just don't tell your mama." Followed by her bellow of a laugh, sending a flood of happiness through Rachel as she skipped to the kitchen with her hand in Mabel's.

Life was exciting in those days. Her parents smiled more before her father became a senator. The house bustled with busy people preparing for a campaign or the start of a new term for whatever office her father had been the victor of. It was joyful, and she'd adored him in the early years. A man bigger than life, with people moving quickly around him and showing him great respect. And he mirrored that adoration, plopping her on his knee, even with camera crews readying for an interview or shooting a campaign ad. She thrived on his love; it was real then. Witnessing and receiving his affection gave her warmth at night as a child, but greed and hunger for power slowly killed that carefree man who slipped her butterscotch treats before dinner.

As a child, she never knew loneliness. By the time the teen years descended on her, things changed for her and Mabel, who found it insulting when her father started having his assistants serve his meals. Even though Mabel appeared to take it in stride when the senator was around, the opposite was mumbled under her breath when her father walked from the room.

"I'm not sure why your daddy thinks that bimbo can serve his meals better than I can?" she would whisper to Rachel.

Rachel would giggle discreetly, then Mabel would wink at her, and they would laugh together.

But those happy feelings had been drowned out by emptiness. Now, she couldn't even force the blues away by remembering Mabel's famous hugs and their late-night chat sessions. Imagining Mabel's pain in believing she was dead made her heart ache. Jeannie shook her head, dislodging the angst of the past. Looking around at her nothingness, alone in a suburb of a suburb of Houston, reality grabbed at her and pulled her under, reminding her she was no longer Rachel.

Outside the walls of this strange new house were rows of houses stamped from molds, identical and boring and offering up a chance at a brand-new undefined life, yet all she wanted at the moment was for Mabel to take her hand and lead her to the place where it was quiet and out of the way of the chaos. She frowned at herself for the heavy thoughts; it was time to grow up. Life had been siloed down to herself, and the only company she had in this new reality was her damned integrity.

Chapter 7
The Senator

Senator Jay Rose sat comfortably on the dark leather sofa in his office, his feet planted firmly on the Persian rug his wife purchased during a European vacation. The shipping alone was a small fortune. He didn't particularly care for the pattern or the colors, but she insisted, and he recognized her taste far surpassed his, even if he wouldn't admit it. Still, he had put his foot down on the early English furniture she'd suggested and opted for the rich, masculine leather grouping. A wise choice, he thought as he admired his surroundings, everything except the photos scattered across the reclaimed barn wood coffee table.

Sliding the photos apart, he picked up the first one, trying to discern the family scene played out on the shiny paper. It was clear he attended the event. His image was captured in faded color and staring back at him, but he had no recollection of any touching familial moments that were portrayed in the image. He studied the photo of himself and Rachel. She was about eight, which must have been around the time of his first run at senator. She smiled proudly and held his hand. Written on the back were the words "Daddy's little girl" in Rachel's handwriting. He moved his finger across their faces, remembering the first time he held her.

She never had eyes of a newborn. From the first day she entered this world, her eyes were bright and wide, and distinctive, and as she grew, they became full of laughter and curiosity that endeared her to him. But now, the curiosity that once was an ethereal blessing had become a curse that nearly destroyed the family and almost sealed his fall from grace.

A slight hint of rage rose in his heart as he tried to pinpoint the moment in time his daughter turned against him. Slamming his fist on the table, sending photos flying to the floor, he released his vengeance.

Why? He had given her everything, hadn't he?

There were no logical answers to the questions swirling in his mind. The one thing he knew was that she hadn't died in a plane crash. It was a sloppy attempt at faking a death. There were no bodies recovered at all, not one. He had known the truth from the first moment the report came over the airwaves. Besides, the media heard first, not the family. They would have notified the family immediately if she had truly died, a technical blunder by the inept FBI but strategic to keep him away from the crash site as he dealt with the media frenzy. With his connections, it was easy enough to confirm the ruse. It had taken one phone call to Senator Randall Billings from Utah, whose son was a rookie FBI agent. When Randall balked at pumping his son for information, a gentle reminder about a questionable sexual escapade in Billings' early senatorial days that his wife certainly would not approve of and who in a split-second would take her family money that supported his campaigns and cut and run, had done the trick. He knew all the sordid details and reminded Randall of that fact, prompting the Utah senator to get the deed done.

Senator Randall Billings plied his young son with liquor

in a quiet celebration of his new FBI appointment and found out Rachel was still alive and well. So much for FBI confidentiality.

After an immediate call to his private investigator, the best money could buy, Jay had all the evidence he needed to prove Rachel was not gone. His investigator had a track record for being the best at digging up information and also the best at burying it when needed. He'd never let the senator down and delivered accurate information with discretion, on time, keeping the senator's hands clean during the process. Part of being good at this dance was knowing when to step on the floor and when to sit one out. As a multi-term senator, he had learned to dance well, not getting his toes stepped on yet, except by his own daughter.

Jay moved toward the wall of windows overlooking the professionally designed lap pool that was rarely used anymore. The water sat still as glass except at the far end, where the waterfall slid into the pool in smooth sheets. Ghosts of his children playing in the pool, swimming in and under the cascade before popping through the wall of water with wide grins, brought no comforting memories. It only made his bones seethe with disappointment and anger. There was no way to turn the clock back, and what Rachel set in motion so many months ago had to be finished, no matter the outcome. But this time, it was between him and her. A simmering anger surged below the surface of his skin as he thought of his "unstable" daughter, as the media conveniently labeled her, and all the damage she had caused.

He returned to the sofa, collecting the photos, stashing them out of sight inside the hidden pop-up drawer under the top of the coffee table. He shut the drawer and carefully replaced the enormous book of presidents on top. Sliding his finger along the front edge, he locked the custom table drawer with his fingerprint, since it also contained his gun.

Settling back on the sofa, forcing himself to lower his blood pressure, he picked up the coffee-table book. A present from Rachel many Christmases ago, when she still believed in him and joined in his dream to occupy the Oval Office.

He flipped the pages open, landing on the bio of John F. Kennedy. A president he admired and mourned, all the while harboring a secret aspiration to be the next JFK. Bile rose in his esophagus thinking of his daughter's betrayal and how she could have destroyed his road to greatness. The plan had always been for him to rise to the most influential political position, earning his page in the revered book. His mother's dream was that the Rose clan would rival the Kennedys in fame and power, but so far, the Roses had only produced a scandal which, in truth, made them "Kennedy-like."

Snapping the book shut, he rose from the sofa and moved to his desk to quell his anxiousness. He mused that one day soon, he would restore his path and legacy of political greatness. It was his deserved place; he told himself, and nobody was going to mess that up, nobody, not even his own spawn.

As the only son, he alone controlled the family's destiny and counted on the political backbone throughout the country built from the sweat of his forefathers. It had been drilled into his psyche his entire life. His own late father and grandfather, having laid the groundwork and taught him well to follow in their impeccable footsteps, the proper schools, the proper connections, all bestowed upon him. They trained him to walk the line on both sides of right and wrong, but how to appear as if you were always on the right side. They had been masters at it, but Jay Rose knew his skill far exceeded theirs.

The anger that shot through him moments earlier morphed into adrenalin that ebbed through his veins as he sampled the power in his mind. Knowing the influence the Rose name carried and the instant status it commanded, despite battling the foreboding voice of his ghost mother, reinforcing her assertions that he was inferior. All that mattered now was that respect for him poured in across the nation, recounting the recent bump in the polls.

In his youth, he'd embraced his father's use of political sway and money to grease the palms of those necessary to guide him down the path to greatness. It was his birthright to attend the proper schools and hold influential and impressive jobs while working his way up. Even riding the wave of sympathy when his father passed away one month before his first bid for public office. He was young and hungry then, right out of law school when he ran for Attorney General in Boston. The death of his father secured the election that he was otherwise losing in the polls.

With his father's coattails cut off forever by death, he became ruthless and serious in his stand against crime, a position his father would have scoffed at. A position that would secure votes when he made his political steps. It was beyond his imagination that now his party had shifted to lessening the stance on criminals, but he needed the party, and he shifted with them even when it went against everything he truly believed. It was politics, and his personal thoughts on the matter were simply irrelevant. Only the voters counted. That was the public statement, anyway. That's who he played to, while placating the party to siphon their money and capitalize on fundraisers. And if the polls revealed the voters had shifted their opinions on the issues, then he would switch like the wind.

There was a time many years ago when he thought Rachel would be the one to carry on his legacy and use his reputation to assure her rightful place as a Rose. But painfully, she had rejected all that was related to the Rose family except his money.

His son Scott, who was the logical choice in the Rose bloodline and was good-looking enough to attract public favor, was a brick shy of a load, and it would have cost a fortune to secure an office for him. But Rachel had the grit and intelligence necessary to handle the pressures of public office. She was the only choice. That's why he brought her into his inner circle to begin with, to start her indoctrination, to continue the family name despite her frivolous insistence she wanted to be a history professor. It had been a clever idea to let her in; he reassured his own ego. It was a defect within Rachel that made her go rogue.

He had raised Rachel right, so he knew he wasn't to blame for her lapse in judgment, and he knew exactly who was responsible for turning her against him and everything the family stood for. It was Roger, that good-for-nothing fiancé. It wasn't until Roger came along that Rachel began challenging the family's beliefs. Wondering if there wasn't too much government interference in the nation already. That was the first hint of warning that Rachel was swaying.

"That's typical Republican rhetoric to excise the uncaring from taking on the social ills," Jay had argued with her at dinner one night. She had become relentless, urging him to consider her latest ideas and attitudes. Ideas that he knew only the conservatives would have introduced into her psyche. It was Roger and his pious family who brainwashed her.

Reaffirming his absolution of any responsibility for the decline in his relationship with his daughter, he shook the newspaper open along with his memories and resumed his morning ritual—coffee, and his papers.

"Did you find her?" Jay didn't look up from his paper when Scott entered the room a few minutes later.

The last thing the senator needed this morning was to be interrupted by his incompetent son. There had been too many distractions already, which were only compounded by his avalanche of memories. All he wanted at this moment was to forget about the turmoil his children created in his life and to read the paper in silence before his day exploded with constituent responsibility.

"I'm sorry, Dad. We tracked her first move to Kansas, the second to Oklahoma, and there appears to be a third move, but we've not been able to track that yet. The trail goes cold. They have her hidden well."

"You're such a bumbling idiot. Can't you do anything right? I told you to find her. I want her found. The investigator gave you all you needed to keep tabs on her. That was your only job. This isn't over, you know, not by a longshot. I want to know where she is and what she's doing. Is that clear? If you aren't up to the job, get the PI back on it. Remember, you wanted this mission, so don't fail me."

"Yes, Dad, but I don't understand why. Our life is fine now. The world thinks she is dead and crazy. Your ratings are higher than ever. In fact, if the reports are right, maybe she is dead after all. The only thing we've found is a paper trail and not a live person."

Scott shifted his weight to calm his nerves. His father was not a forgiving man and had the power to get whatever he wanted. It was clear how his father felt about him, that he was inferior and no match for his father or Rachel. All his life he'd been compared to Rachel, who was exalted for being an intellect and clever, something never assigned to Scott when his father introduced him to friends or associates. And even though admittingly Rachel was smart, even she'd been outsmarted by their father.

Scott knew better than anyone that his father, Senator Jay Rose, was most definitely a force not to be trifled with. It would take years of careful planning to dethrone the patriarch. The timing and the planning had to be perfectly executed, and only the most cunning would ever defeat his formidable father. That knowledge could only come from someone who had learned firsthand how to be ruthless and cruel with the ability to take that cruelty to a higher level. And while Rachel was book-smart, she was neither cunning nor cruel. Those were traits left to others, not princess Rachel.

"As I've told you, those reports were fake. I can't even believe you fell for it. You traced her to two cities, and you still believe she is dead?" The senator threw his paper to the ground and huffed across the room to stare out the window again, not focusing on the view. He ran his stern fingers through his thick hair, trying to push away the annoyance caused by his children.

Scott knew it was his cue to leave. "Maybe the feds wanted us to think she was alive to set you up again." Scott thought it sounded completely plausible as he presented it to his father. "After all, the media reported Rachel's death, the feds would know you would find that suspicious. The media's not in on this cover up, I've already tapped my connections there," he reasoned.

Rachel was dead as far as Scott was concerned, and even though he knew he couldn't convince his father to let it go, his mother was different, weighed down by the pain, drowning in misery too dark to think about him or life moving forward. The notion of Rachel still walking the earth was kept from the ears of his mother, and to him was secondary in importance to his goal of his mother forgetting his sister. But despite all his efforts, she claimed she could still feel Rachel's presence.

Scott didn't want to feel it. He didn't want to feel anything toward his sister. In his mind, Rachel needed to stay dead. She'd only caused problems for the entire family, derailed plans, and undermined his rightful place in the family even more. The unforeseen drawback was, as the days passed, Scott was the looming target of his father's ever-changing moods. The only bright light in all the chaos Rachel created was that his father's political trajectory had been accelerated, and his move-up couldn't come soon enough for Scott.

"Why don't you leave it alone?" Scott suggested. "With the public sentiment like it is, this would be the perfect time to announce your run for president. Let's leave her dead. She won't come out of hiding." Scott didn't want his father digging around, chasing after Rachel.

"Scott, don't offer your asinine opinions to me. Is that understood? Do your job or I'll find someone else to do it." Jay turned on his heel and glared at his son, though he reluctantly admitted to himself that he half agreed.

The prudent thing to do would be to focus on his life and

political goals and forget about his daughter and stop letting her actions bore under his skin. Pretend she were truly dead and move on. But Jay knew his daughter and, when wronged, wouldn't rest until she proved herself right, even if it put her life in danger.

The cartel had delivered a clear message of displeasure with the mess that he was still attempting to smooth over, and he couldn't take any chance that she'd pop up at the most inconvenient time and destroy his empire. He'd lost enough time and money.

"Yes, sir, I think she's dead, that's all." Scott responded, knowing he had no choice but to treat his father with fake respect.

The sad truth of his life was, he was trapped and would never find another cushy position like the one he held with his senator father, where all he had to do was smile and do the bidding of the devil. There was no title. He was an unofficial staff member receiving an unprecedented salary. The only way he could improve his status was to take over his father's position, not as a senator, never hungering to play the corrupt game of politics. But he could oversee the drug business he knew his father was still operating. That was the shiny jewel he wanted in his crown.

Who cared that it was a corrupt business? The money was more than he could dream of earning in his lifetime as a staff member for a senator. But it could all capsize if his father insisted on locating Rachel. Discovering her alive would only mean trouble for everyone. It was better to persuade his egomaniac father to get on with his life and his ambitious political agenda and let Scott get on with his secret aspirations and continue to climb the corporate ladder. A ladder that needed a couple of rungs removed to fast-track his journey.

"Excuse me, sir." The voluptuous receptionist, who had questionable brain power but loaded on the young and pretty side, a job requirement by the senator, opened the door. "There's a man here to see you. He has an appointment this morning," she almost sang privately to the senator.

"Certainly, Tammy, show him in, please. Scott, you need to go. You have work to do."

The sugary tone his father used with the airheaded girl was another intolerable quality Scott resented. Since he was a young boy, he'd observed the most disgusting behavior of watching this man stalk his prey year after year. With his father's advancing years, it added a layer of disgust that Scott couldn't wash away at the end of the day. It didn't go unnoticed this morning, but it certainly remained unmentioned, as always. Scott knew how his father operated, and he also knew his mother endured it. Who could blame her? Like Scott, her life was tucked tightly into a little box that his dad held the only key to.

"Okay, Dad." Scott turned to leave as the man entered the room.

"Scott," his father called after him, "don't call me Dad during business hours. It's Senator Rose," he scolded his only son in front of Tammy and the waiting man.

Scott narrowed his eyes, regretting not having testified against his father and putting him away until the end of time, but that would have been suicide in more ways than one. Rachel had cursed at him and called him a coward when he told her he wasn't going through with the testimony. But he wasn't stupid and had wisely learned one thing from his father over the years: to look out for himself. The last thing he needed was his father's assets to be seized by the government. How would that have benefited him?

Success and power were expected from the Rose men, and Scott knew the only way to achieve it was to stay aligned with the man on top until the precise moment when he could cast him aside. The mere thought of that moment had Scott salivating. A tight grin forced its way across his handsome face. The Rose blood turned cold in his veins as he eased the door closed behind him, shutting out the bitter old man.

"So, Mr. Ramirez, what brings you here at this early hour?" Jay's tone was cordial and inviting as he watched Tammy leave the room.

Mr. Ramirez was a longtime associate of the senator. They had been engaged in business since Jay made his way to California to vie for attorney general decades ago, a strategic move made publicly out of concern for California's climbing rate of crime and consumer scams permeating the west coast shores.

In reality, it was a move to position himself for the Senate seat behind the ailing incumbent. Jay had spent weeks constructing his plan. Plotting to endear himself to the incumbent senator and eventually slide into his space. He played it patiently, and it panned out. When the ailing senator finally passed on, Jay was appointed in his stead for the remainder of the term. Easily winning the special election a few months later. The constituency leaned his way and most voted party lines; the wins were routine year after year. After that, his senatorial position remained unopposed and locked in for decades.

"We have business, unfinished business, Senator," Mr. Ramirez said in his familiar heavy accent, smiling as he stroked his thick mustache, first one side then the other, his thumb and forefinger working in harmony.

"Oh yes, we certainly do, but right now is a touchy time for me, you know. The death of my troubled daughter and the sham of the trial and all. It's really quite tragic and has taken a heavy toll on the family." The senator put on the face of a brokenhearted father.

Mr. Ramirez saw through it. "Yes, yes, quite sad. My associates send their condolences. They are also considering a sizeable donation to your campaign, or even to one of your charities." The men exchanged glances and covert communications. Smiling in unison as unspoken agreements passed between them.

"Well, next week there will be a benefit to raise money for cancer. Quite an impressive cause, I assure you. Perhaps you or one of your associates would like to attend the benefit? I have some individuals you should meet, the big donor type. I, myself won't be there. I'm not sure if my work in Washington will be done by then. My son will attend in my absence." The senator motioned to the closed door as if to remind Mr. Ramirez of his son's earlier presence. "It's only been a few months, and my wife believes it's too soon for her to appear in public. But soon."

It had been eight months since the supposed death of his daughter, but his wife was still distraught and barely left the house. Her grief was real.

Mr. Ramirez knew his signal. "Of course, we would love to help with the cancer research cause. My own mother suffered from cancer. I will inform my associates, and they will decide who will attend. I will send word."

"Very good, then. Call my secretary with the details, and

she'll make the necessary arrangements." What he didn't confirm was their meeting to be held soon about business that could not be discussed in his office.

The men rose. Jay towered over the slighter man. He placed his hand on Mr. Ramirez's shoulder to confirm their agreement, shook hands, and concluded the spoken and unspoken terms of their deal.

When the man was gone and the office door shut, Jay sank into his large leather chair to brood about his future. His eyebrows crinkling together as he fumed over not knowing the whereabouts of his turncoat daughter. She was a threat as long as she was alive, and he feared she had the photos of the unrecognizable dead girl. He didn't even know where they had come from, but the girl could be traced to him. He was certain it was Natalie. It was true he wanted her sent away and taken care of, but he never ordered her to be killed.

Those photos threatened his plans and his life. He couldn't afford to have them popping up in a run for the presidency. How would he explain them and his connection to the dead girl? Weathering one scandal in his career was fortunate, but two would undo him.

Retracing that day in his mind when he found Rachel with the photos still brought no clarity about his reaction, backhanding her in a fit of rage. The flash of what he had done wouldn't leave his mind. Grabbing the papers from her hands as she scrambled to maintain consciousness. The blood dripping from her mouth was a memory he couldn't erase. He'd never struck his daughter ever until that nauseating moment.

It was no wonder she fled and tried to take him down. He'd sped after her to apologize, but she peeled out of the driveway, not giving him a chance to utter a single word. With the confusion and the words between them, and his shock at his own behavior, his focus on the photos had been diverted momentarily. He'd torn his office apart when he returned, but the photos were gone. Rachel had to have them. There was no other conclusion.

The puzzling question was why she didn't use them at the trial. It was a relief, but he didn't trust that they wouldn't surface one day. He'd been so preoccupied with recovering from the drama, he'd not devoted time or attention to finding out who took the photos or why. There was a long list of suspects, perhaps another senator looking to even the score, but the source was irrelevant, knowing his digging into the matter could set off more alarms and potentially shine the spotlight on himself. It had to be pushed aside for now and hope that Rachel would leave it dead and buried.

His sole goal now was to find the photos, then find out who took them and how they'd ended up in his office and make them regret it. But to do that, he had to find his daughter. The cartel wouldn't tolerate another slip-up. Which left two options where Rachel was concerned: to be permanently silenced or become an unsuspecting player.

A sly smile eased its way across his face, recounting the secret satisfaction of having beaten her at trial. Watching her face when the Judge pronounced the not-guilty verdict to the packed courtroom, another small gratification. It had to be gnawing at her moral sanctity then and now; he knew his daughter well. He also knew that being swept away from her life couldn't be sitting well with her, and that enough time had passed that she had to be getting lonely. The thought comforted him.

His smile spread wider at the idea of what he knew was a growing discomfort in her new life. His brooding was over.

Chapter 8
Settling In

Unpacking boxes and arranging and rearranging furniture ate up the entire afternoon. Jeannie had carefully assessed the setup from every angle, but nothing seemed to fit right. Her instinct was to pick up the phone and call her mom and ask for suggestions of the best layout to fit an oddly shaped living room, which flowed into a dining area with an adjacent breakfast nook. How could she optimize the space, create flow, and yet also have it remain cozy and comfortable? These were questions she had no answer to, but her mom would know if only Jeannie could reveal she'd not died in the Nevada desert.

The growing absurdity of the entire scenario was epitomized by the ridiculousness of agonizing over the traffic flow in her home at all. It wasn't like she'd be entertaining anyone. What did it matter if it was aesthetically pleasing or even functional?

With a heavy sigh, she shoved the sofa across the room with her thighs, knowing they were stronger than her arms, tugging on the back of the sofa to realign it like she had it three rearrangements ago. The ache in her arms confirmed this was where the couch would stay.

The only true decorating criterion she had was a clear

view out of the large picture window while relaxing on the sofa. Ensuring a front-row seat to get the jump on anyone who might be lurking outside her house. Even though this strategic configuration would make TV placement impossible, there was no solution in her mind for her layout dilemma as she stared at the blank wall. Abandoning the idea of the TV in the living room, she struggled to lift it, then laid it flat on a sheet and dragged it to the bedroom.

Flopping on the bed with exhaustion, she closed her eyes, trying to force out the realization that she could never again call her confused, socialite mom, whose greatest accomplishment was marrying into a wealthy, influential family, securing her exotic vacations and endless shopping sprees. The truth created a nasty taste in her mouth.

As polar opposites, Jeannie wondered how she had developed such ambition when her mother had no desire to live in the real world. Though the long list of differences didn't negate a bond they shared, perhaps only because they were women. It was impossible to understand how her mother had ignored her father's flirtatious escapades, his multiple affairs, his icy distance from her unless public eyes were following his every move, and his brutal treatment of his adult children.

The resentment she'd been hoarding for years about her mother's nothingness slid over her. Quietly, she yearned for her mother to put her foot down and either divorce her father or stand up for herself. Losing count of how many nights she lay in bed vowing never to become a woman like her, a kept woman. That was the only way Jeannie could see her, especially after the trial.

Her mother appeared content to tend to her own

business and activities, distant from affection and love. Not Jeannie. She needed those emotions in her life. It was more than a need; it was a want. Her mother's ability to live without intimacy bordered on abnormal. Ironically, now Jeannie was the one being forced to live a life void of affection and intimacy. How close could you get to someone if you could never tell them who you were? The question rippled along the base of her skull daily, taunting her in this new life.

Looking at the empty cardboard boxes stacked next to her bed, Jeannie couldn't help but draw some sense of similarity with her mother at the moment, both having given up their lives, and each left with nothing real. The difference was, Jeannie had no choice, but her mother did. Jeannie had to choose a castaway life to stay alive, but her mother made the choice to maintain her country club lifestyle and designer labels. The saddest part was the wasted talent and flair for design her mother possessed but never used. Many years earlier, Jeannie had encouraged her mother to pursue a career in interior design. Her wealthy friends already called on her for advice. She could make a decent living if she tried. But her mother wouldn't hear talk of such ideas and accepted the compliments with a giggle and a smile.

"Oh, Rachel, why in the world would I want a job?"

"To have a sense of accomplishment. To have something of your own," she'd countered.

"Really, darling, I have plenty of my own, and my schedule is horrendous now. I can't imagine trying to juggle a career."

She'd always tried to encourage and support her mother's independence, believing her mother would do the same for her. In fact, when the trial started, she expected support, but it never came. The last true discussion was not something Jeannie could easily forget. Her mother had cornered her one afternoon when she asked her to drop by and said, "Rachel, this nonsense has to stop. All you're doing with this case against your father is causing the family pain. And what if he actually goes to prison? What then? What would happen to us?"

"Mom, you of all people should want Dad to be accountable for what he's doing. Don't you care that he's breaking the law? Dealing drugs? That can't be acceptable to you. And we will be fine if Dad goes to prison."

"You really have no proof of the allegations you're tossing around. Besides, this is a family matter, and I hate that the public has become aware of our skeletons in the closet. It's not right. Your and Roger's breakup was enough of a scandal. I recently stopped having to explain that situation at the club. Why do you want to add more gossip to embarrass us?"

"I'm sorry you don't understand, but it's illegal, and it's wrong. If you won't stand up for what's right, I will."

Her mother had shrugged and walked out of the room without another word. In her mother's circles, "family matters" were anything that might cause embarrassment or worse yet, accountability, and included affairs, rehab, abortion, illegitimate children, and now, drug trafficking. Soon after, the only subject they discussed was the weather and the latest social gossip about other's "family matters." When the trial started, they stopped talking altogether.

Jeannie rolled herself off the bed and headed back to the living room to examine the furniture one last time before forcing herself to be satisfied with the placement, concluding it was a sterile situation with new boring furniture. *Probably chosen by a male agent.* It was so...brown. She sighed and went to the kitchen, where organizing only required space and not design talent.

Putting away the minimal kitchen items she owned prompted the creation of a list of additional shopping items. The refrigerator and pantry were pre-stocked with the basics. At least the agents didn't leave her to starve to death. Her growling stomach reminded her that food was still a necessity, even in her new life with her new identity. She perused the food stashed in the pantry and chose the Raisin Bran Crunch cereal. Her appetite had dwindled to nothing since the trial. Thanks to Mabel, she had reasonable cooking skills, but life had soured her appetite.

Digging through the array of utensils, she plucked a lone spoon and a bowl out of the box. It was a far cry from the fine dining she had grown accustomed to during her five-star life. She shoved the remaining utensils into the drawer and out of sight. There would be plenty of free time later to sort through and organize them. Maybe she wouldn't remain a neat freak like she'd always been. Maybe instead, she would live like a slob and never pick up anything or put anything away until she absolutely couldn't stand it anymore. Knowing that would never happen since the mere thought of all the utensils in the drawer left to their own devices and not separated properly was sending irritating prickles down her arm.

Roger had once told her that her spirit animal was an ant, methodically orchestrating the minute details of their lives.

"An ant?" she'd questioned, expressing her hurt at the comment.

"It's not meant as an insult. Ants are busy, hard workers, always trying to build something. It makes me think of you. Persistent and clever. When there is one obstacle, you find a way around it until you've built something quite majestic. Have you ever seen the intricate tunnels ants build? They are nothing short of an architectural masterpiece."

"And people despise them and step on them."

"Nobody is going to step on you. You're too crafty." Roger had assured her with a kiss on her forehead.

Rachel hadn't been convinced by Roger's explanation about her spirit animal. "There's nothing wrong with being organized or persistent," she'd argued.

He'd hugged her tightly and told her that ants never quit, and that's what he admired most about her. Her fighting spirit. But she hadn't fought for their relationship in the end. She had run fast and far with betrayal and pain and sharp words intended to cut him to shreds. And now she was alone.

She resisted the urge to identify with her spirit animal at this moment by placing the utensils into neat little stacks and instead sat down to eat her cereal minus the milk, since there was none. Reading the cereal box several times as she ate in solitude, the ticking of the oven clock reminding her with every click that she was alone and would be for the rest of time.

Sinking into self-pity, she shook her head, then refocused on the list of ingredients and questioned how one could partially hydrogenate soybean or why and what polyglycerol esters of mono- and diglycerides could be. Was guar gum really an ingredient? What was guar gum? And didn't BHT sound more like a pesticide than a preservative? Strangely enough, there was a tiny spark of comfort in pondering the chemical makeup of her cereal instead of the ingredients of her life.

Lost in a blur of unproductive thoughts, she stood at the sink scrubbing the spoon and bowl far beyond clean until the water became scalding and snapped her back to the present, pulling her from a dead-drop into a time-warp with Roger's face in focus. Over the years she'd mastered forcing away the images of his handsome face, but now, with this move, her thoughts gained intensity. The further they moved her from California, the more the gravitational pull of her former life tried to suck her back in.

Get busy, she lectured herself.

Pulling the kitchen chair out from the table, she sat back down to assemble her shopping list. Lists were a path to organization, and a way for her thoughts to direct themselves back to sanity. Lists eliminated anxiety, at least they did for her. Maybe the rest of the world managed in chaos, but one trait she'd carried with her from being Rachel Rose was her *To Do* lists. The first item on the shopping agenda was a utensil tray. With no tape measure, she used her arm to measure across and deep to make sure she purchased the right size. She'd learned about the intricacies of endless choices at Walmart on her maiden shopping voyage for the last house. That was the one place she felt comfortable meandering freely, certain nobody who shopped there paid attention to politicians or their crazy daughters. The next item on her list was a tape measure.

Deciding to settle into this house and this life, as long as the government didn't say otherwise, the list grew longer as she ambled in and out of the rooms, noting all the things she didn't have but most certainly needed. When she finished, she picked up her government-issued cell phone and placed a call to the preset phone number labeled "Account Info" listed in her favorites, presumably put there by Marshal Gagne.

"This is Jeannie Smith," she informed the operator on

the other end.

"ID number, please."

Jeannie grumbled silently. She'd been forced to memorize the number and never write it down, she replied, "7432509081."

"Yes, what can I do for you, Ms. Smith?" The woman was polite but distant.

"For some reason, all my belongings didn't make the move. I'm sure it has nothing to do with the competency of the agency." Jeannie rolled her eyes. "So, I need to do some shopping today, and I want to make sure that my account is set up." Jeannie felt like a kid with an allowance from a government bucket of money.

Most of her own assets were in a trust set up by her father for tax reasons, all reverted to him on her "death." She had died in an airplane crash, after all. What she had access to was a solitary bank account she'd set up privately when she and Roger became engaged. Those funds were transferred to her new identity prior to the "crash." And the FBI took care of the subsequent name changes, though it was a process layered with every color tape she could imagine, bright red being only one of them. Now, she depended on the government to supplement her life.

Her checks were supposed to be deposited automatically, and then she could establish her own budget, but the process was steeped in broken promises. Until they worked it out on their end, she needed to inform the keepers of the witnesses how much she planned to spend. A new procedure, Marshal Gagne had told her with a hint of satisfaction.

"One moment, Ms. Smith, I'll connect you to Marshal

Gagne. He can help you with this."

"Thank you," Jeannie started to say but was already in phone transfer hell; dumped right in the middle of Barry Manilow belting out a torrid love ballad. Before Barry could finish his serenade, Marshal Gagne cut his throat.

"Marshal Gagne." His voice was curt and on full alert.

"This is Jeannie Smith. I'm checking my account status."

She pulled the new bank card from her wallet, reading the foreign name of Jeannie Smith. It hadn't connected to her subconscious yet. Barely remembering the other names assigned prior to this one, which also felt foreign, as if parts of herself had simply vanished into thin air. The first forty-eight hours of each new persona required a concentrated effort to say the name over and over in her head until it sounded somewhat normal when it spilled from her mouth.

"Your account is all set, Ms. Smith. Is there anything else I can help you with?"

Taking a mental pause before answering and heading off the powerful urge to rattle off a list of demands, her first impression of this less than helpful agent slid over her. She wanted to convince herself to trust him while internally battling her instincts, but every attempt to move past herself was failing fast.

"Could you tell me what exactly I'm supposed to do with my time?" she finally answered.

"Ms. Smith, maybe you should relax, buy some books, and enjoy some downtime for a while. Start a hobby. The last eighteen months have been quite difficult for you. How's your anxiety level? Have you spoken with your psychiatrist lately?"

The word triggered a surging rage followed by her blood

skyrocketing through her veins, straight to her head, melting into a thump, thump from temple to temple. The overpowering urge to curse sat precariously on the tip of her tongue. *How does he know about the psychiatrist?*

The sessions with Dr. Franklin were supposed to be confidential, and this revelation confirmed her doubts that any part of her life was her own. The doctor had encouraged her to open herself up to terrors lodged in her body, the body remembers, he'd told her. Purging herself within the sanctity and safety of his office would relieve her of the burdens she was trying to shovel dirt over and bury, he said. Reminding her multiple times that the problem with memories being buried inside her was that one day, they would erupt.

They met twice in his office initially, then spoke weekly for the first six months after that, and she'd made progress. Then, he abruptly sent her off with a prescription for anxiety, and the sessions stopped. Supposedly, the medication had no side effects, but her mind floated around in circles within an hour after taking one. It made her feel lost and vulnerable, and increased the number of times she looked over her shoulder, feeling eyes poring over her and drilling into her back. It was intolerable, so the pills remained in the bottle.

Dr. Franklin had managed to pry some information from her during a particularly vulnerable virtual session. It had been raining that day, and she'd felt gloomy, wanting to be back in California and to have her life back. It felt as if there was no hope that day of surviving any of it. So, what would matter if she told a stranger the details?

"Tell me about your father and what you found when you were going through his office," he'd prompted.

"Well, I didn't find much. What I heard was proof of his connection to the drugs. I'm not sure whom he was speaking with. It sounded like they were talking in code. He was speaking about the weather. I didn't understand it until my father said the drug shipment could increase on the next transport."

"Was there anything else?"

"My father also promised to 'take care' of any problems with senators who wouldn't cooperate with him in getting the 'coffee shipments' into the country." Rachel disclosed, dropping air quotes around the words "take care" and "coffee shipments."

"How'd that make you feel?"

"What do you mean? It made me feel scared. And angry. And disappointed. The rug had been pulled out from under me. My father is a powerful man. I needed the truth, so I followed him and watched him meet with men in the shadows."

"Were you able to get any photos?"

"No, it was dark, and I stayed far away so he wouldn't see me."

She excluded the parts about dangerously riffling through her father's office, trying to uncover dates and times when the illegal shipments were to arrive. The little she uncovered, she handed over to the federal agents, and they set up the sting, but arrived too late. She'd told no one about the photos of the dead girl, though, not even the prying psychiatrist. It was too mortifying to visualize. It had taken months to get those images out of her mind. And she couldn't prove there was a connection.

The doctor continued the inquisition, wanting to know how the operation was run, which she thought was odd, but she'd indulged him.

"Supposedly, the cocaine was transported with the coffee on the ocean liners, offloaded to Java Connection trucks, then transferred to the linen company trucks which were leased to Java Connection but owned by an independent group of investors of companies with no knowledge of the drugs, except my father who orchestrated all of it. At least that's what the prosecutors told the jury."

"How much money do you think he was making in this operation?"

"I have no idea. According to him, there was no operation." Jeannie remembered the counseling session that day, and how the questions the doctor asked always seemed to twist back to her father and details of the operation and away from her emotions or anxiety.

"So, you followed your father? How long did you do that?"

"Yes, basically I stalked him," she admitted, "and tried to overhear his conversations."

"Would you say you became obsessed with proving his guilt?" the doctor asked bluntly.

The string of curse words that flew from her mouth was something she regretted.

The doctor continued pressing. "Have you considered that perhaps you created the idea of his guilt in your mind, and your father wasn't really involved in smuggling drugs?"

It was then she considered that her obsession had blurred her objectivity. After all, she was the one who'd guided the feds to the possibility of a drug ring, even though there were no red flags before her phone call.

By then, Jeannie was angry at the psychiatrist, feeling that he believed she was delusional. So, she shut down, refusing to defend herself or tell him about the threat her father made against her. How he described in excruciating detail the slow and painful way cartel informants die. Promising that anyone stupid enough to go against a powerful organization such as the Colombian cartel would certainly be taking their life into their own hands. Then, he quietly assured her he had no connection to such barbarians or illegal activity.

Jeannie never believed her father, but the mere possibility she was wrong created an anxiety that settled in her brain, lurking there and ready to strike at will.

During the initial investigation and the pre-trial interviews, her dad's attorney had planted the seed of doubt in her own thoughts with the insinuation that she was imagining everything. Then carried that seed of doubt to the jury, and it all conveniently unraveled after that, leaving her holding the proverbial bag.

Unimpressive connections to a few charitable donations to questionable organizations that the investors in the linen truck companies were involved with were the only other tidbits of anything illegal the feds could uncover. Middlemen padded the envelopes holding the large legitimate checks with even larger amounts of cash, presumably for off-the-book favors, all conspicuously and graciously trading hands at stuffy fundraiser dinners and cocktail parties. After all, who would suspect powerful and handsome men in tuxedos at boring charitable fundraisers of bribery, money laundering, and drug deals? She knew the reality; the trouble was proving it. That…she'd not been able to do.

The evidence against the senator was sketchy at best and

full of holes when he was indicted for drug trafficking. The prosecutor said, in retrospect, he never should have brought the case without more evidence. They were relying heavily on Rachel's testimony and insider knowledge. The defense team hammered away at her credibility, making her look as if she were delusional.

Nothing about the trial went as she had imagined. Initially, the prosecutor had the testimony of the truck driver in addition to her testimony and diligently constructed a deal where the driver would testify against the senator. But before the truck driver took the stand, he'd flipped his story and took the blame for the entire concoction, claiming it was a onetime deal for a buddy. In the end, he pled guilty to a low-end trafficking offense, a parole violation for a gun found in his truck and opted to serve his time in a federal penitentiary with three squares a day.

Jeannie knew someone had paid him off or threatened him. It was too convenient. The testimony he gave ended up helping the defense when he claimed he didn't even know the senator, and as far as he knew, Senator Rose had no knowledge of how the trucks were being used.

While useful in providing the link to charities and the investors of the trucks, she couldn't unveil the smoking gun or even a tiny whiff of smoke showing the contributions were improper and traceable to Java Connection. Without it, the jury couldn't connect the dots.

Snapping her thoughts back to the question Marshal Gagne had asked her, she tore back at him. "How do you know about my medical history?"

"If I'm going to protect you, Ms. Smith, I have to know everything about you. That's all. The stress you've undergone would naturally affect anyone. I would worry more if it hadn't affected you." Marshal Gagne said soothingly.

Jeannie felt somewhat diffused by the sincere concern in the Marshal's voice, but she was unsettled knowing this surly man was sitting around reading about her personal life and medical history. Of course, there was no use complaining, certainly not to Marshal Gagne, so she gave in and played along.

"I'm feeling a lot better, thank you. If I need anything else, I'll call you." Jeannie started to hang up, but said, "One more thing, Marshal."

"What's that, Ms. Smith?"

"Are you watching me all the time?" Jeannie wasn't sure if she wanted the answer to the question, but she had to ask.

"Don't worry, Ms. Smith, you are safe. Get on with your new life. Go do your shopping. If you need me, call."

Marshal Gagne didn't wait for more questions. He knew from personal experience that people got jumpy when they felt they were being watched. He needed Jeannie Smith to trust him, relax, and go about her business, not imagine danger in every bush and behind every corner and hounding him twenty-four, seven with her paranoid concerns. And if the rumors were true, that she was unstable, thinking he was following her might only increase the paranoia. And he needed her to feel comfortable so he could take care of the rest and do his job. One day soon, she'd find out exactly what that job was.

Chapter 9
Follow – I'll Lead

The conversation with Marshal Gagne and his non-response didn't sit well with Jeannie, recognizing a brush off. Truth was, if they were going to get her, they would accomplish it with or without an agent nearby. There were many scenarios of her own demise that tumbled through her mind. One of them had to come true.

Grabbing her purse and the keys to her new car, she exited through the garage door, carefully setting the alarm as she left. The non-descript silver SUV was not exactly her dream car, but it would do. In fact, the lipstick-red Mustang sitting in her father's garage was her dream car. She grimaced at the thought of her immature brother squealing around Malibu in *her* car. Okay, so Daddy had actually paid for the car, but it was a gift to her after the break-up with Roger, an emotional token of sympathy from her father and a bridge to endear her to him again. That was three years ago. Seemed she'd been treading in an ocean of water under that bridge since then.

Jeannie pressed the open button on the garage remote, started the SUV, and adjusted her seat to begin her exploration of the sprawling city awaiting her. After backing into the drive, she purposely watched the garage door close, then sat for a few moments doing a mental inventory check on whether she locked the door leading from the garage into the house.

What about the patio door? Surely, she locked the front door. Her thoughts somersaulted, finally halting when she checked the car door locks one last time and reassured herself the house alarm was on. She continued backing out into the cul-de-sac and wound her way through the wide streets leading out of the neighborhood to the main avenues. Venturing out into the public-eye was dangerous, especially considering the constant media watch throughout the trial that made her infamous.

Each house she passed looked like the next: bland and mundane. Nothing exciting or scandalous happened behind the doors she was eyeing as she drove through typical suburbia with cookie-cutter designs, varying only in the four subdivision floor plans and landscaping.

Feeling a little directionless, she tried to pick out an anchor in the sea of houses that opened up in front of her. Without one, finding the three steps leading to her builder-grade beige front door could be a challenge. Especially if she found herself sitting alone at a wine bar, toasting her loneliness with more than one glass of wine. Once she'd weaved her way through the maze of houses, it would be simple to walk into a stranger's house. That was a danger she didn't need.

As she drove and scanned the houses, no landmarks stood out. All the neighbors appeared to be in lockstep with the HOA requirements. The length of the long block came into focus in her rearview mirror, making it look endless as it stretched as far as she could see. She eased the car to the intersection, stopping at the sign. One Pepto Bismol colored flowerpot placed carefully on the front porch of the corner house caught her eye. Blue and yellow flowers spilled over the edge of the pot. That would be her anchor.

Once she'd emerged from the subdivision, she set her GPS and headed north until she located the first strip-center, flagged by a Super Walmart on one end and Ulta on the other. Smiling, she designated it as her first happy place in Houston, Texas. She would do all her shopping and pick up the makeup she needed. If only she could access her Ulta reward account she had as Rachel Rose, with hundreds of points and free gifts ready for redemption, this day would be perfect. Now they'd sit there until the end of time, lost, the same as Rachel Rose. Her shoulders relaxed before being swallowed up by the rows of cars and hordes of people. Somehow, being surrounded by innocent bystanders made her feel less conspicuous.

After a few "hellos" from strangers. She decided Texas was brimming with overly friendly people. Not the pretentious sort back home in Beverly Hills. Texans said things like, "excuse me, ma'am" and "pardon me, ma'am" and "let me get that for ya, little lady" and "howdy" followed by a chorus of twangy "y'alls" from every direction. It was impossible not to smile when that Southern drawl landed on her so poetically. She even tried out a few y'alls here and there. Maybe she would become a real live southern belle. Her grin continued to spread, sending a tickle of joy down her spine. It felt nice, capturing a moment of joy, even if it was short-lived, and only momentarily brought a tiny relief to her battered soul.

Meandering from aisle to aisle, and spending money that wasn't hers, something that felt natural, further raised her spirits. The thought of her high society friends frequenting Walmart was a vision that made her laugh out loud, garnering a half-smile and a quizzical look from the woman standing next to her, scrutinizing the shampoo. Still, it was a safe escape. Nobody glared at her, mistaking her for a street person or a loon. They smiled as if they understood and went on about their business.

By the time she stood in line to check out, dodging a few extremely tired and cranky children, she had almost drained herself of energy and good humor, concluding wisely that trips to Walmart, while initially joyful, must remain short and concise. The clerk made her smile though when she said, "y'all come back now, ya hear?" Jeannie giggled quietly all the way to the car. It was too stereotypical to believe, yet it was real, and this was her life now. The laughter was the only thing that could force away the tears that were perched precariously under the surface, so she embraced it.

Decision making on the makeup and hair products was easier. A jaunt through a drive-thru to pick up dinner, and it was time to retrace her path back to the house. Though the exit from the strip-mall appeared quite different from the entrance and she hesitated with which direction to take before darting onto the freeway ramp. It wasn't rush hour, but the traffic was heavy and reminiscent of California, perking her heart up a little as she switched from lane to lane with skilled maneuvers.

Having located her subdivision without too much consternation and no GPS, practicing in case she ever needed it, she began the search for Meadow Lane, the street she now called home. Checking her rearview mirror at the four-way stop leading into the subdivision, she spotted the tail. Jeannie was sure the dark Cadillac, three cars behind, had been at the shopping center. She wiped her hands, one at a time, on her yoga pants to remove the slight wetness that was coating her palms.

There was no way she was driving directly to her house and lead the enemy to her front door. Instead, she aborted her left turn towards home and detoured quickly to the right, climbing a hilly stretch of asphalt to the slightly higher-rent district. The houses were less uniform in this burb, more custom designed. The dark Cadillac maintained its course behind her. Taking a deep, slow breath, she took a sharp left and increased her speed down the meager hills, around the man-made pond with a fountain gracefully sending water catapulting through the air, into the next adjacent area where the houses loomed even larger and more luxurious. Long brick driveways appeared, inviting entrance to each mini mansion set back hundreds of feet from the narrow two-way street. Further down the road, she spied an entrance blocked by automatic gates.

Jeannie felt her breath quicken and her heart react, attempting to keep time with her shallow breath. She wiped her palms again, continuing to check and recheck her mirror. The dark Cadillac maintained its speed and continued following her lead. Jeannie turned to the right again to avoid the dead end she was barreling towards, not knowing if this counter-direction would be another trap inside a confined, wealthy neighborhood with no way out. As the traffic dwindled to a rare car, she felt a stir with the vibrations of shaking bubbling in her gut. The Cadillac had gradually closed the gap between them but still lurked behind with a comfortable distance.

She grappled with herself, as fear was determined to take control, but she straightened her shoulders, gripped the steering wheel, and retook command over her senses, lowering the window slightly to replace the air that was somehow magically sucked out of the car. Once her breathing slowed, she rolled her window back up as the car behind her edged closer. Turning without warning onto a long driveway, she punched the brake hard. An unexpected squeal escaped her tires when she locked them down. *Good, maybe they'd know she means business.* It was time to face her fear and her followers.

Massive trees lined the drive and sat in front of an eight-foot brick wall, allowing her no escape. She took a deep breath and exhaled slowly, grasping her cell phone, pausing her finger on the redial button to Marshal Gagne, and waited.

The dark Cadillac moved slowly on the street behind her, almost coming to a stop directly at the rear of her silver SUV. Jeannie twisted her neck, hoping to glimpse the face of the driver, but the dark tint on the windows hindered her view of the two men inside. The Cadillac bolted and increased its speed as it passed the driveway and disappeared from view. Jeannie dropped her head onto the back of her white knuckles clutching the steering wheel, took a slow breath, and composed the last shred of her nerves. She checked the locks again, still down and secure. Thankfully, the shaking drifted away.

She backed slowly out of the drive, checking both directions; the Cadillac was nowhere in sight. She placed the car in drive, then backtracked her route until the plush streets finally disappeared and the indistinguishable houses on Meadow Lane surrounded her.

Dozens of questions sped through her mind: Who was in the Cadillac? Had her father found her? Was it the FBI or the Marshals? The not knowing who was out there was the catalyst making her feel as crazy as her father's attorney claimed she was.

Finding her house with more ease than anticipated, she stared at the front porch, contemplating adding her own distinctive planter, while impatiently waiting for the garage door to open. She pulled in abruptly; the nerves climbed her spine quickly, forcing her to reflexively smash the close button, leaving no room for any uninvited guests to sneak in behind her.

Clumsily, she exited the car, bouncing off the doorframe as she made her way into the house, weighed down with shopping bags, collapsing on the sofa with her arms full. But instead of dissolving into a whimpering mess, this time she burst out laughing, a crazy, uncontrollable, soul-soothing laugh.

Chapter 10
Putting on the Ritz

Charles, the concierge at the Ritz Carlton, greeted the familiar senator with a warm hello. A routine of exchanging pleasantries they'd been performing for over thirty years.

"Hello, Charles! How are things going today?" Jay replied, extending his hand, grasping the man with a firm handshake.

"Fine, sir," he said as usual. It was his practice to tell all the guests he was fine, even though it was only true on rare occasions.

Relieving the senator of his bag, he signaled the clerk behind the desk, who, without a word between them, handed Charles the coveted key to the senator's suite before signaling the bellboy to deliver the senator's bag to his room.

"Your usual room, sir?" Charles said with a wide smile, pressing the card into the senator's hand. An implied wink was shared between the two men.

"Your usual tip?" Jay delivered a real wink at Charles, who accepted the money and slid it into his pocket.

"Are you expecting any guests, sir?"

"Yes, two constitutes will join me around eight p.m. and then my assistant will drop off some work."

"Very good, sir. I'll make sure you're not disturbed."

The two men went their separate directions, the senator off to his suite, which sat across town from his plush home, a regular destination to escape the eyes of his family to conduct business he'd rather not share with them. The other man to protect the senator's privacy and his own tips.

A perfectly prepared steak dinner, medium rare, a gold bucket with a bottle of chilled champagne, the glass already filled, bubbles still rising to the top, sat ready for him on the table in his suite flanked by the wall of windows overlooking the bay. All arranged for his insatiable appetite for the finest meals. Jay smiled, sat, and cut his sizzling steak while taking in the city view. Feeling his importance for the first time today. And to further lift his self-importance, he knew there was a waiter standing outside, down the hall, prepared to remove the table and empty plates at exactly 7:30 p.m.

Full and relaxed, sipping a whiskey-neat, the first knock on the door came precisely at eight. Jay swung the door open and greeted Mr. Ramirez and his associate. The men exchanged insincere pleasantries and sat down in the business area of the massive suite, eager to manage their shadowy dealings.

"As you know, we had to suspend our business arrangements with you while the trial played out and we were assured the operation was not compromised by your daughter's accusation. In fact, as you also know, my boss has been utilizing another supplier who's been managing deliveries for the past year and a half, and he's pleased with their service," Mr. Ramirez explained.

Jay was used to Mr. Ramirez and his dramatics, but he'd never met the other man, and he sat back to size him up carefully.

"Can your friend be trusted?" the senator asked Mr. Ramirez as if the other man were invisible, drawing an unpleasant look from Mr. Chavez, his small dark eyes suspiciously drilled into the senator.

"Absolutely. Mr. Chavez is an equal of mine. He comes with the same authority as I do. He's in charge of operations and I am in charge of distribution," Mr. Ramirez laid out in his heavy Colombian accent.

Mr. Chavez raised his hand to Mr. Ramirez, interrupting and taking over. "Please let me fill him in. Senator Rose, our operation depends on stable suppliers, delivery, and distribution. Now, in the past, you have provided a consistent line for distribution, and you've been able to do that discretely. But when the federal government had you under its eye, so to speak, it was not in our best interest to continue our association with you."

Jay uncrossed and recrossed his legs, listening patiently for the man to finish his spiel, knowing that somehow this was all leading to a cut in his percentage of the operation. The men continued explaining how the Colombian drug lords were taking greater risks of exposure every day, far greater now with the heightened awareness. He had created an almost impermeable system until his nosy daughter had been determined to undo him and tip off the feds. If not for her, nobody would have been any the wiser about his drug trafficking business. The senator remained calm and listened until he'd heard enough.

"Mr. Chavez, cut the bullshit."

The two Colombian men initially appeared shocked at the senator's stance, but there was an unspoken respect for his candor.

"You and I both know that you have no increased risk.

Besides, gentlemen, you are immersed in a risky business. I turned my head many times as attorney general in the early days when I should have come down on you. As far as your new supplier is concerned, I own him. He's under my control, something nobody has discovered, apparently not even you. So, you can continue with your current supplier, which is me, and to whom you are paying a higher percentage, or you can return to the original distributing arrangement with…me so I can get rid of the front man and reduce risks for all of us. Of course, my percentage will now increase since you've offended me in this way. So, gentlemen, it's really your decision. You can do business with me or do business with me."

Jay didn't need to smile. The smugness of his words was enough to send crimson climbing through the faces of the dark-skinned men.

"You are not a trustworthy man, Senator," Mr. Chavez sputtered.

"Compared to whom?" Jay's voice boomed through the room. "Mr. Chavez, I take care of myself. I watch my back and mine alone. You should watch yours." He sent his threat without a veil.

"What about your daughter?" Mr. Ramirez sat back in his chair, hoping to find either a way out or a way to salvage the meeting.

"My daughter is dead," Jay said without emotion edging his words. Though he considered her a loose thread, one that needed tying up. But he wouldn't discuss that with these business associates.

It grated on him that Rachel had the potential to destroy him. He needed to find her before anyone else did. Recalling the look on her face when he'd caught her rifling through his personal files in his home office, he was certain the look on his face at the time gave him away as well. She thought he was still in D.C., but he'd come home early to catch her in the act. Turning his anger loose in an uncontrolled explosion, losing his composure for a split-second, that's all it took.

"My daughter is no longer a threat, gentlemen, I assure you. Now, are we going to continue our business or not?"

The two men excused themselves as they conferred privately, voices raising ever so slightly, arguing in their native tongue. Finally, they appeared to agree and, with tones simmered, returned to join the senator, who was waiting calmly.

"Okay, Senator, we have a deal. We will continue with the arrangement in place at the prior percentage, plus a slight increase. Make sure there are no more slip-ups," Mr. Ramirez scolded.

"Wise choice, gentlemen, and a profitable one." Jay rose and gathered the champagne and glasses. He poured each man a glass. With clinking glasses, they toasted their continued profits. "To Java Connection," he said. The men nodded in agreement and smiled. After toasting, sipping, and exchanging idle chat, the men returned to business.

"Okay, gentlemen, I'm sure you're aware our government has recently put tighter restrictions on imports. I don't think any of our business will be affected. There's a bill pending in the Senate to increase security checks at certain ports of entry and imports from particular countries. Colombia is one of them. The bill has been tabled for now but will come back in front of the committee when we reconvene next week. You need to arrange for your ambassador to speak with Senator Marks,

Senator Gray, and Senator Willis. They are important committee members and the ones who will reformulate the bill."

The men leaned in and listened intently, making mental notes of the contacts. All details had to be committed to memory. Paper trails had undone many operations over the years.

"I'm familiar with Senator Gray. He and I have a history. I'll get a meeting with him," Mr. Ramirez said. Mr. Chavez nodded in agreement.

Jay didn't acknowledge the comment and continued explaining what he was orchestrating. "I'm asking to be removed from the committee so there's no appearance of any impropriety. The Ambassador needs to agree to increased security checks, but we need to suggest that to ease the U.S. burden, all Colombia imports come through six ports of our choosing, three east coast, two west coast and one in the gulf, instead of the more than 500 locales the ships can head into now."

"And we assume you have a plan for those ports?" Mr. Chavez said with a touch of sarcasm in his voice. Sitting back in his chair, he pulled his phone from his pocket, stared at it, and ignored the senator.

"Yes, I have a plan," Jay responded sharply. "You continue to ferry the cocaine on your private submarines off the Colombian coast to the steamers. Your captains haven't been consistent, and it's too risky with all the available ports. I have my underlings ready to keep our business off the radar. Once my security team is in place, I'll make sure the ships pass through the ports here. You handle matters on your end."

"How will you do that? This is a fool's plan. There are too many unknown players we're relying on to make this work."

Mr. Chavez said, his voice rising higher and higher before arguing in Spanish with Mr. Ramirez.

Jay sat back, staring at the man. He didn't particularly care for Mr. Chavez. An uncomfortable air fell over the room as a hushed silence settled. The men stared suspiciously at each other.

Without warning, Jay lurched and grabbed Mr. Chavez by the collar, shoving him backwards until the wall slammed their motion to a halt. He ripped the man's shirt open wide, sending buttons flying to the floor, exposing his bare chest.

"What are you doing?" he heard Mr. Ramirez scream behind him.

"Are you wired?" Jay screamed at Mr. Chavez, inches from the startled man's skinny face.

"No, I promise," he gasped as the senator's grip tightened around his nimble neck. So nimble that an enraged senator could easily snap it into.

Pressing the man tightly against the wall, Jay could see the fear in the man's dark, tiny eyes. Satisfied it was the truth, he released Mr. Chavez, straightened the torn shirt, patting him in apology.

Mr. Chavez gathered his composure, tried to reassemble his buttonless shirt, crossing the tails over each other, and tucked it in his slacks. Both men returned to their chairs as if nothing out of the ordinary had occurred.

The duo continued to listen intently as Jay finished laying out his plan. Mr. Chavez was still skeptical but opted to take it up with his associate after they left the volatile senator.

"I'll send word about when the inspections will be done and by whom, and your boss can time his deliveries to accommodate the schedule," Jay said.

"When will this go into place?" Mr. Ramirez asked.

"Soon. Get your distribution streamlined, so this will appear routine," Jay ordered, garnering satisfaction in handing out instructions and controlling the entire operation. He was the heavy on the U.S. end, and a nameless and faceless Colombian boss was the heavy on the other end. They were a good team. He took a long sip of his champagne and silently congratulated himself.

"One minute." Jay left the living area of the suite and walked to the bedroom.

The men glanced suspiciously at each other. Mr. Ramirez's knee bounced up and down in rapid, tiny movements.

Jay returned to the living area with a T-shirt in his hand; he tossed it to Mr. Chavez. "Put this over your shirt. You can hardly leave with a bare chest," he said without remorse.

"Thank you," Mr. Chavez said, catching the shirt. Opening it to see the silkscreened words "Washington, D.C." on the left breast pocket.

"Mr. Ramirez, please enjoy the cancer benefit. Here are the tickets I promised."

"Thank you, Senator. I'll be in touch after the event." He reached up as if to tip an imaginary hat.

The men nodded to the senator and rose to exit. Mr. Ramirez purposely positioning a black briefcase under the chair. Jay was familiar with the green content. He smiled in appreciation.

"Pleasure doing business, gentlemen," Jay said as he opened the door to his suite.

"And with you, Senator." The men disappeared into the

stairwell.

Jay placed the briefcase inside his own leather bag and prepared for his next visitor. He stripped off his suit, loosened his tie, and slid it from the crisp collar of his starched shirt, stepped out of his Italian shoes, and dropped the silk-lined Armani pants to the floor. After a refreshing hot shower, he wrapped himself in his new robe, a present from an old friend, and waited.

Tammy arrived on schedule. Jay cracked the door; it opened slightly, enough for her to slide into the room wearing a fur coat, as he'd instructed. It was November, after all. She waited for his command, then smiled and complied. As he told her to do, she wore nothing underneath. A crafty smile slid across his face. Tammy would get a raise tomorrow.

"Good girl, now come to papa." And she did.

Chapter 11

A Cup of Joe

For three days, Jeannie stayed barricaded in the house, not trusting the door locks, leading her to slide the bookcase against the front door while peeking through the blinds every hour to see if any suspicious cars were lurking about. The peculiarities she once assumed defined paranoia now sat solidly within her bones. The difference being that paranoid people had no good reason to think they were in danger. There were real people wanting to kill her, even though there'd never been an actual physical attempt on her life. But she knew it was only a matter of time before they found her. Sitting behind a barricaded door was being pragmatic, not paranoid.

Reporting the tail straight away to Marshal Gagne was the protocol she agreed to follow, but she'd convinced herself it wouldn't make a difference and ignored the rules. Today, after looking out the window too many times, she felt like a caged animal. A prisoner in her own home, surrounded by monotony. A monotony she had to escape before her mind circled in on itself one more time.

Grabbing her keys and locking everything tightly and double-checking each entrance so she wouldn't worry later whether she remembered to lock the doors, she set the alarm and stepped inside the garage and climbed into her SUV. Removing herself from the house instantly relaxed her muscles and lessened the pulsing behind her eyes.

Maneuvering the car out of the garage with caution and her head on a swivel, she edged down the driveway. Fortunately, seeing nothing unusual. Relaxing the grip on the steering wheel and exhaling in relief, she casually took notice of her surroundings.

The next-door neighbor was outside watering his lawn. It was fall, but the temperatures in Houston seemed to bounce up and down between pleasant to hot. The flowers were still in bloom, which brought a bit of happiness, but she still missed the temperate climate of California and the bougainvillea with its sweet honeysuckle-like fragrance that climbed on the arbors in the quaint backyard of her beachside condo.

The man gave a cautious wave to his strange new neighbor. Mentally, she noted he was about six feet tall, blonde hair, mid-forties, not unfit, but no bodybuilder, probably a golfer, eyeing the sock tan line circling his ankles. Maybe tennis, or the newest craze, pickleball. Lifting her hand in a half-hearted attempt at civility, she returned the wave.

Instead of exploring the direction toward Walmart that she'd already visited, after she reached the main highway, she spontaneously darted in the opposite direction. As the mall came into view, she cursed out loud and swerved across three lanes of busy city traffic to reach the exit that came upon her faster than anticipated. The car behind her lay on the horn at her maniacal driving.

"Oh, get over it," she shouted at the car, raising her middle finger. A behavior she never would have exhibited a few years earlier, but this new life was under her skin and breaking down her norms.

The mall parking lot seemed unusually busy for the middle of a workday, but it was Houston after all, with more than two million people, so it made sense that there could be many people off work. She rolled slowly into a parking space that provided a clear view of her car from the exterior of the building, so if anyone was waiting when she left the mall, she would spy them first.

Making a mental inventory of the few vehicles parked around her before she left the safety of her car in the barren parking lot, a wave of vulnerability surged through her. When her foot hit the pavement, the urgency to quicken her pace pushed her forward. A desperate need to reach the door of Nordstrom's pulsed through her head. Sucking in a deep breath, she lengthened her steps, only exhaling when the glass door shut firmly behind her.

The familiarity of the store helped release her anxiety. Landing in the shoe department further eased her mind. She released the last gasp of the breath she'd been holding. Picking up a slingback taupe sandal, checking the price, she smiled and leaned into the soothing environment, refusing to think of her budgetary constraints or her new faux life.

Having spent an inordinate amount of time in malls in all parts of the country, striding through the stores brought grounding intoxication. Feeling the pulse of the escalator rising to the top level, she watched the people below her, scanning faces, not knowing who she was looking for. Finally, her shoulders sank down as the safe environment melted over her, fashioning a firm decision that she would be a frequent visitor to enjoy the change of scenery and feel a bit more like herself and halt the destruction of the pieces of herself she once loved. The delicate pieces that were now feeling guilty for the rude behavior on the freeway.

As she mapped out the mall, she launched her adventure at Nordstroms, planning to walk the entire mall first, then return to Nordstroms at the end of her outing, so she didn't have to carry any bulky packages that might slow her down if she needed a quick escape. With the tension gone, a lightness returned to her skin as she walked through the wide corridors.

After enjoying a quiet and delicious meal at a faux bistro set in the middle of the foyer, and sipping a latte, the emerging Christmas decorations caught her eye. Considering the holidays was not a path she could venture down. Certain it would be a repeat of last year, alone with her microwave meal and remote control. There was no protective custody during those dark days, but there might as well have been with the trial underway and her family exiling her. The joyful days of the past her family spent together on holidays were a distant memory.

Closing her eyes, trying to force the thoughts away, was no use. Her mind couldn't help time-tripping to laughter and spontaneous grins when the family attended the Macy's Day Parade on Thanksgiving. Sweet memories from her teen years. The meaty fragrance of gourmet catered turkey dinners, the teetering piles of presents around the tree at Christmas, and the hot rich cocoa with Mabel's homemade whipped cream lining her lip as she sipped. Then further back to the most precious holiday memories many years earlier, when the family still held hands and bowed their heads in prayer, giving thanks for their good fortune. She would still give thanks this year, thanks that she was alive.

Forcing her holiday nostalgia out of her mind, she continued her cheery stroll until bright colors adorning a window distracted her. Focusing on the sign, it filled her with intrigue: Java Connection, the now famous, globally expanding coffeehouse. Serving overpriced coffee and pastries erupting on every street corner and mall in all the yuppie neighborhoods throughout the nation. It was also the same coffeehouse her father was using to smuggle drugs. The day she discovered the truth smashed into her, recalling the glimpse of the name as her father caught her red-handed and smacked her across the face. She touched the spot; the pain reoccurred momentarily, then disappeared.

Insidious anxiety surged in and out of her, piercing her nerves, not landing heavily as it usually did, instead bouncing around indiscriminately. Her stomach felt like Jell-O, yet a sudden curiosity filled her in a fresh way. She stared at the sign in the window. The hope of recovering her life flashed through her mind as she read: *Help Wanted.*

Moments ago, her inner self began believing she was content to walk away from it all, to let her life go on as well as the lives of her family, take up gardening, and cross-stitch, and live a peaceful and unnoticed life, but the sign beckoned her.

Pacing slowly outside the store's wall of windows, and biting the inside of her lip, she considered something dangerous and wild. A decision that could complicate her life tremendously and possibly get her killed if she was right. Maybe it was the Rose blood flowing coldly through her veins that told her she couldn't let it go. Maybe it was a suicidal tendency, or maybe she couldn't stand the thought of letting her corrupt father, Senator Jay Rose, win. Whatever it was, Jeannie stopped pacing, marched determinedly through the entrance, and asked for an application from the disinterested barista behind the counter.

"I saw the Help Wanted sign. I'd like to apply," she said.

"Sure," the kid said, continuing to stare robotically at his phone, pointing to the iPad on a stand at the end of the counter. "It's electronic, just tap it and it should pop up."

"Okay, thanks," she replied, moving to the end of the counter, activating the iPad to fill out the application with her new fake information.

When she arrived at the previous employment and educational background section, she panicked, then, without regret, lied, providing two fictitious employers, scribbling Marshal Gagne's phone number for one and skipping the contact information on the other. Finishing the application, typing in her real educational background with the wrong university. It was a history that would certainly raise eyebrows. She would have to alert Marshal Gagne to her little white lie; he could figure out how to cover her trail. She wanted this job. It was the perfect way to get inside. If she hadn't been able to do it from her father's side of the action, penetrating the business from this angle might do the trick.

Her hand quivered as she hit submit. She turned back to the bored, prickly boy standing behind the counter. "Do you know when I might hear from the manager?" Jeannie asked, using the most pleasant voice she could conjure.

"Yeah, the manager comes in about one. I'm sure he'll look it over then. He'll probably hire you tomorrow, cause I plan on quitting today." The pimply-faced barista sat down on the stool he had dragged behind the counter. Not standard operating procedure, Jeannie surmised.

"Well, if so, I could start right away. I moved here recently, and I need a job sooner than later." She wanted to sound eager, but not desperate.

"Okay, I'll let Tommy know, but it goes straight to his email. You're lucky. Typically, we only accept online applications that go to corporate for the screening process, and we never even see them. Corporate is a black hole though, so Tommy thought he better do the hiring himself if he wanted to find someone. Yours is the only application so far."

Tommy! Is everyone in this town twenty-one?

She wanted to grill the young man vehemently about the business. Instead, she said, "Thanks," and excused herself. Surrounded by youth, her natural instinct to obsess about her looks kicked in, not wanting to appear too old for the job. She needed a makeover and to treat herself to a shopping spree. Some retail therapy was in order and would make her feel better. This she knew was a proven fact. All the research she'd done on her own over the years proved it never failed.

Struggling with package upon package to get to her car with her new wardrobe violated Rule #13 of the "stay alert and wary" relocation handbook. It wasn't smart carrying so many bags, tying up both hands, and she knew that, but she didn't have any option, having gone overboard a bit. But when there's a sale, it would be foolhardy not to take advantage of discounts.

She scooted into the seat after struggling with the door, tossing the bags into the floorboard and onto the passenger seat. After locking the doors, she made an excited call to Marshal

Gagne. She punched in the security routine, then finally heard his depressing monotone voice.

"Guess what?" she said with preteen excitement.

"What?" He was not equally excited.

"I've applied for a job, and I think I might get it." There was no response at the other end of the line. "Did you hear me? I'm getting a job. Isn't that great?"

"You don't need a job. If you need more money, tell me and I'll see what I can do," the agent replied, clearly irritated with the news.

"It's not about the money, well maybe a little, but mostly I'm really bored. I need to meet people and talk to people. I need to be out in the world," she said enthusiastically. It was the first hope she'd felt in the past eight months. And it was true. Being locked up in the house gave her too much time to think, and too much time to visit ghosts.

"Not to rain on your parade, but I don't think this is a good idea. You need to lie low for a while. Give it some time, take up a hobby or something, not a job," Marshal Gagne barked.

"Look, I'm getting the job and you're going to help me," she ordered. The tone in her voice sounded similar to her father, causing her to recoil.

"Where is the job?" Marshal Gagne asked, hearing the determination in her voice.

Jeannie hesitated, knowing her next answer was not going to be received well. She said, "It's a coffeehouse."

"A coffeehouse?" Marshal Gagne said suspiciously, "What's the name of it? As if I don't already know."

There was no way around it if she wanted his help, so she told him the truth, "Java Connection." She waited for the explosion.

"Are you crazy?" he blustered.

She moved the cell phone away from her ear so her eardrum wouldn't rupture from the volume of his voice.

He continued shouting at her, "You are not working there, do you understand? You stay away from that place."

"Look, Marshal Gagne," she replied calmly, suppressing the anger simmering under the surface. "I don't even know where you are. We've met once for a brief minute. For all I know, you're sitting behind a desk in St. Louis or some other place, which does me absolutely no good. Three days ago, someone followed me. Did you know that? I didn't think so," she said, not waiting for an answer. She was providing her own answers. As she raged, she continued, "I don't trust you, and I certainly don't trust my slimy father. Now, you can either help me with this or you can sit behind your desk and pretend that I'm going to be okay if I wait around. I'm not going to be all right. And I'm not waiting idly by for him to come get me. Now, the question is, are you going to help me or not?" Her voice was shaking from her hysterical ranting, but she didn't care how she sounded. Nobody was going to deter her plan. She'd been playing by everyone's rules for far too long.

Marshal Gagne had been listening to all she said. He smiled sadistically at the other end of the phone, knowing she couldn't see him. The plan was unfolding as his boss predicted. It was only a matter of time before someone connected the dots and figured out where Jeannie Smith, aka Rachel Rose, was living. The information had come down to him that an investigator had been nosing around and been in the first two cities of placement, so the timeline had been accelerated.

He didn't tell her he already knew about the car following her a few days ago because it had been his men who got a little trigger-happy and wanted to scare her. That was not part of the plan. And since decisions were being made from above, he did what he was told, which was to keep her happy and get her back to California, so that's what he was going to do.

"Okay, Jeannie, I'm going to help you, but we're going to do this by my rules, especially if this gets dangerous. If you turn this into anything other than a stupid job, I can't promise I can protect you. And I'm to be informed every step of the way about what you're doing. And no digging into anything other than coffee grounds. I want to know how many lattes, double espressos, and cafe mochas you make every day. You got it?"

"Thank you, Agent Gagne, thank you. I promise, I'll play by your rules," she told him, knowing it was a lie.

She gave him all the pertinent information from her application so he could construct her fake life in case her background was checked. Her fake employment included his phone number and the info number as the reference contact. He'd better ensure that he answered the call.

Jeannie was reeling with glee when she hung up. She had no interest in making over-priced designer drinks, but everything else about Java Connection interested her greatly.

Marshal Gagne typed out the text message:

Subject proceeded as anticipated but faster than expected. Will continue watching until plans to lure her to CA are in place.

He hit send and watched the text fly away to his superior, then settled back to wait for further instructions.

Chapter 12

Get the Picture

He watched her sitting in the SUV, wondering why she hadn't started the car. But he was patient and could wait her out. It both amused and excited him to see her carelessly stroll to the car with her arms full. Oblivious of how close she was to becoming extinct. A big package-wielding target in the wide-open with no apparent witnesses around.

He'd deactivated the parking lot cameras two days ago after "vandals" did their damage. Jeannie, aka Rachel, thought she was clever, but she'd let her guard down, falsely assuming the government was protecting her. He was right when he'd suggested to his superiors the mall would be one of the first places she'd go. This might be easier than he thought.

He opened the envelope, the black gloves scraping the thick manila material. Pulling the photo out, he compared it to the woman in front of him. Certainly not much resemblance anymore, except for the body. The body was fit, supple, and inviting. A lustful grin slid across his thin face when he thought of the body. The hair was too short for his taste, but who cared? He preferred the long blonde hair, but the new brunette style would do.

He already knew which direction she'd take when leaving the lot, having done surveillance a few days earlier when she went on her wild scramble, trying to shake Gagne's flunkies when they tailed her. Now he snapped photos of her inside the SUV. His boss would be ecstatic when he produced this proof of life. Though the assignment confused him, wondering why the order had only been to acquire photos of her and not finish the job. Why the delay?

They'd known where she was since the day after the inept marshals whisked her out of California. His boss quashing his questions, only telling him that "timing was everything" and "it would be handled at the top." Ironically, it was killing him to wait. He fought his instinct to sneak into the back of the SUV and quietly break her pretty little neck instead of pressing the button opening and closing the shutter of his camera, compiling a trove of digital images.

Finally, she started the car and pulled from the lot. He waited to follow, watching for any other tails. He would trail her in good time, turning off before she suspected anything. There were no apparent agents watching her today, at least none he could make. In spite of his frustration with his assignment, he was a good soldier. And his boss seemed to know the answers to his questions. Not divulging the information to a low-level like him was standard operating procedure.

Besides, in the organization, doing as you were told and keeping your lip zipped was the only path to earn your stripes and move up. It was time to move up. After serving as a lackey for two years, he was getting impatient. This moment was no different. Watching the careless girl was more than he could bear. She must really be crazy, he decided, as she nonchalantly meandered home.

With the information gathered, he diverted his path, exited, and headed for the airport, back to California. As far as finishing off Rachel Rose, there was nothing to do yet, not until he got the signal. He'd waited this long for the senator's daughter. What did a few more days matter? Maybe if these photos were good enough, the next time he saw Rachel Rose, it would be face-to-face. Then, he could explore that body, not just admire her in photos.

Chapter 13
The Senator - D.C. Moves

Senator Rose landed in Washington, secretly glad the session was resuming so he could escape the prying eyes back home in California. The games of D.C. and the hobnobbing he was required to do on behalf of his constituents suited him. After-hour cocktail parties replete with eager young interns, anxiously waiting to be educated by the knowledgeable senators, made his days worthwhile and appropriately stoked his ego. D.C. was also full of financial opportunities for the industrious like him.

Gazing around at the monuments as the limo delivered him to Capitol Hill for his meeting, he knew the traditions like trading votes on issues, sometimes for money under the table, sometimes for other favors, were also embedded in D.C. history.

The committee sessions he was returning for were long but only attended by a select group of senators. He'd been part of that select group beginning decades ago when he learned who to suck up to. The meetings were an opportunity to formulate game plans to advance the party's particular agenda.

Sitting at the long conference table, he analyzed each colleague, recalling the history and indiscretions of each. Tucking away his valuable mental notes. Nearly all the senators and the representatives had their share of indiscretions, some more than others. And some, more public than others. All had an Achilles' heel, and he'd found it on each and every unsuspecting public servant.

He first surveyed Senator Billings, a man with a lust for the new young male staffers. His vote was locked up. It was shocking that Billings had kept his secret for the past seventeen years. It wasn't the worst behavior Jay had seen in a senator, but he was grateful for the proclivity, so he could exploit it without remorse. And something he'd stumbled upon innocently enough when the controversial debate over policies about gays in the military hit the floor.

An unplanned late-night visit to Senator Billings's office to discuss the bill led him to the discovery. The lights were off in the outer office, but the doors unwisely unlocked. After entering the private office, expecting to find Senator Billings behind his desk, ironically adorned with pictures of his wife and kids, he instead discovered Billings precariously perched on the conference room table in an extremely compromising position with a young male staffer fresh from the Ivy League.

Truth was, nobody cared about what Billings did in his private life except his wife, who would divorce him and pack up her substantial trust fund when she moved back to her palatial family estate in Connecticut. Mrs. Billings was the wind beneath his wings, or technically the green beneath his wings, and responsible for supporting everything that created Senator Billings and kept him in office. Without her, he had nothing except disgrace and banishment from his family. Her ruthlessness was common knowledge, as was the fact that she ran the marriage. From Jay's point of view, Senator Billings should feel indebted to him for continued silence about the entire incident.

The next senator was Willis, a plump, ruddy-faced man who liked to play both sides against the middle. He was a hard one to figure out; it was anybody's guess which way he would vote, and he appeared to be overly considerate about the heart of the issues instead of being a political operative, but he too had a weak spot waiting for Jay to exploit.

Even though Willis was a conscientious advocate for his voters, he was a lonely man. His appearance was not one that attracted the ladies, and while he was good in front of a crowd, his one-on-one with the opposite sex was painful to watch. Enjoying the gifts Jay periodically sent to him had done the trick over the years, with Willis being the trick. Jay would pull the trigger on that resource when necessary.

Senator Gray was next, and easy to work with if your issue fell on his side of the aisle, a pure party-line guy, right down the Democratic line with no coloring outside of it. Standard operating procedure for Gray during the past seven years he'd been in office. There would be no surprises with him. The party would support the import inspection issue, and Senator Gray would understand how limiting inspections from Colombia to only six ports of entry would maintain the impression of cohesive international appeasement yet satisfy the need for national security checks. He would vote for it since the bill was being introduced by the Democrats.

The only wild card Jay saw in all the men sitting across from him was the party leader, Johnstone, who had come out publicly against the bill prior to the meeting. Of course, now that Jay was back in D.C., he could explain to Johnstone the important details of the bill. They were drinking buddies after all, and as the drinks added up, Johnstone always became more persuadable. If that failed, he would secure support the good old-fashioned way: money.

Their families had been engaged in the reciprocal practice for as long as both had been in politics. The summer vacations at Martha's Vineyard partaken strictly to settle scores and to give the media juicy, exclusive photos with an occasional bipartisan soundbite for the news, particularly in election years.

The last on the list was Waters, a party-line Republican. He would be the hardest to roll because of a logistical issue: no information on the man. There were no rumors on the floor or in the halls about indiscretions. The photos of his happy family appeared to be real; a beautiful wife, two perfect kids, one boy and one girl. Of course, Jay knew better than anyone that looks could be deceiving. He had similar photos sitting on his desk of his now fractured family. But there had to be a way to get to Waters. Jay was a master at performing discreet digging and would eventually unearth any torrid details if they existed.

The conversations were taking place among the committee members while Jay ran through his alternate options in his head. He'd stopped listening to Senator Johnstone, who was droning on about a security issue out of the Middle East. Jay planned to excuse himself from the committee vote when the topic of the import inspections came to the table. Until then, he would work the senators quietly behind the scenes. For now, he was bored.

"So, why don't we wrap things up for the day, men?" Jay suggested.

"Great idea," Senator Billings agreed, glancing at the staffer who had just delivered fresh coffee.

"Let's go to The Watergate. There's an informal cocktail party over there for our welcome back," Senator Johnstone offered.

"Shall we, gentlemen?" Jay asked.

With everyone in agreement, they adjourned to the Watergate to meet the fresh group of interns and the other legislators who had returned to work. Jay put his hand on Willis's back, patting him encouragingly as the men went to mingle and drink. Many deals were cut over cocktails, and it was an unavoidable part of being a senator.

Jay had perfected his own method in playing this game, pretending to drink a lot, filling the young newbies with alcohol and then listening carefully as they divulged more than they should. It was entertaining to watch their enthusiasm to make their mark on the world, an enthusiasm that usually increased with each drink they downed. Having endured one session by now, they thought they had a handle on the process and the system.

They weren't necessarily wrong, just naïve. Jay knew there would also be seasoned skeptical senators lurking about, wondering if he was a drug lord, but he liked to believe most of those dark days were behind him as he re-solidified his place in the senate.

At the first session a few months ago following his acquittal, sympathy was the most common emotion shown by his colleagues on his side of the aisle. The other side exhibited disapproving glares but soon extended him more and more latitude and understanding as time passed and with the news of Rachel's demise. Surely by this session, Jay and his alleged ties to the Colombian drug lords would be old, forgotten news. If he were lucky, a new juicier scandal would erupt, and it would be business as usual. If one didn't present itself, perhaps he would create one.

The media is an extremely fickle and gullible animal. The more personal and outlandish the drama, the more they want to fuel it and report on it, especially if the word Russia or racism is embedded in the mix. In the old days, the years when his father was in office and Jay was young and still believed in honor, the media protected certain political families, including his. They didn't report on infidelity; it was a private and common issue, or about buying votes through outlandish trades and compromises. Even the increasing power of lobbyists was watered down.

But now, any story that furthers the covert agenda of corporate media and has tabloid quality and can generate social media views, likes, and comments is fair game. It's been proven, the more controversial the story, the more the media jumps on it. Controversy, and getting the public fighting online, drive social media analytics through the roof. Division of the people sells news. Division makes money. Division builds conglomerate empires.

The media moguls, with their outlandish salaries and extravagant perks, encourage the sharks to continue the bloody kill with the creation of fake news stories and slanted opinions to gain an edge over the competition. The climbers and wannabes stepping on or sleeping with whomever necessary to get the big break that will send them to the top of the pack. All driven by the bottom line. The corporate boys watch it play out with encouragement of the ruthless cyclones to keep their pockets fat.

In the "information age" it is more difficult to find and

maintain a scoop for any length of time. Once it hits one wire, it burns through platforms like wildfire. And by the time it rolls through, the lead story that started as a wisp of smoke within one news cycle erupts into a five-alarm fire. Driving the feeding frenzy over and over as the original reporters dig harder to get more evidence, better experts, and produce spin doctors to boost their Nielson ratings.

The media being one of the most corrupt players of all in shaping public opinion and influencing the wave of sentiment across America. A freight train headed downhill with nobody to stop it. Their power supreme after acquiring company after company, building indestructible monopolies to control opinions and influence thought. Nobody daring to take them on. They have the power to make or break you, so it is wiser to play the game. Sadly, journalism had taken a nosedive over the years and landed face-down in the gutter. Jay Rose had done his best to avoid the sewage filled gutters.

Jay smiled as he sipped his scotch. "So, what do think, Charlie?" he asked Senator Gray. "You think we can get our bills pushed through this session without too much wrangling and horse-trading?"

"I think so. The issues are pretty cut and dried, not too much to fight about."

"I hope not. I'm not in the mood for a fight these days, at least not this session." He didn't want to spend all his time behind heavy wooden doors pondering a stack of bills that would be buried before a vote. He knew the import bill would make it out of committee and to the floor because it was being pushed hard as part of a security package the president was endorsing.

"Well, it's nearing an election cycle, so I wouldn't count

on anything being too easy or predictable, at least not for the next year or so." Senator Gray said.

"Oh yes, the glorious election years, putting our jobs under a microscope. Let's hope this is one of the smooth years," Jay smiled, tossing back the last of his drink. "I think I'll go mingle and see if I can hear anything that might cause us late nights," he joked with the senator.

"Always keeping your ear to the ground. It's helpful, Jay. Glad you're back and all your struggles from last year are behind you. I think of how painful it must have been to lose Rachel," Senator Gray told him, shaking his hand as they departed.

"Thanks. It's a lot to handle but staying busy helps." Jay sighed, knowing it was a temporary pain, at least until he found her.

Jay spotted the women gathering at the bar across the room. Even with their designer dresses and handbags, he knew they were all high-dollar escorts brought in for such events. He was familiar with them, and they him.

"Hello Marla, why don't we get out of here," he discreetly whispered in the ear of a leggy brunette, as he leaned to set his empty glass on the bar behind her, knowing it would magically be filled without a word.

She tucked her dark hair behind her ear, allowing a discreet kiss to be placed on the nape of her neck. None of the other senators were paying attention, but it was important to try to appear somewhat respectable. Over the years, it seemed the other congressmen and senators had lost interest in Jay's fidelity, probably because Jay didn't care if they knew what he did in D.C., most likely because they, too, were engaging in their own extracurricular activities.

He scooped up his new drink and made his exit, moving toward his apartment on the top floor of The Watergate. Marla was intimately familiar with the routine and would follow in half an hour. She didn't particularly enjoy the senator's company, but she was afraid of alienating him. He wielded a lot of power in Washington. Besides, she'd heard the stories about Natalie, who was exclusive to the senator a few years ago, before she disappeared.

Natalie was sweet, but too trusting, wanting to find her white knight. Marla had spent many evenings listening to her talk about living in North Dakota, missing the simple days. Natalie was a lost girl. That's how Marla and her friends categorized her type, the naïve ones that ended up as high-dollar callgirls because they had no other plan to survive. The truth was, they were all lost, but some more than others. A few finding they had no choice, others finding "the life" too easy to refuse.

Natalie, with her natural girl-next-door beauty, had been on the streets since the day after she turned eighteen, her family dirt poor. Scraping to send money back home as often as she could and feeling guilty for the high life she had been moving toward, though not feeling guilty for how she was earning the life of shiny trinkets. It was a necessity.

It had taken her ten years to become a regular on the D.C. circuit, and her work sufficiently provided for her family back home, who never questioned where or how the money appeared. At least until Natalie vanished, and the money stopped. Then the questions didn't end. Nobody had seen or heard from her for more than a year, maybe two. Marla had lost track as long days and longer nights morphed together, contorting the years that passed too quickly, but also too slowly.

Consoling themselves over Natalie's disappearance, the regulars rationalized, for their own sanity, that maybe she'd gone back to North Dakota.

Maybe she found self-respect.

Marla knew neither was true. Natalie's cousin had come around asking about her whereabouts, most likely out of concern about the money, showing a photo around, finding nobody who would admit they knew her. The police were too busy to help find a missing hooker. Marla had consoled the cousin for a few moments before wishing her well with the search.

After tossing down the last of the bitter drink before leaving to meet the senator, Marla pulled out her compact and touched up her lipstick, staring a bit too long as thoughts of Natalie webbed into her heart. Nobody knew the truth.

One rumor circulating was that Jay had tucked her away on a little island somewhere with a stack of money. Counter to that was another, more realistic rumor that she was dead, but her body hadn't turned up, which gave Marla emotional license not to believe it and instead chalk it up as a famous D.C. tall tale. Besides, it had been so long now that most people had forgotten about Natalie, everyone except Marla, even as much as she tried to erase that sweet smile from her memory banks. There were no more conversations or speculation about where Natalie was. It was dangerous to ask too many questions, a skill she'd also learned over her past twenty years in D.C., so she kept her questions to herself.

Scooting off the comfortable bar chair, Marla headed toward the elevator. She found the senator's preference in sexual escapades particularly distasteful. He enjoyed domination gimmicks, most of which she thought were degrading and sometimes painful. But he was a dependable customer and, if he liked setting women up with a new life on a private island with suitcases full of cash, she was willing to be his next victim. Plus, she had a price, and it was high, and tonight it would be doubled.

Reluctantly, she pushed the button to the penthouse, releasing an anxious sigh. Counting the money she would receive by morning while mentally listing all the pretty things she would buy tomorrow afternoon. One-by-one, the floors ticked off as she ascended to meet the senator. She sighed again as the elevators opened, hesitating momentarily before sinking her designer stiletto into the plush carpet of the hallway leading to the despicable Jay Rose.

Chapter 14

Business as Usual

Marla pushed the senator off her legs. He was deadweight. The irritation his snoring was inflicting upon her was enough to make her consider quieting it with the pillow knocked to the floor earlier in the night. Finally, deciding it was a poorly formed idea because he was certain to become combative, overpower her, and kill her instead.

Slyly, she extricated herself and slipped into the bathroom. The cold water she splashed on her face didn't seem to faze the lingering effects of the vodka she had so easily sipped last night. But it was a necessary ingredient to spend the night with Jay Rose. She rubbed her sore wrists. The gradient lines caused by the rope darkening by the minute.

God, I'm a fool.

She scolded herself, examining her neckline for any remnants of last night's escapade. Fortunately, there were none. Quickly, she dressed, brushed her hair, and repaired the makeup that hid the deep lines and weathering of her advancing years. Despite all her efforts to keep the years at bay, she knew it was only a matter of time before she'd be forced to retire. Her youth had slipped away, a death knell in her profession. She tiptoed out of the bathroom to make her getaway.

It was hard not to feel nauseous while she stared with disgust at the sleeping senator. Perhaps he wasn't worth the trouble. Spying his wallet lying exposed on the dresser, she couldn't resist the temptation. Like the expert she was, she peeled the leather open without a sound and browsed the contents. She removed an extra three hundred for the wrist burns and replaced the wallet cautiously, then eased out of the room, gingerly closing the door. She was an expert at silent departures.

Jay woke slowly. The sun hadn't been up long; the room was beginning to come to life. He was typically awake before now, but last night Marla cramped his style.

He checked the opposite side of the bed; it was empty. Relief shot through him. Sharing the dark of night with Marla was one thing, but he had no intention of entertaining her in the daylight. The last thing he wanted in his ear was the voice of that woman. With no obstructions to his daily plan, he rolled out of bed and strode to the shower.

Refreshed and ready to participate in his favorite pastime, making money, he connected his laptop and withdrew Mr. Ramirez's business card from his wallet, noticing that Marla had lightened it. It was not unexpected, but he had more pressing business. He would deal with Marla later.

Holding the card flat in front of him and examining it carefully in the light, he finally located the hidden raised numbers. He logged onto the Internet and entered the numbers on the Java Connection webpage. The screen flashed, and a secure private portal opened before him. Within seconds, a second private chat room appeared. The person on the other end was waiting for his entry.

Jay typed in his code, and the chat began with the unknown individual he'd been trying to unmask for the past year. All he knew was the screen name: BogataOne. A disadvantage since BogataOne knew his screen name: BostonPop along with his real name and true identity. It didn't sit well with the senator to be at a disadvantage. That's not how he managed his life.

"Is everything set up?" Jay pecked out on the keyboard.

"It's ready. Here's the link." BogataOne typed back, providing the link in the chat.

The senator anxiously clicked on the coded link. After the security check and scrambling of IP addresses, the screen lit up with lines and lines of inventory and corresponding currency available from the cartel distributor points across North America.

"Thanks. Let me review this." Jay sent his message.

"Ping me when you're ready to continue," BogataOne responded.

Jay studied the list as most men do the stock market page in the daily paper. Excitement pulsed through his veins as he stared at the screen and considered the dangerous game he'd been playing, not letting that diminish his rush while calculating the money he would make with a single stroke of the computer key. He had become a pro at money laundering and was turning profits month-over-month. Java Connection had been the perfect front. And the money was far more than he would ever make by debating legislative drivel in Washington.

The electricity surging through him now mirrored that of the campaign trail many years ago. The power, the prestige, the doors that opened which would have otherwise slammed shut in his face. He beamed at the ingenuity of his newest business venture. If only Rachel had been more loyal, he would have shared this perk of the Rose family ingenuity with his treasured daughter.

For years, Jay had taken Rachel under his wing, taught her, spoiled her, all to bring her to the pinnacle of his world. His heart became full of pride at the thought of his beautiful daughter overtaking him, only to be deflated by her betrayal. Unfortunately, Rachel inherited her mother's cautious virtue, and Roger had intensified her do-gooder persona.

It wasn't fair that his only son, Scott, was lacking in ambition and intelligence and that his daughter was the recipient of those gifts. He could have shaped Scott into a mold of himself, but it was too reckless to chance with his unpredictable son. A boy who was simply not bright enough or sturdy enough to take over crafty endeavors, a momma's boy. He'd told Linda when Scott was born not to spoil him, to make him tough. But she insisted on pampering him and giving him everything he wanted. It was when the teachers implored him to place Scott in special education for an attention issue that Jay had given up.

That's when Linda swooped in with her tutors and her mothering, and Jay lost the boy completely. He accepted the fact that Scott would never be the successor to the high and mighty Rose family. With full attention turned to Rachel, she flourished and impressed him. Graduating valedictorian and summa cum laude from Harvard. His chest still expanded when he recalled the press release he spent hours working on, the fatherly pride shouting through each word he carefully crafted.

The memories wrapped around his heart, then ripped it open again as he pictured her face staring at him from the witness chair. Her disappointment was obvious, and on display for the world to see, the anger in her eyes, the coldness. It slapped him harshly, particularly given all he had done for her and the life he'd provided. For Christ's sake, she was his princess, and she still plunged a knife wickedly into his back. When she spoke in the courtroom, each word burned a hole in his heart until it fell away in ashes, her pretend tears washing the remnants away forever.

When Linda confronted him regarding the allegations, he had even convinced her that Rachel had gone mad. In the end, Linda finally believed her only daughter had truly broken with reality, and hopefully, she now believed Rachel was gone. He pitied his wife and her blind acceptance.

"Perhaps if you had listened to me and not coddled Scott, you would have been around to have observed Rachel more," he told her after Rachel's supposed death.

"You're a cruel man, Jay Rose. When did you become your mother?" She'd slung her arrows back at him before succumbing to her reclusive mourning, retreating further from Jay, which pleased him.

He shook the thoughts from his mind; all pointless now. Today, he was back on top of his game; a satisfaction that months ago, he wasn't certain he would experience again when the trial began. He'd manipulated his family into the positions he wanted, all except Rachel. He'd lost control of her but would soon regain it. She had committed the ultimate betrayal a daughter could against a father, gouging a wound deep in his heart, worse than any other in his life, and the deepest cut a man could possibly endure. A father betrayed by his own blood.

The flashing cursor snapped the senator back to the task at hand. There would be plenty of time for nostalgia in the days to come.

With a click of the mouse, he opened the drop intercepts, committing the dates and destinations to memory. The routine was the same: Java Connection trucks meet the ships to offload the coffee, transport it to the warehouse, separate the drugs, load the cargo into the linen trucks owned by the senator, though the trucks were now labeled *Growley's Bakery*, then drop the drugs at select restaurants to the dealers who knew what to do.

It ran like clockwork. Once a week, every week, he pedaled cocaine. Long ago he'd been offered a chance to jump into the fentanyl market, but even his immorality had limits. Cocaine was the choice of bankers, computer geeks, CEOs, and senators. It was his world. He had no intention or desire to kill unsuspecting innocent teenagers. He magnanimously steered clear of the fentanyl game.

"Inventory on the fourteenth needs to reroute through Miami. Snow expected in New York," the senator sent the message to BogataOne.

"Confirming weather report. Will try Miami on the thirteenth unless rain is in the forecast. Otherwise, Galveston will be the final port," BogataOne answered.

"Seattle expecting clear weather on the twentieth. All ports closed to inspection that day."

"Twentieth confirmed. Order will be processed. Thanks for your report." The final message from BogataOne read.

Jay logged off the web portal and switched to his favorite site: Whitehousedolls.com, the most popular porn site for all self-important senators.

BogataOne enjoyed his exchanges with the clever senator. He reviewed the list of dates and drops. He was proud to be the creator of the cartel's most innovative communication system. The state-of-the-art scrambling of the web, the private chat rooms for business transactions. He'd developed AI technology preventing hackers from tracking his business and allowed the cartel to monitor its own members down to the fine details of their lives and every move they made on websites, phones, and email, rooting out any informants who became greedy for DEA reward money. If they made a keystroke, it was documented and tracked. Members were trusted only until they left the sight of the bosses, then, they were watched.

Since the trial and the snooping around of agents from every alphabet soup agency, he'd developed a new AI dark-web program that allowed constant wiretapping of all communications by the cartel, whether phone, text, or email. Calls were continually re-routed to avoid traces and control their members' receipt of information. The only activity the cartel could not completely monitor was person-to-person communications, but of course, it never got that far. Uncovering turncoats and thwarting in-person meets or ensuring they were final meetings was how the cartel dealt with traitors.

The last DEA agent that tried to infiltrate the inner circle didn't live to tell the tale. Instead, his ashes had been scattered across the rugged terrain of Colombia in the company of many others who believed they could outsmart the higher-ups. Some met their fate slowly, depending on what kind of information they were planning to divulge. Others were of such little consequence that a quick bullet to the head and a drop into cold shark-infested waters did the trick.

BogataOne smiled, satisfied with himself. Nobody had to know he didn't do the actual programming, but sat as the mastermind behind it all, the one who found the perfect geek to create what he needed, assuring his ascension to the top of the organization. Particularly since he'd earned the trust of Julio Leguardo, the head of the cartel, who had faith in his abilities that others doubted. In fact, Julio had so much confidence in him that he graciously assigned him the latest mission, Senator Rose. The boss treated him with respect and pride, like an adored son. And as BogataOne, he would complete this challenge and receive a handsome reward. A bonus paid on delivery. First the senator, then the lovely daughter.

He propped his over-priced high-tops on the large oak desk and stared out the window at the majestic California surf.

Chapter 15
Brew and Seek

Jeannie's cell phone vibrated, the screen lighting up with an unknown number. A likely probability, with only two contacts on her phone. She weighed the decision to answer, but the anticipation of the call being about the job overrode her paranoia of being discovered.

"Hello, this is Jeannie."

"Jeannie, this is Tommy from Java Connection," he said between nervous gasps of air.

"Yes, Tommy. I was hoping to hear from you," she said.

He cleared his throat. "Good. I'm calling about the job. I've reviewed your application. You are way overqualified for this job. You do know it's a barista job, don't you?"

"Yes, I know. But it's exactly what I need right now. It isn't a problem for me if it isn't a problem for you." She couldn't let this chance slip away.

"No, it's fine with me. But it only pays minimum wage. You understand that as well, right?"

She couldn't decide if he was trying to talk her out of the job or afraid she'd quit on day two of the job. "I know. It's fine. I assumed that was the case," she said, trying to remain optimistic.

"Okay. You can work as much as you want. I need all weekday shifts covered, no weekends. I have a college student that works weekends and a couple of nights. You would open in the mornings. I'll close. Of course, I'll be there in the mornings as well until you get acclimated."

"That sounds perfect. When would you want me to start?" she said, trying to contain her excitement.

"If you can come today. It's eight now. We open at ten, but I had a barista quit without warning, and I'm shorthanded," he told her, a heavy sigh hidden behind his words. "Normally it will be nine to six with an hour for lunch."

"Perfect. I'll get dressed and head over." She smiled, feeling a surge of giddiness as she hung up the phone. The plan was falling into place. It had to work. There was evidence somewhere, and she was going to prove to the world that she was not the "*Troubled Daughter*" of Senator Rose.

Grabbing the bags from the mall, she dumped the spoils of her shopping trip onto the bed. Picking through the new slacks, she selected a black pair and a turquoise top, one of the Java brand colors. A tickle ran through her, not spurned by anticipation for the job she was about to undertake, or serving lattes, but the job she'd be doing out of the sight of observant eyes.

Dressing quickly, she jumped into the car, barely remembering the drive to the mall. She'd pushed aside her normal safety precautions of acute awareness, her mind instead preoccupied with calculating how to gain access to the information she would need.

She parked on the desolate side of the mall, forgetting rule #7 of not frequenting dark, isolated areas, since her walk back to the car would be under cover of night with the sun setting just after five p.m.

Jeannie strode into the mall, down the corridors, and through the doors of her path to liberation. "Good morning. I'm Jeannie." She shook Tommy's hand.

"Hi. I'm Tommy. Welcome to Java Connection. Thanks for being on time. That's unheard of for my typical employee."

"Well, that won't be a problem for me. I actually have a bit of a hangup about being punctual."

"You'll be employee of the month then, probably employee of the year." Tommy handed her an apron with the script letters of the company name and logo silk-screened across the front. She tied it on, running her hand over the words Java Connection.

Following Tommy closely as he oriented her to the forty-by-forty square feet of the satellite location, she listened intently as he meticulously explained the ins and outs of the supplies, the vendors, where the baked goods were to be placed, and how and when to restock. Delivering all details with a hushed look of seriousness, as if he was divulging the codes to the nuclear bomb. When he moved on to how the machines worked, he suggested Jeannie take notes, which she did to appease him, even though she confirmed there were instruction and recipe cards sitting at the base of each machine.

Tommy spoke fast, and she had to commend him on his knowledge of how to create a multitude of beverages with limitless combinations of ingredients needed to produce the overpriced drinks. All from memory.

Jeannie picked up the business end of things easily, but the actual blending of the specialty coffees gave her pause. When the doors opened, she was genuinely nervous, faced with the reality of performing the job of a barista. The morning flew by as she tried to remember how much to measure, pour, blend, shake, and sprinkle in the magic concoctions. She felt more like a coffee bartender than a barista. Having to depend heavily on the recipe cards and her young boss with his fountain of knowledge. By lunch, her rhythm was flowing as she began to master the art of coffee, with the ingredients for the most common orders popping into her mind without looking at the cheat sheets. Yet still grateful when an order consisted of a simple coffee with cream. Understanding the never-ending combinations as customers rattled off their favorite drinks was further complicated by deep southern drawls; many orders became lost in translation.

Tommy must have decided she was capable because he congratulated her on being a quick learner and told her he'd be back before the afternoon rush, mostly commuters partaking in a quick pick-me-up for the drive home.

"But what if I have a question about something?" She rushed after him, inserting herself between him and the exit.

As if he took mercy on her, he retreated back behind the counter and down the short hallway to his office, emerging with a white binder covered with a colorful logo on the front, and handed it to her on his way back out the door.

"All the answers are in here, and anything you can't find is in the computer. This book even tells you how to get on the computer. Bye now." He was gone before Jeannie could protest. Staring at the massive binder, a warm feeling of success ebbed through her.

Everything I need to know is in the book.

Jeannie flipped the cover open to the first page, finding the instructions to access the computer neatly typed at the top of the page. Haphazardly placed yellow sticky notes revealed the passwords. Jeannie smiled. Tommy's lack of concern about company security worked in her favor. She turned the page and found Tommy's password for the manager portal, hand-scratched in the margin.

With no customers lurking about, she went straight to the computer and typed in the password. The screen blinked, the hard drive hummed, and the page pixelated the scrolling words of Java Connection and reformed into the words *Welcome to the Inner World of Java Connection.*

Weighing her page navigation options, she tapped the corporate structure button, leading her to the company organizational chart and bios of all the top executives. She printed them quickly so she could study them later. Clicking on the world icon, it took her to the worldwide distribution map with schedules for both the United States and the limited European locations, mostly airports. She printed both. Interrupted by the door chime, she peeked out, seeing a customer standing at the counter. Forced to log out, she snatched the papers from the printer, folded the pages, and crammed them into her pocket.

A steady flow of customers continued until Tommy returned to the store that evening. The rush ended along with her shift. She hurried to gather her things and retreat to her house, where she could study the information and log on to her own computer and continue searching for the connection to her father that she'd failed to find the first go-round.

Jeannie scampered through the parking lot. The sky was

dark, a fact that took her by surprise as she crossed the desolate asphalt.

Glancing from side-to-side as she walked, she plunged her hand into her purse to find her keys and retreat to the safety of her car, then pulled her jacket tighter as she walked, bracing herself against an unanticipated chill. The closer she got to the vehicle, the harder she concentrated. It hadn't seemed so far away when she'd parked this morning, but now it was miles. The darkness swallowed her with each hurried step, feeling as if she was running from someone; she checked behind her. There was nobody in sight.

Jeannie forced her scrunched shoulders down and reassured herself she was safe, but the shaking nagged at her relentlessly. It started in her hands, rattling her keys with each vibration of her steps taking her away from the protection of the entrance to the mall. Hustling faster, she added a half-run every few seconds to cover more territory. Finally reaching her car, with hands shaking uncontrollably, she fumbled for the unlock button on the remote, forgetting if it was on the top or bottom.

Steadying her right hand, holding the keys with her left, she attempted to push the button on the remote. It wouldn't release. Jeannie's throat tightened, hoping her eyes would quickly adjust to the darkness so she could make out the buttons on the remote and figure out which was "lock" and which was "unlock." She pressed the second button but accidentally squashed the alarm button. The screeching of the siren jolted panic in her gut as her hands shook violently. Frantically, she groped at the remote, hitting the right button this time, silencing the deafening noise.

Looking around to see if anyone heard, she saw nobody,

which was not comforting. Holding the remote at an angle so the parking lot light lit up the buttons, she finally found the magical unlock sensor. The second the door lock popped, Jeannie scrambled inside, slamming the door behind her and smashing the auto-lock button. Gasping for air as she released her tight breath, the electricity of her fear slowly melted from her body.

With hands still shaking, she jammed the key in the ignition, fired the engine to light, and bolted from the parking lot. She wanted to surround herself with people and traffic, needing to flee the secluded parking area. As she turned the corner of the building, a sea of cars, milling families, and early Christmas shoppers packed the area. After a few slow, deep breaths, the shaking subsided. She weaved her way through the lines of cars and located the exit. Tomorrow she will park on this side of the mall, she lectured herself. She bit her lip to steady her mind, gripped the steering wheel a little tighter, and merged onto the freeway.

~

Jeannie didn't completely relax until she was safely inside her home, clad in her silk pajamas and slippers, a mug of chamomile tea in hand, and had turned some calming music on, sliding the volume high enough to overtake her thoughts. The relaxing yacht rock gradually pulled her soul into a smooth mode, releasing all the demons she battled for most hours, particularly when she was alone and wondering if killers were lurking outside.

As relaxation soothed her, she let the music pull her back to lazy days on Roger's boat as they bounced past ocean waves to glassy blue water and anchored. Lying on the deck for hours, fishing periodically, but mostly listening to music and planning their life together. Soaking in the California sun.

Her heart tugged at itself, threatening to come undone with the resurgence of the pleasant memories. It was exhausting trying to keep them at bay; but tonight, she let them roll over her and happily absorbed the comfort of the idyllic memories. When the heartbreaking thoughts of Roger's betrayal threatened to drown out the pleasant images, she redirected her focus, rewarming her tea before plopping on the sofa and positioning her laptop across her thighs.

After carefully unfolding the creased papers, she went to work on her new project. The first person on the list was Rudolpho Velasquez, CEO of Java Connection. A web search for information only turned up a boring personal and professional bio. There wasn't even a hint of corruption or criminal allegations. Not the drug lord she'd imagined he would be when she ran his name through her mind over and over.

Frustration surged from not finding an easy connection to the cocaine smuggling. Of course, she told herself, if it was that easy, the feds would have found it long ago. Clicking the mouse, and typing in each corporate officer's name, she delved into the research, trying combinations of the name, locations, attaching it to the corporation, finding relatives, and spiraling down rabbit hole after rabbit hole, for every corporate officer she could pull up that was ever employed by Java Connection. All fruitless. Only producing mounds of press articles praising Java Connection for philanthropic activities in Cali, Colombia, where the company was born.

Jeannie rubbed her strained eyes and checked her watch. It was already three a.m. and the ache in her heels reminded her she'd spent the bulk of the day on her feet. A day that was now officially swamping her with weariness, prompting a heavy yawn.

She'd never held a retail job, not even as a teen. The long hours were physically draining. And since there was no point in continuing her search tonight and the workday would dawn in a few hours, she logged off and reluctantly closed her laptop. Maybe she could find something more promising on the company computer tomorrow.

Folding the paper and stuffing it in her purse, she trudged sleepily to her room, gladly sliding under the plush, heavy comforter. It had been a long day, full of excitement she hadn't felt in a long while. Hopeful that attempting to sleep would be easier when her body couldn't stand to be awake anymore, she sank deeper into the mattress. It accepted her and swallowed her exhausted body. The sleep came fast and remained undisturbed from her own thoughts for the first time in months.

Chapter 16
Moving on Up

The thrill of finding time to dig through the database as soon as Tommy ran off to who-knows-where he went every afternoon had Jeannie arriving at work thirty minutes before opening. Sitting in her car waiting for time to pass gave her a chance to formulate a plan. Without Tommy hovering, there would be plenty of time to investigate. Her late-night research was a bust, turning up nothing of importance and, in fact, the information she found made the board of Java Connection look like a troop of boy scouts. The accolades for their philanthropic activity stretched a mile long, with donations to prominent charities and worthy causes.

The long list of recent donations included some of her father's questionable favorite causes, but there were so many other charities that had no connection, it would be a weak argument to allege money was being funneled through those groups. Besides, there were comptrollers and boards that accounted for the donations, not her father.

Not seeing much activity in the nearly empty parking lot, Jeannie rethought being positioned in her car like a sitting duck. She grabbed her new purse and headed to the mall employee entrance. Arriving before Tommy, she stood in the broad walkway outside the storefront, waiting for the chains covering the entrance to be raised.

A man sitting on the bench outside the store lowered his paper and smiled. Jeannie responded with an insincere reciprocal smile and a suspicious twinge. Prompting her to memorize details about him like Marshal Mayer had taught her, situational awareness, he'd told her, use it.

The man wore wrinkled khaki slacks, which appeared to be two sizes too large, rather worn boat shoes, frayed sleeves on his plain white button-down shirt, and pudgy fingers wrapped around the pages of the newspaper. She couldn't see it, but she imagined a stomach equally chubby rested behind the paper. His proximity to the coffee shop told her he would soon be inside the store, gobbling down a few creamy pastries.

The chains finally rattled, bringing her eagerly scuttling under the gate and into the store. "You're late," she scolded Tommy, who didn't react or take offense.

"I should get you a set of keys so you can open the store. Then I won't have to rush so much in the mornings." Tommy replied with a yawn. "Your ID badge should be ready tomorrow so you can come in the back door."

"Keys would be great." Jeannie's mind whirled at the possibility of being able to have unfettered access to the computer.

"I'll get them today. In fact, why don't I do that now?"

"What about the morning rush?" she asked, wheeling around to confront Tommy. A surge of panic shot through her. It was going to be a busy morning judging from the small crowd, mostly other mall employees, gathering outside the chains, waiting for their first daily jolt of caffeine.

"You'll be fine. You've picked up everything so quickly, I'm not worried." Tommy flashed a weak smile and fired up the iPad system used for orders.

Jeannie grimaced and hurried to place the fresh pastries delivered the night before in the cases. "You know, it would speed things up in the morning if we did this at closing," she complained.

"They wouldn't be fresh if we did that," Tommy replied without cracking a smile.

She shot him a look he never saw, then resumed the opening routine and turned on all the machines and readied the filters. They were supposed to be there an hour early, but today they only had half an hour to get everything ready.

"I'm sorry, I'm exhausted. I know it's only your second day. I'll help with the morning rush, but I bet you can handle it tomorrow. You've picked it up quickly." Tommy raised his arms in a stretch, followed by another yawn.

Jeannie looked at Tommy and his unkept hair, appearing as if he hadn't slept at all. "You need some coffee," she smirked.

"You're right. It was a bit of a rough night."

Jeannie presumed he must have been partying all night with his buddies. "Late night on the town?"

Tommy looked at her with surprise. "No, a new baby in the house."

Jeannie shrunk before the eyes of her new young boss, overcome with guilt for making such a negative assumption. Though in his apparent state of bleary-eyed sleep deprivation, her comments didn't faze him as he continued the morning set-up without a pause. After an awkward moment, she tried to make amends. "Congratulations," she offered.

"Thanks," he yawned.

The crowd thinned out by ten-thirty, except for the man with the newspaper, who had moved inside the store from the bench he'd been parked on in the foyer. He seemed consumed with yet another paper as he sipped his coffee, carefully folding each section of the paper once he'd completed reading it from top to bottom. She couldn't help but be reminded of her father and his newspapers.

"I think I'll take off now," Tommy told Jeannie.

"Okay, I'll be all right," she assured him, still feeling guilty about her misjudgment.

With Tommy gone, the tickle of excitement surged. It was time to get on the computer. If only the stranger would leave before the lunch crowd descended. Glancing at her phone to check the time, there was a small window of opportunity, but the stranger had planted himself and didn't appear to be going anywhere soon. She tapped her foot anxiously, watching the man turn each page with no regard for the rest of the world.

"Can I get you anything else?" she asked the concealed man. She waited for a response, but he was oblivious to her question. Circling the long counter, then scrubbing a few tables until the finish almost came off, she edged her way back toward the man. "Do you need anything else, sir?" she asked louder.

He lowered his paper and drilled a look through her. Earlier when they met, there wasn't much to notice, but now she looked more closely at his features. Nothing about the man stood out as memorable. Curly brown hair, brown eyes, and a face found on any street corner in America. The round belly she had pictured wasn't there. In fact, he appeared rather fit. An unusual combination of features, but nondescript just the same.

"I'm fine, thank you," he replied.

A sudden reminder of her true identity crashed into her reality, as if it was being unraveled by the man's stare. She looked away to reclaim her balance and turned her back to wipe another table. "If you need anything, please let me know…uh, otherwise, I'll be working on the computer." She excused herself. Turning to take a last glance at the man, who'd resumed studying his paper.

Safely out of sight, she logged onto the computer and entered the password, feeling relief when the main page came into view. Plucking various pages out of lists and searching every link and icon available, her hopeful enthusiasm to learn something useful faded as nothing out of the ordinary immediately jumped out. Completely absorbed in her frantic hunt, she didn't even notice when the man left the coffee shop.

The lunch crowd dribbled in a few patrons at a time, stretching out over the next two hours, making it impossible for Jeannie to continue searching. Not that there was anything to find. Each click on the company website took her to a different page, only to be brought back to the home page again. The circular treasure hunt was exhausting.

The afternoon brought bleary-eyed patrons, most seeking steam to make it through their dreary jobs and boring lives for another few hours. Sipping their drinks happily as they waited to escape to their homes before recycling their daily life drudgery the next day. And while she smiled as she went through the motions of providing the fuel, Jeannie's mind was still floating around, focusing on the lack of information gathered so far. There was no answer to the puzzle and no discernable link between her father and Java Connection. When Tommy returned, she abandoned the frustrating quest for the day.

"So, Jeannie, how do you like Java Connection?" Tommy asked before her shift ended.

"I like it. I think I'm getting the hang of making coffee. There's a lot to learn, more than I realized." Jeannie was sincere in that. She never knew the sheer number of combinations and flavors possible with caffeine, milk, air, cream, chocolate, cinnamon, vanilla, and ice. People had definite ideas about the exact measurements and ingredients that must be in their coffee to make their day livable.

"I have some news. I think I'm getting transferred to a location on the north side of Houston, which is much closer to my house. The district manager asked if you would be interested in training for the manager position?"

Jeannie stammered, unable to formulate a response. An offer of a managerial position was the last thing she expected to hear from Tommy and the last thing she truly wanted. Especially considering it was only her second day on the job. "I guess so." She finally broke through the shock of the proposal.

"There's a mandatory two-week training session at the corporate headquarters in Santa Monica, California."

California! Had he said there would be a trip to California for two weeks? A mandatory trip?

The news hit her hard, like a squarely delivered punch in the stomach. Staring at Tommy, trying to understand what was happening, warning herself that it might be a trap, she squeaked out, "Really?"

"Yeah, it's pretty boring actually, but it's great training on the computer system for inventory maintenance, tracking, and reorder issues. Also, the bookkeeping process for receipts, expenses, payroll, all of that. It would also be a pay raise. So, you interested?"

In her mind, she was already packing her bags and heading for the corporate computers. "Isn't this kind of unusual to offer someone a management position on their second day?" she asked.

"Well, it's kind of unusual that someone with an Ivy League education wants to work in a coffeehouse for minimum wage," he answered back.

"That's true," she said, realizing it was better to stop asking questions if she wanted access to the computers, scolding herself internally for not lying better on the application. At least she did say Yale and not Harvard, she pathetically rationalized.

"I think you can handle it, Jeannie," he continued.

"I'm absolutely interested." She diverted the conversation from her past. There was no cautiousness in her tone now.

"I'll let the district manager know. You would leave on Sunday and spend two weeks in training and be back before Thanksgiving, which is as close as I can cut it with Christmas coming up. My actual transfer would be January first."

As he spoke, she stared back as if she were carefully listening to each word, but she couldn't filter Tommy's words because she was rehearsing her discussion with Marshal Gagne in her mind. Maybe she wouldn't tell him, go and come back and see if they even noticed. It would serve them right. Nobody was watching her back. She was certain any protection of her life was going to come from herself. Getting to the corporate office would give her access to the information she needed, and her father was probably in D.C. for the session, so she should be safe. Promising herself that once she arrived in Santa Monica, she would go nowhere except the hotel and the office. The conversation with herself continued, rationalizing that with the crowds of people living in the area, it would be easy to get lost in the masses. Last night, she had located the corporate office on a map; it was a relatively new building, one she wasn't familiar with. Still, she felt comfortable with the area.

The friends she ran with when living in Santa Monica didn't frequent the downtown area, and it was far removed from the country club, so the odds were in her favor of not running into anyone she knew. With one exception. The corporate offices were situated across the canal near Roger's apartment. Somehow, even that fact didn't make her pause, convincing herself that she was invincible and could slip in out of town as if she wore an invisibility cloak, prompting her to blurt out, "Make the arrangements, I'm in."

"Okay, I'll let corporate know. I'll send you all the information tonight."

Her stomach fluttered at the possibility of being that close to Roger, not certain if it was a happy flutter or a remnant of anger. Whatever it was, on Sunday, she would be packed and ready to return to California. It couldn't come quickly enough for her.

Chapter 17

Can you Manage?

Jeannie stared at her cellphone sitting on the table. She knew what had to be done. The dreaded call to Marshal Gagne, no matter the consequence. All her mental wrangling over the decision had led her to conclude she had to do the right thing and let the feds know where she was going. As much as she'd rather disappear and let them worry about finding her, that wasn't who she was. At least it wasn't when she was Rachel Rose. Rachel followed the rules and dealt thoughtfully with people. With a sigh, knowing that even though her name was no longer Rachel Rose, she needed to cling to the person she used to be and make the call or lose herself forever.

Reaching to retrieve her phone, it slipped from her hand, tumbling precariously under the sofa. Cursing, she scrambled to the floor, finally finding it a few inches underneath the couch. She retrieved it and tried again, gripping it while she punched the contact button, it connected immediately.

"Yes?" the marshal answered.

"Marshal Gagne, this is Jeannie."

"What can I do for you?"

"I wanted to let you know I'm leaving Sunday for Santa Monica." Jeannie tried to sound casual.

"You're not authorized to go there, you know that." His words were stern, but he maintained his composure.

"I know. But it's mandatory corporate training. I really don't have a choice."

"You aren't authorized. You can't go, it's too dangerous."

"I'm going. You can go with me, or you can stay here. I really don't care anymore. I have to do this. I have to find the evidence I missed before, and that the FBI missed as well." Jeannie's voice raised, her determination unmovable.

Agent Gagne was quiet, thinking about Jeannie's predicament. "You could be signing your death warrant. You know that, right?"

"I know," Jeannie's voice calmed. She knew better than anyone this decision could trigger her world to explode, with deadly consequences.

"I have to tell you something, Jeannie." Marshal Gagne hesitated. "Like I told you in Arizona, there was a credible threat against you. We have certain information that someone is attempting to track you down. Our intelligence says they've tracked the first two cities you were in."

"Is it my father?"

"We're not sure yet. Maybe. We can't be sure."

Jeannie took in the news. There had been so many nights that she played out the scenario of being discovered in her mind. It was almost anticlimactic at this point. And even though she knew this day would arrive, she hadn't planned on it coming so soon. She tapped her fingernail on the back of the phone and bit her lip, waiting for what was next.

"We can move you tonight, if you want," Marshal Gagne

offered, knowing she would decline.

The feds had moved her so many times she had to remind herself the city she was living in and under what name. No more. There would be no more hiding. She was done. "I can't run anymore, Marshal Gagne. I don't want to run. I'm tired of running." Saying it out loud was freeing.

Holding her arm straight, eyeing her hand, she searched for the familiar tremor, waiting for the chill to climb up her backbone as her fate unfolded before her. But all she saw was a steady hand, the shaking noticeably absent. A smile forced its way across her face. *Good for you!*

"We have a twenty-four-hour watch on you, and we have for a few days now. In fact, you met one of my men in the coffee shop. We are taking care of you. I'd like to meet with you face-to-face before you leave, and I'll escort you to Santa Monica. Give me the flight information so I can make the arrangements."

"That was your guy?" she asked.

"Yes. I told you we're protecting you," he added. The lie necessary to pull on the predictable heartstrings. So far, Jeannie was behaving as his boss had anticipated. Making it easy to manipulate her and get her back to California. All he had to do was resist a little, and she dug her heels in deeper. Easy money. He smiled as he twirled his pen and waited for the flight number and time.

Jeannie had no reason to distrust Marshal Gagne. After all, he was a federal agent assigned to protect her, but her inner thoughts jumbled, screaming at her that this trip was a death wish. She bit her lip again, contemplating whether to disclose the flight information or not. She figured he probably already knew it if he was doing his job well. Although there was a growing sense of relief with the knowledge they had been protecting her, so maybe she could trust him, she argued against herself. Scratching the back of her neck, she looked around at her house, spotting two boxes still taped shut.

Is this the life she wanted to live?

It was time to trust someone, so she told him, "The flight is American #245. It leaves at seven forty-five p.m. from Intercontinental Airport on Sunday. Where do you want to meet?"

"There's a Motel 6 off the interstate near the airport and a convenience store next to it, a 7-Eleven. I'll text a pin. Let's meet behind it. Pull off at five-thirty p.m. into the hotel back lot where the dumpsters are and raise the hood of your car. I'll stop and help you. I'll have some items for you."

Jeannie calmed the other questions swirling in her mind and accepted his instructions. She dimmed the house lights and peeked out the window, spotting a dark SUV a few houses down. *They were watching.* Exhaling, she rolled her neck and stretched her jaw and finally relaxed. Then double-checked the locks, reset the alarm, and went to her bedroom to pack.

Sunday evening arrived at a snail's pace, despite her pacing impatiently all day long and checking her watch every ten minutes. Jeannie tossed the government-issued suitcase into the back of the SUV and headed for the airport, trying to time it and arrive at the motel parking lot exactly as Marshal Gagne had laid out.

She spotted the motel easily but mistimed the offramp, forcing her to drive past the exit. The next access was two miles down from her original ramp. Irritated by her mistake and the time it was taking to find the turnaround and come back under the freeway, she ran through a litany of curse words. Finally spotting the bright sign of 7-Eleven next to the motel, she exited. Noting the time, ten minutes early, even with her unplanned detour, she forced herself to relax. But nothing felt right about this meetup.

She meandered across the bumpy asphalt, spotting the dumpster, as Marshal Gagne described. Fighting the urge to gun it and head straight to the airport instead of sitting in the dark alone, waiting for a man she despised, she rolled the car to a stop, turned the engine off and held her breath. A careful survey of the area painted a picture of what she already knew. It was a perfectly deserted spot to wind up dead. Nobody would discover her until morning.

All she could see in front of her was a large dumpster holding a partially burned sofa, standing straight up. The desolate parking lot suddenly felt further from the freeway exit than when she turned into the lot. The sign of the Motel 6 barely lit a small portion of the blacktop. It might have been brighter if the "t" and the "l" weren't burned out, leaving only "Moe 6" on the sign.

Jeannie started the car again, moved the gear back into drive and continued cautiously past the long building, closer to the beckoning dumpster where the light from the "Moe 6" sign faded into blackness. The usual starlit Houston sky was missing tonight, hidden by clouds forming a line of showers across the city, the light of the stars trapped on the other side. Darkness overhead and darkness on the ground engulfed her. A lone streetlight lay on the ground in shattered pieces. Her headlights bouncing off the fragments provided the only beacons of safety, which were weakly keeping her fear at bay.

Settling on a parking space next to the light pole, despite the lack of light, she turned the key and killed the engine, then pulled the lever with the hood picture on it until she heard the heavy lock pop loose. She took a deep breath, letting it out slowly, hoping it would ease her nerves before she left the artificial safety of her car. It didn't help one bit. She released her grip on the steering wheel, tucked her phone in her back pocket, and climbed out of her SUV.

The putrid odor of the burned mattress stung her nose the minute she opened the car door. She covered her mouth and nose with her sleeve and tried to adjust her senses to the charred air. The sound of her heart pounding rang in her ears. The volume of the beats increased as she moved towards the front of the car. She cleared her throat, forcing the uneasy feeling out of her chest, holding her breath to stop the urge to breathe more rapidly. Taking one last look around behind her, eyeing the open side of the dumpster, she carefully raised the hood. Fearing the worst, she glanced over her shoulder for the second time and checked her watch. There was no Marshal Gagne. It was five-thirty exactly.

Jeannie moved to the edge of her vehicle, her eyes darting back and forth to the shadows. Headlights scooted by on the frontage road at the entrance of the hotel, but no cars came her way to deliver the agent.

Five-forty.

She paced a little, being careful not to step too far from the car door she'd been clinging to for the past ten minutes. She heard the crunch of glass under her feet and glanced up at the dark streetlight following the path back to the glass sitting on top of the weeds. A recent break, Jeannie deduced. She fought the urge to check the time, knowing she'd have to leave soon or miss her flight. Her phone alarm went off, sending her heart into her throat.

Five forty-five.

She couldn't wait any longer. Jeannie turned and raised her arms to shut the hood.

She never heard the person behind her as a wide hand clasped her mouth. Her arms flailed wildly; her mind had created this moment hundreds of times. Pain surged through her shoulders as both arms were pulled tightly behind her back. The grip tightened as she struggled.

"Shhh, shhh," the masculine voice whispered in her ear.

Jeannie tried to calm herself, knowing she needed to think and not panic as her mind raced through all the previously imagined scenarios that kept her awake into the wee hours of the morning.

"It's okay. It's me, Marshal Gagne. Relax and don't scream or do anything crazy and I'll let you go," he said.

The words should've brought relief, but with her arms still bound behind her, she instinctively wanted to wrestle herself free. But as he said he would, he lessened his grasp. Jeannie stopped fighting, relaxing her arms as her captor released her and revealed himself.

"I'm going to take my hand away from your mouth. Don't scream," he told her.

With her mouth now uncovered, Jeannie stretched her lips but did as he asked and didn't scream as she wheeled around to come face-to-face with the agent who had accosted her.

"Was that necessary?" she cursed under her breath at the

agent. Trying to get a better look at him in the dark. They'd only met once at 3:00 a.m. but his face looked different. Not quite as she remembered. It had been a hurried night, and she had been groggy, so she could remember him wrong.

"Calm down. I parked down the road and walked up the back road so nobody would spot us together in case one of us was followed. I was behind you and didn't want you to panic as I walked up."

"You could have said, 'hey Jeannie, don't freak out, I'm behind you,' instead of grabbing me and scaring the wits out of me," she scolded, rubbing her shoulders.

"Consider it practice for real life. We need to schedule some self-defense classes for you, because if that had been a true attack you'd be zipped in a body bag right now. Let's get down to business. There's not much time before the flight. Here's the plan." He handed her a lapel pin in the shape of a coffee cup. "Nobody will suspect this. It is a camera, kind of like a body cam, so we can record all that is happening when you get inside Java corporate for the first day of training."

"Can we communicate through this? Will I be able to talk to you or hear you?" Jeannie was confused.

"I'm getting to that," he told her. "You'll need to find the computer room, log into the system and read off the system configuration information to me so we can find out if there is a hidden backend." He handed her a small black jewelry box.

"Okay, that will be in the morning." She was still sizing up Marshal Gagne after being hog-tied. Her instincts were in a tug of war, with mistrust winning out. She took the box and opened it to reveal earrings.

"Earrings? I don't understand. What am I supposed to

do with earrings?"

"These are not ordinary earrings; they have a two-way transmitter and microphone built into them. You'll be able to hear me give you instructions, and we'll be able to hear you. Our computer expert will walk you through their system to locate the information we all need."

"Stylish and functional," Jeannie remarked.

"The last thing you will need is the phone I gave you. It has a locator on it, and I'm the only one who can track it, so keep the location on. But, Jeannie, if anything happens and you feel like someone else is tracking you, turn your location off. And no getting on social media," he said with a tight frown.

"Like whom? Who else could track me other than the marshal's office?" she asked.

"I don't know. Probably nobody, but just in case." He wanted to tell her more but knew it would be his life if he did.

"Okay, I understand. I don't have any social media anymore, anyway. Don't you remember Rule #4 of the protection handbook?" she asked him, staring at the items he'd handed her. She looked up to ask him about other details of the plan, but when she did, he was gone.

"Okay, guess I'll stand in the dark by myself," she blurted. Annoyed at his perpetual habit of disappearing.

Jeannie hurriedly slammed the hood, climbed back into her car, and headed to the airport. Panic shrilled through her, the idea of stepping foot in California becoming a reality as she rushed through traffic to the airport. What if TSA recognized her at the airport? She'd not flown since this entire ordeal began. She had a fake driver's license, a fake name, a fake life, and now she was going to have to smile and put on her best performance. Her knowledge of being a fraud ballooned her fear to an almost conspicuous level. Presenting an ID with a fake name, a non-existent person, Jeannie Smith, surely was detectable when the scanner sucked it in for verification. What if they were using facial recognition? She'd heard about that recently. The outcome depended on the feds having done their job well. Her confidence sank.

Approaching the ticket counter and boarding area, she searched for Marshal Gagne, but she never spotted him.

"You have to remove your shoes in this line, especially the boots and your belt."

"Really? The boots?" Jeannie asked.

"Metal on the toes or the heels. It will alert every time, plus it's regulation."

She'd never owned a pair of cowboy boots; an impulse buy she now regretted. So much for trying to fit in, she thought, promising herself to slip on a pair of tennis shoes the minute she landed in California. At least everyone around her was suffering the same fate of prying boots off their feet. Thinking ahead, she'd been smart and worn new socks, as her mom had trained her, clean socks and underwear. After all, you never know.

It had been years since she'd traveled without TSA pre-check and CLEAR, so she could breeze right through security with no hassle. There were no luxuries now. Fingerprints and background checks would undo her. She'd been relegated to processing through security checks without convenient efficiencies.

"You're clear." The stern TSA agent told her as she stepped through the x-ray in her stocking feet.

"Thanks," Jeannie said, breathing a sigh of relief. She'd

made it through without anyone questioning her identity. As the agent motioned her to move along, a heavy weight melted from her shoulders. Soon, she'd be in the air on her way back to her stomping grounds.

Gathering her items, she shoved her feet into the boots and stuffed her belt in her purse, not feeling the need to have the mini-sized Texas belt buckle on. Grabbing her carry-on bag idling at the end of the conveyor belt, she checked the gate on her app and headed off. One step closer to getting back to her hometown and, hopefully, one step closer to finding the truth.

The plane jerked and jolted as it maneuvered onto the tarmac for the journey to California. Relaxing into her seat with earbuds firmly in place and her playlist tripping through her favorite power songs, women singing proudly about strength and courage, something she desperately hoped to find before landing, she closed her eyes wanting to block out the world for a few minutes as her thoughts calmed. The music lured her into a half-awake state, and even with all the motivation surging through her ears, self-doubt drifted into her subconscious, dredging through the questions that haunted her for the past eighteen months.

What if her father hadn't been part of the cocaine transport? What if he was only taking kickbacks from campaign contributors, as he tried to explain when he found her in his office? That he wasn't as corrupt as she had painted him out to be. Perhaps it was only a one-time thing, and other senators had done the same or worse, including her grandfather and great-grandfather.

Focusing on the lyrics of her "go get 'em girl" song, she

drifted off until the pilot's announcement of the pending descent into the city woke her with a jolt. She grasped the armrest, knocking the arm of the passenger next to her off the slender metal.

"Sorry. I didn't mean to do that," she said. The man next to her looked at her with irritation and readjusted his arm.

Jeannie looked out the window, straining to see the city coming into view in the far distance. The questions she'd been battling in her sleep rolled through her mind again, popping in rapid fire, along with the images of the dead girl. Forcing the images away, as she had done minutes after she saw them, she fought to convince herself that her father could have anything to do with a murder. The wasted body, bloody and beaten, was something she couldn't bring herself to confess to the federal agents. She hadn't disclosed it to the psychiatrist either. Besides, as far as she knew, her father had the photos. There was no actual proof without them. The psychiatrist theorized in his medical jargon that she was holding something back, contributing to the anxiety attacks, and promised her that until she dealt with it, the shaking would continue. Jeannie discounted his theory, because secretly he was right.

Without that information surfacing at the trial, her father's attorneys manipulated her words and information, claiming that Jeannie was a disturbed young woman. Even she hadn't been able to trace the so-called kickbacks to anyone connected to the Colombian cartel. And when the sources of the money were located, there was always a reasonable explanation for the senator receiving a payoff, as her father had calmly explained to the jury. The senator paid back the one and only unexplainable transaction, but it was of such an insignificant amount it seemed rather innocuous, more of an accounting oversight than a criminal action. Regardless of reasonable explanations, her soul wouldn't release the thought that there was a connection between her father, Java Connection, and the cartel.

Jeannie unbuckled her seatbelt, wanting to check on the whereabouts of Marshal Gagne before they landed. "Excuse me," she said to the passenger seated next to her, patiently waiting for him to lift the tray, stand and move aside for her to exit the row.

Stepping into the slender aisle, she strode cautiously to the back of the plane. Examining each face row by row as she passed. There was no way to tell if anyone was aware of who she was. Inquisitive eyes landed on her, scrutinizing as she passed, making her feel as if her true identity was embroidered across her chest for all to read. The last row on the right held the face she was searching for. Her eyes diverted immediately to minimize blowing his cover. He did the same.

Relief washed over her as she finally arrived at the back of the plane, able to abscond to the small lavatory where she hurriedly locked the door. Her hands began shaking, betraying her desire to remain in control, increasing as the plane dipped slightly, sending her stomach up and out of her body.

Sitting on the closed toilet lid, gripping her hands together, she willed the shaking to respond to the counterpressure and subside. The seatbelt light flashed on with a ding. The cold water she splashed on her face helped calm her nerves as her thoughts raced. Soon she would step back into her city, back in her hometown, back to Roger's neighborhood, and not far from her own condo. Back to herself, she hoped.

Returning to her seat, she gave a quick side-eyed glance

to ensure that Marshal Gagne was still with her; he wasn't. She felt her hands turn to ice.

Chapter 18

California Dreaming

Jeannie shifted restlessly in her seat as the plane descended into the airport, fighting the urge to stand up and look back to see if Marshal Gagne was in his seat. Watching the plane rock gently and level itself, preparing for the landing, a tinge of a thrill pulsed through her body. Unsure if it was from being back home, or her mission ahead, she let it wash over her. Whatever the source, it was bittersweet.

The familiar city lights lining the coast came into focus. Clustered twinkles moved away from the shore, designating ships headed out to sea, bound for their cross-ocean deliveries. Jumbled thoughts snuck upon her as she watched the familiar scene. This had been a dream for months after being forced to bury the roots of her childhood that were planted here.

Missing the familiar streets, sights, and especially the sugary fragrance of spun cotton candy on the boardwalk in Santa Monica. Everything that gave her a sense of belonging, of being real. Hot, nostalgic tears welled. Blinking purposely, she forced them away. This was her home, and she shouldn't have been driven away. A new determination sparked within her as the lights grew larger and brighter. She had to redeem herself, prove that she was right, and not crazy.

The plane leveled and slid easily across the tarmac, gracefully shifting from the back tires onto the front wheel, before the brakes engaged, slowing the plane enough to taxi to the gate. It all felt so routine and normal, like any other flight she'd taken on autopilot, not having to consider the significance of her arrival.

Fighting the urge to search again for Marshal Gagne as travelers stood, waiting to deplane, she fidgeted with the buckle on her backpack. The departure was slow, as the unloading process seemed to halt every few seconds for no apparent reason. Passengers gathered items from the overhead bins, searching, fumbling, unable to remember where the bags they had placed above had ended up. Others were poorly navigating the narrow seats and walkway, banging bags against armrests, ricocheting themselves down the aisle.

Sighs of impatience mounted all around as the dam of people brought the exit to a trickle. Jeannie seized the opportunity to study faces, analyzing the men around her and trying to locate the marshal, but his face was nowhere to be found.

As she stepped into the hustle of the busy airport, familiar sounds brought a welcome comfort to her soul as she hustled to the taxi pickup lane. Ride apps had been disallowed in her new world. Taxis were her transportation of choice during her captivity. She stared at the eager drivers waiting for tourists to be scrambled around town, searching for passengers who wouldn't know the long way from the short, racking up a few extra dollars. Jeannie realized this tactic when her own driver went the long way unnecessarily, not knowing that Jeannie was perfectly oriented.

Consumed by the anxiety of being recognized rested in the back of her mind, forcing her to remain silent, fearing some revelation of her former identity if she drew too much attention to herself. Catching her own reflection in the rearview mirror made her want to shrink from sight. She slouched down into the cheaply repaired vinyl seat, still silent, allowing the driver free rein to bilk her for a few more dollars.

Finally arriving at the hotel, she threw the fare through the cutout in the plexiglass barrier and exited the cab, tucking her remaining cash in her pocket, not offering any tip, an unknown punishment for wasting her time.

The check-in was relatively painless, but Jeannie avoided eye contact with every individual she passed. It was protection for her mental comfort, knowing the risks of being back in California, back home.

Once she was safely inside her hotel room, she leaned against the closed door for the stability it offered and to compose her thoughts. A deep sigh shook the remnants of the discomfort that assailed her the minute she'd stepped into the lobby and further grew during the ascent of the elevator. She relaxed and took a breath, a normal breath, not the tight, pressured, up and down of her chest that she'd become hostage to over the past several months. But a real breath, like she did autonomously before the craziness infected her mind and her life.

Crossing the room to the window, she slid open the glass door and meandered onto the balcony, embracing the sounds of the city. She already knew what the view held, but she needed to see it, to know where she stood in her emotional reincarnation. And to let the moist salty air touch her skin.

Glancing at the too familiar scene, she forced her eyes to gaze at Roger's apartment building across the canal. Lights illuminated the structure, beckoning her to look harder at the floors and undraped windows. Emotions and loneliness shocked her heart. An ache soaked into her muscles as she stared at the lighted window of the apartment of the man she once loved…the man she still loved if she could climb over the pain.

The next moments were not thought through clearly. Impulsively, she picked up her phone and dialed his house number, wondering if he still had the landline. It was the only number still committed to memory.

The second ring brought a gentle voice to her ear and her heart to a halt.

"Hello," the voice was deep and masculine. The sound soothing and warm.

"Roger," she barely whispered into the phone.

"Who is this?" He had heard her, but the recognition of her voice was not immediate or expected.

She reassessed her impromptu action but couldn't muster an ounce of regret. She longed to hear him speak again, to take in the sound of a voice that once brought her so much warmth and security. If only the clock could be forced back, so she could hold Roger and love him for the rest of her life like they once planned. The urge to profess her sorrow and ask him to come inside her inner circle again gnawed at her.

Can I trust him? Jeannie asked herself honestly, then, knowing the answer, awkwardly hung up the phone, ducking quickly back inside the room.

It had been a foolish move in a moment of weakness; one she knew couldn't happen again. There was nobody to provide a haven of respite, she scolded herself. It was up to her to be her own harbor.

She tossed the phone across the bed and moved away from it and back onto the balcony, unable to look away. The lights in his apartment still shone. A figure moved toward the window. Jeannie slunk back into the shadows, away from the light of her own room, and watched as he approached the window and drew the shades wider, looking out over the city. It was a scene Jeannie had gazed at many days and nights, years ago, in happier days. Remembering the endless nights, she spent with his arms wrapped around her, admiring the view of the ocean and planning a future of happiness together.

Is he thinking about me? She wondered as she stared at him, his shape obvious, his face much too far to read.

A tear escaped and lazily dripped down her cheek before she felt the pain in her heart. It had been so long since a man had touched her, held her, kissed her. All the trauma and stress she'd endured had been managed solely on her own. With her back to the wall, she slid to the ground, clutching her knees for the sole purpose of feeling a human touch. The tears disappeared without her willing them away, but the pain in her heart remained firmly in place.

Roger retreated inside his apartment, drawing the shades, followed by lights being extinguished one-by-one. Remaining on the balcony, Jeannie stood to face her city and the past. Fixated on the town, she glanced up the hill to the area where her parents' home sat. She knew her father would be in D.C., but her mother was there. Probably alone, sipping the third glass of wine for the evening, coupled with a prescription drug for sleep, lost in a torrid romance novel, still void of reality. Somehow, it made

Jeannie feel stronger, measuring herself against the reflection of her mother's weakness. Promising herself she would never succumb to the same fate that was her maternal life example. There was a satisfying pride in her own strength and independence, and from knowing she was the exact opposite of her mother. And as much as Jeannie knew her mother was weak; it would have been nice to have someone to lean on. But she was alone. No Roger, no family, and no friends.

There were a few women she had maintained friendships with over the years, but most of her life was spent in the clutches of working with her father and keeping his political career moving. When Roger came along, he became the epicenter of her world. Splitting time between her father and Roger became a battle, with her father demanding her attention, trying to loosen Roger's grip on her. But when a heart is captivated, lessening the hold on it could only be done with dynamite. And as hard as her father had tried to separate them, it was Roger who blew it to kingdom come, not her father.

Once Roger was gone and she was alone with time smothering her, Jeannie attempted a reconnection with some of her girlfriends, but they were absorbed in their own lives, married, having children, or pursuing careers in other cities. The only choice was to find her own comfort in knowing she was strong enough to make it on her own and heal her heart through gritty determination. And now, she was back, still alone, and she would finish this game, even if it killed her.

Chapter 19
Can't Forget and Can't Remember

Roger was puzzled by the phone call, mainly because he thought the voice was familiar, but he couldn't decide for sure. He examined the caller ID. The number read "unknown." Why he still had his old landline was a mystery to him. But his mother insisted, to be assured she could get in touch with him if there was ever an emergency. Cell phones can die; she told him. Making no difference to his mother that he had the latest smartphone. Aside from his mother, nostalgia stopped him from getting rid of it. He'd had the phone number for years. Other than one of his law partners or family, he rarely seemed to receive calls on it, so the call had to be from someone who knew him well and for a long time.

It was partly his own fault nobody called him anymore. He had purposefully created an isolated life after the breakup with Rachel. Losing the gumption to be seen back in bars, back in the singles scene. Not wanting to explain what everyone had already heard through the grapevine, but not from Rachel. She never explained it, even to her closest friends. He knew it was to protect him, not herself. It was Rachel's father who made sure the word spread about his infidelity.

His future father-in-law had especially enjoyed making a

visit to Roger's father, showing him the photos and handing him the thumb drive containing the video, stressing the embarrassment and anger the Rose family felt when the information was hand-delivered to their doorstep. Providing some contrived consolation to the shocked Judge Williams, the tactful Senator Rose reminded him that the damning evidence could have just as easily been sent to the media.

Judge Williams had agreed with the senator that it would have been devastating and expressed his gratitude for the discretion. But the Judge's disappointment with Roger continued long after the senator left the Williams's front step, mainly because the senator appeared to have the moral high ground in the situation. Though secretly, Judge Williams was relieved the relationship was over and he wouldn't be tied to the Rose family for the rest of his life and share grandchildren with the man he detested.

Roger went to the refrigerator and sighed, annoyed he couldn't relieve his mind of the thoughts, opting for a beer that had been left behind by his legal team at last week's deposition prep. He'd sworn off alcohol the year prior, but tonight, his heart had betrayed him and catapulted him down memory lane in a vicious way. He popped the tab and released the constricting top button of his dress shirt, having shed the tie hours ago. Dropping onto the sofa in the dark, he instinctively propped his feet comfortably on the coffee table, staring toward the window and the bay.

Why can't I remember that night? It was a question he'd tortured himself with for the past three years because it was the truth. As hard as he searched for even a slight memory, he couldn't conjure up a single inkling of what happened with the blonde, naked woman. The photos were clear there was something going on; he was naked, and she was naked, and they appeared to be wrapped around each other.

Roger drew in a deep breath, followed by a long pull on the salty beer, and thought about it again. Forcing himself to search for some recall of the memories he'd carefully locked away since Rachel's death, but tonight it besieged his brain and tugged at his heart, sending guilt surging through him.

Setting his beer down in frustration, he went to the locked cabinet and pulled the salacious photos from the wedding album he had bought Rachel as a gift. One she never received. He flicked on the table lamp and sat gazing one more time at the photos. He turned them left and right and up and down, but nothing had changed since he first saw them, except now he didn't have to fight the urge to throw up. It was a puzzle he couldn't figure out, and he was always good at puzzles.

As an accomplished trial lawyer, plaintiff cases mostly, he was skilled at probing evidence and pulling out minute details to be scrutinized meticulously. *Why hadn't he been able to decipher the images in the photos? Why didn't he have any memory of it?* Roger asked as he forced himself to reanalyze the photos carefully.

Then he saw something new. His eyes zeroed in on the image of a speck of light. A reflection, a flash, perhaps? Maybe there was a photographer in the room? Why hadn't he thought of the photographer before? If he was in such a compromising position with this woman, he couldn't recall why was there somebody there taking photos? It wasn't like the paparazzi followed him around snapping unscrupulous poses. Who would have cared where he was or who he was with unless the senator had followed him? Something he'd considered multiple times since the incident but never had proof.

Looking at the images now with the eye of a lawyer, concocting strangers in the pictures instead of himself and a destroyed life, he saw it from a new perspective. There were obvious clues, details he should have seen before had he not been so undone by the destruction of his relationship with Rachel. Details he would have seen if he hadn't taken to numbing his pain with alcohol the first year after the break-up. Details he should have seen if he hadn't forced himself to conjure up false indignation the second year, somehow blaming Rachel for his moment of weakness. Finally settling into the third year, when he started to put himself back together, throwing away the alcohol and consuming himself with fitness and work, and locking the photos away instead of punishing himself night after night with the strange images.

When the circus of the trial played out daily in the media, he laid low. Then she was gone, killed in a plane crash. With that news, he sealed himself away in his mind and his heart, seeking numbness anywhere he could find it. He dove into work, cut everyone off, even his family, and buried himself in anguish, despair, and overwhelming shame.

Now, as he stared at the photos with a clear eye, it was evident he wasn't there by mistake. Somebody made sure he met the woman. Racking his brain, trying to pull grainy pieces of meeting the blonde from the cobwebs in his mind, all he could clearly recall was waiting at the ocean bar for Rachel. They were supposed to pick out china patterns, something Roger had reluctantly agreed to after his mother had given him an earful of expected husbandly duties.

The blonde woman sat beside him at the bar, but he paid

her no mind except for a polite hello. That much he remembered. After that, he found no other minutiae in his brain. The next flash was inside his apartment, disoriented and groggy, a terse message on his answering machine from his enraged fiancé, whom he had unknowingly stood up.

Roger rubbed his head, stood and paced across the living room, hoping to force the ragged pieces of that night into view. Re-running the scenes over and over again. At the ocean bar he had sipped his beer, not paying much attention to the woman, even turning his back away from her to gaze out the window waiting for Rachel. Usually his memories stopped there, but tonight he pushed himself to go past that point of his recollection.

The woman spoke to him, asked him what he did for a living. He'd chosen not to answer that question and instead informed her he was waiting for his fiancé. It was crystal clear he was engaged, ensuring there was no misunderstanding of his status. After all, Roger was a handsome, upcoming legal star. There had been other women who had made a run at him during his engagement with Rachel, but he had always been true.

What happened? Roger decided it was time to face the demon. It had to be a setup. The only way to find out the truth was to find the blonde.

Settling at his computer, he typed in escorts in the search bar. It was a long shot, but he had to unravel this for his own sanity. The server loaded up thousands of sites. Inappropriate site names populated. He reluctantly read a few; hotbabes.com, barelylegal.com, youngandhorny.com, comenow.com. The nauseating list went on and on. Roger clicked on the first site. Tiny square photos popped up on the screen. Roger double clicked, launching the images to page size. The first two women were blonde, oversized breasts spilling onto the screen, legs spread wide, revealing everything proper women should keep private. Roger tried to concentrate on their faces. Neither was the blonde he was searching for.

After an hour of looking at naked women posing provocatively, women with women in semi-aerobic positions, women performing pleasurable acts on parts of men, he decided he had enough. He angered at his arousal by the surreal images and the realization that there were more pornographic websites out there than he could look at in one lifetime. It was hopeless. To find this girl required resources. He scrolled through his contact list; it was time to engage some old college and law school buddies for help. *They won't mind!* Roger smirked weakly before he made four calls, waking a couple of buddies on the east coast who were sleeping next to their wives.

"How would I explain this project to Shania?" Joe whispered into the phone, not wanting to wake his wife. Roger hadn't thought about that. He heard the same concern from Brian.

Fortunately, the interest from Chuck and Wally was the opposite as they joined onto a group call, so Roger didn't have to explain the nauseating scenario more than once. A project searching porn sites was the least they could do to help a buddy out, they had both chuckled.

The trio reminisced about the crazy days of college and law school, and sleepless nights of studying and having fun in between exams. The three of them agreed during their sophomore undergrad year to apply to and attend the same law school. Wally was the one who broke the agreement, unable to get accepted to Princeton like the other two. And, ironically, Wally was the one pulling down the most money now, making partner two years out of law school at one of the most prestigious firms in San Francisco.

After Wally dropped off the call to catch some sleep, Roger finished his call with Chuck. "Hey, sorry for the late call. I assumed you'd be up working on some important political underpinning of the nation." Roger said.

"Hey, Buddy. You know me, I'm always up late. Something told me this wasn't a social call to catch up on my legal genius." Chuck laughed.

"You still working for the party?" Roger asked.

Chuck had opted for the D.C. political life, doing research for the Republican Party. Not the typical-looking research guru with his overpowering stature and two-hundred-and-forty-pound solid frame. Perfectly satisfied never to step foot into a courtroom.

"You bet. You wouldn't believe the number of lawsuits that fly back and forth, ridiculous suits at that. But it's job security." Chuck bellowed. "I'm sorry about all this turmoil in your life. Hopefully, we can find something, and you can get some closure."

"I can't let it go. I know it's been a few years. But I have to know what happened that night and if the senator was somehow involved. It's making me crazy again."

"I tried to warn you about him. But love is love, and I'm glad you and Rachel found each other for a while. I'm sorry you're still being tortured by that relationship. I thought since Rachel's death, you might get past those dark days. I guess not."

In spite of Chuck's warnings that the senator's reputation

as a ruthless, underhanded son-of-a-bitch was common knowledge on the streets of D.C., Roger had been in love and naively thought love overcame everything, even politics.

"I need help to track that blonde woman. She has to be a professional."

"You mean a hooker?"

"Yes, I guess. I can't remember anything. And I have full confidence in your sleuthing skills."

"That's why they pay me the big bucks. And anything to help you and possibly take that asshole down," Chuck said with his reassuring baritone laugh.

Roger felt sure if anyone could find the blonde bombshell, it was Chuck. Roger forced a smile as he hung up the phone, walked to the window, pulling the drapes aside, wishing Rachel were still alive so she, too, could know the truth, whatever that truth might be.

Chapter 20
Find the Link

The morning broke, sending slivers of light through the gap in the curtains, spurring Jeannie's enthusiasm for her mission to get to Java Connection corporate offices and began her quest.

After changing outfits twice, finally settling on a power pantsuit, she stepped out onto the sunny streets and walked past the buildings, not bothering to notice the street names, keeping her eyes focused on her destination. It had taken three return trips to the bathroom mirror to assure herself that remnants of Rachel Rose were not detectable in her face or eyes.

Tugging on the large gold handle of the glass doors leading into the corporate office, she'd finally reached the terminus she'd imagined for the past seventy-two hours. Stepping onto the shiny marble slabs inside the two-story foyer of Java Connection, she swallowed hard and steeled herself for what she was about to attempt.

A perky receptionist sat waiting to greet the new recruits. "Welcome to Java Connection. Are you a new manager?" the young woman chimed.

"Yes," she told her with a forced smile.

Behind the receptionist sat large clear windows edged

with multi-color neon lights moving colored liquid through the distinctive tubes, a customized version of the lava lamp. The globby colors flowed along the edges, into, through, and out of the letters that spelled out the word Java. It was the same treatment as the store signs, a Java Connection original concept.

On the other side of the glass were offices, where people made important hand gestures and were busily speaking on headsets, pacing as they negotiated. Silent laughter was recognizable by the tossing of heads as deals were made with exaggerated nodding followed by wide smiles, confirming victory. There were brief looks from the wheeler-dealers to the corridors, where young women bustled with files in hand, moving purposely to some unknown destination. It was a contagious atmosphere of importance.

"Your name?" the receptionist asked loudly.

Jeannie wasn't sure how long the young girl had been asking the simple question.

"I'm sorry, a little jet lagged I guess," she tried to excuse herself. The girl smiled, waiting patiently for a response.

"Jeannie. Jeannie Smith."

"Here we are, Ms. Smith, your name tag. If you go to the third floor, you will find the training room and the instructors," she informed her, handing the printed name tag to Jeannie and directing her to the brass trimmed glass elevators that rose and descended behind the reception area.

Unable to formulate a response, Jeannie's thoughts froze as she mentally took inventory of the items in her purse, the plan, the possibility of getting caught and losing this opportunity forever, and worse, her true identity being exposed. She picked up the name tag, but didn't move from the spot where she stood, oblivious to the other new manager trainees stacking in a line behind her.

"Excuse me," the young man behind her finally said.

"I'm sorry," she apologized as she emerged from her disoriented fog. Seeking safety, she fled to the elevator, pushing the close button immediately as she stepped in, locking out the approaching manager trainees. All in a last-ditch effort to gather her composure, watching the bustle below her as the elevator climbed.

When she reached the third floor, the doors slid open with a modest ping, delivering her into a large, expansive room. Young men and women were milling from table to table, gathering reading materials and Java Connection promotional items. Taking a seat, she offered a weak smile to a tall, fresh-faced guy settling in beside her. A long table fixed against the wall of windows was covered with bagels, fruit, packets of snacks, beverages, and, of course, Colombian coffee.

"Welcome to Java Connection." The presenter boomed through his microphone. "We are excited to meet you all and we hope you soon feel like an integral part of this vast family. It's not only a corporation that makes the best coffee in the world, but it is truly an environment, a culture, and a mission worthy or your skill, knowledge, and time."

With a push of a button, the shades lowered, and darkness shadowed the enthusiastic faces, absorbing all that was being delivered by the energetic executive, who disappeared after the inspirational film clip from the founder of the company began spooling.

As she watched the video, the words lost meaning. Instead, she fixated on the founder's eyes for clues to his corruption, but there was no villainy, only kindness. The same as the internet searches she'd fruitlessly done. The lack of obvious guilt sent a flash of anger through her tightened chest, hoping this would be an easy mission, knowing logically, it would not be. What was it her father had always told her? Nothing worthwhile is easy.

Intentionally avoiding conversation with other trainees, Jeannie immersed herself in the literature while plodding along through the day trying to absorb the "meaning" of the company, the "mission," her "motivation," and the "purpose" of the existence of the coffeehouses. It wasn't a business, but a dream. A dream of a poor coffee bean picker, who over the years planted and propagated his own coffee plants, carefully splicing and experimenting with the plants until he finally achieved the perfect genetic recombination and thus the finest coffee beans ever to be grown. He was well into his sixties by then and his health was failing, but his three sons joined together to carry on his dream.

They sold the beans locally in the beginning and from there, the popularity of the rare beans spread like the plague.

A Colombian businessman who, years earlier, made his home in California, uncovered the valuable beans on a trip back to his homeland. He immediately threw money at the boys and brought the beans to the land of opportunity. The family retired wealthy, and the old man's dream, as interpreted by his sons, was fulfilled. The rest is, as they say, history.

Michael Long was the trainer for the group. A tall, lanky man in his early thirties, with wire-frame glasses slipping off his pointy nose. Not the typical California muscle builders who pepper the beaches of Santa Monica. It was questionable whether his milky skin had ever seen the West Coast sun. He was, however, extremely bright, and knowledgeable about Java Connection.

Jeannie tracked his information all afternoon, hoping to extract a helpful detail. It seemed he droned on longer than need be, enjoying the spotlight, something she was certain he never had outside this particular forum. Thinking she couldn't muster one more ounce of energy to become one with the company, Michael Long finally wrapped the presentation.

"That's all for the first day. I'm passing out a training link to each of you in pre-prepared packages made specifically for your region and demographics. It's self-prompting and will take you through virtually every management scenario you may encounter. We'll be going through each step this week with an expanded discussion. Next week, you will focus on the financial management of your stores," Michael informed all the eager newbies. "If you want to look over the site and you don't have your company laptop issued yet, you may use our computer lab in the adjacent room. There are private cubicles with terminals set up for your use, so help yourself. The lab is open until eight p.m.," he continued.

Jeannie stood up before the others to make her way to the lab and started down the rows of metal chairs but was halted by a perky young blonde who had been chiming in all day.

"We're headed to the beach bar for a drink. Would you like to join us?" the woman asked.

"Me?" Jeannie was puzzled.

"Yes, sure. I noticed you were sitting alone all day and didn't really engage with anyone. I thought you might want to have some fun. I'm really good at social events," the blonde continued as she flipped her hair over her shoulder.

"Oh, thanks for that. It's sweet of you, but I wanted to review some of the corporate information tonight to get a jump start on my job when I get back. But you have fun." Jeannie turned on her charm, patting the girl's arm before she excused herself.

"Oh, I totally understand. I love your earrings. Are those from Tiffany's?" The girl reached up, nearly touching them.

Jeannie flinched, pulling her head back a tiny bit. The girl paused before retracting her hand. Reaching to her earrings instinctively, ensuring they were still in place, Jeannie stammered, then mumbled, "Yes, they were a gift."

Acting as if she hadn't noticed Jeannie's reaction, the girl said, "Well, they're lovely. If you change your mind about joining us, we'll be right up the street at Maloney's Beach Bar. You can't miss it. There's a large surfboard out front." The girl waved down another attendee and skirted away.

Jeannie turned quickly and headed for the lab, escaping the laughing and chatting of the sociable men and women. Most of them fresh out of college, eager to make their place in the corporate world and ascend the ladder of success. Her bitter attitude bit at her emotions. She would prefer to introduce herself, join them at the bar on the beach, have a few laughs and a couple of drinks, forget responsibility. The majority were young and single, undoubtedly pairing up and exploring different hotel rooms during the next two weeks. Jeannie sighed, then scampered away from the jovial youth, back to reclaiming her life so one day soon she could laugh with abandonment at a beach bar.

The lab was empty except for a few technical-looking nerds wearing white lab coats, monitoring some type of data, and chatting nervously. They ignored Jeannie.

She searched for the most private cubicle, moving the coffee mug shaped lapel pin out from under her name tag. She'd hidden it after another trainee wanted to know where she bought it because it was "so cute!" The last thing she needed was someone examining it closely and drawing more attention to it.

Sitting in a brightly colored chair and following the instructions on the handout, the laptop sprang to life, popping open the main website. Entering her username and password, it immediately brought up her private login page with her store information. Combing the site, wondering how to get into the main home area for the entire corporation, she examined each icon, but nothing unusual stood out.

"Are you there?" she asked in a barely audible voice. Silence. "Hello? Marshal Gagne?" she raised her voice slightly, then rose high enough to peer at the surrounding cubicles to ensure nobody was within earshot.

"This is the computer tech." She heard a faint male voice say through the tiny transmitter in the earrings.

"Okay. I don't know how to find the main system configurations. All I've been given is the login to my private page for my store. I think I need to finish some other training before we get access to the main corporate portal."

"Log out and go back to your login page, text me the URL, then login with your username and password," the person on the other end told her.

Jeannie complied, reentering the login information, and giving one more glance toward the geeks who were abandoning their project and filing out of the room.

"Okay, I did that. What now?" she asked the faceless

voice.

"Did you text the URL?" the voice asked.

"Yes, I sent it already," Jeannie was puzzled. There was a definite lag between what the tech was saying and her answers, giving her pause and making her palms sweat.

Her text message alert dinged on the new smartphone, it was from an unknown number, a link was attached.

"Open your text, and let me know when the site comes up," the voice commanded.

Touching the link in the text message, the site opened, producing the Java Connection main corporate intranet. Examining and scrolling through the various buttons and selections, it contained standard corporate materials: managerial quizzes, employment policies and laws, customer dispute scenarios, customer service tips and tricks, and guidebooks for managing store financial reports.

"It looks boring," Jeannie said.

"Keep looking," the voice urged.

Running down the page again, she slowed her scan, taking care to examine each button and search for anything that looked out of place. She scrolled the screen, enlarging it so she could see elements in greater detail. Then she saw something that didn't look right. The V of Java appeared to be a hyperlink, but it was so light it made it difficult to tell. Jeannie touched the V, but nothing happened. She tried again and double-tapped it. The V grew and opened up like a blooming flower as the page turned inside out. A smile slid across her face.

"I think I found something," she whispered anxiously.

"Good," the voice responded.

Jeannie stared at her phone screen for what seemed like

an eternity, then a muddled image popped up, words scattered across the page, reading: **you'll never be safe.**

Jeannie's breath caught as she read the message. Then it disappeared and transformed into what appeared to be a security video with black and white pixels piecing together slowly, the fragmented person coming to life. The date and time stamp revealed itself in the bottom right-hand corner. It was today's date, and the time was now, it was a live feed.

A man sat in a chair, bound by ropes on both his feet and hands. His mouth covered by a gag. His eyes, blind-folded. But Jeannie recognized him despite the partial coverings. It was Marshal Gagne. Jeannie gulped her own breath down, trying to comprehend the picture plastered across the screen.

"Are you watching now?" the voice came over the transmitter.

Jeannie didn't respond.

"Did you hear me?" The words were spoken in a harsh melody.

"Yes," Jeannie hissed.

"Watch carefully, Jeannie Smith," the voice warned.

Confused by the images, Jeannie didn't want to watch what was playing out on the screen, but she couldn't look away. She had to know the truth. A black gloved hand appeared on the top right of the screen, pointing a gun at Marshal Gagne's head.

"No!" Jeannie started to scream, clasping her hand over her own mouth to muffle it, silencing her voice.

Before the protest could come out of her throat, a shot rang out. The distinctive bang echoed in her ears. Marshal Gagne's head exploded into scattered black and gray pixels. His chair teetered back and forth before tossing his lifeless body to the floor. Motionless, black fluid spread its way across the gray floor as the man's life melted away. All she could hear was resounding laughter in her ears.

Jeannie ripped the earrings off and threw them against the cubicle. She slid the screen away and smashed the off button on her phone to terminate the sight of the death she'd witnessed. Arms thrashing with panic as she attempted to gather her belongings, cramming everything haphazardly into her bag. Terror pulsed through her, she sped to the elevator, frantically pushing the buttons. Coming up the elevator, Jeannie hadn't noticed its slowness, now making her muscles contract with frustration.

Abandoning the elevator, she ran to the stairwell, smashing open the door with her full arms, scuttling down the steps two at a time, stumbling every few steps as panic accelerated through her body.

The door on the first floor stuck, then gave way with the force of her adrenalin. She spilled into the dark parking lot, forcing her to gather her thoughts and orient herself. The streets were bustling with people. She sought safety by blending into the masses, searching for the face of evil that had found her.

Images of death chased her with every step, forcing her to quicken her pace. There was only one place she could go. Her horror-struck thoughts now blindly driving her away from Java, away from her hotel, straight to Roger. He was a safe person she could trust, even if it went against all the dark pain and brokenness she'd endured over the past three years.

On autopilot, she found Roger's building but stopped in her tracks when rounding the corner and eyeing the entrance. It was keycard access only. She would have to wait for another resident to come along and shadow them to enter.

Choking back tears now coming from her throat in loud sobs, she ducked out of sight while the emotions rolled over her. The reality she'd dreamed of for years had come to life, bringing with it a desperation to survive, coupled with battling the overwhelming desire to fall apart on the sidewalk.

Wiping the tears from her face, fanning and blotting until there was no emotional evidence remaining, she inhaled slowly, gathering all that she was and forcing herself to calm by concentrating on the task at hand, which was gaining entry into the building without appearing to be breaking and entering.

She rearranged and stuffed all the materials she'd fled Java Connection with into her faux leather shoulder bag and watched the door for the next opportunity.

Spotting two preoccupied women heading toward the door, their conversation evidently hysterical, Jeannie allowed herself a small distance between them. They swiped their card and the doors magically released to let them enter. Jeannie stuffed her hand in her bag, pretending to search for her misplaced key card. "Wait, hold the door, please," she called out. The women weren't interested in the innocuous girl following them into the building and held the door while continuing their clucking.

"Thanks," Jeannie called after them. Thankful for the power suit, giving herself a modicum of credibility. The elevator opened, she pressed the button to Roger's floor, climbed inside, watched the doors close, then collapsed against the shiny mirrored walls while making her escape to safety.

Chapter 21
Bogata One

BogataOne laughed at the blood pooling on the floor. He summoned his soldier to remove and dispose of the limp body.

"Good work, Nicky," he congratulated his employee.

"Thanks, boss. What about the girl? Do I get a shot at her other than with my camera?" Nicky grinned and rolled the dead Marshal Gagne onto his back.

"No, this one is personal. I'll be taking care of this myself. Besides, you've got a flight to catch. You've been summoned to Colombia for a while."

Nicky smiled, knowing he'd earned a promotion. He grabbed the body under the arms, then professionally rolled it in a tarp. A maneuver he had practiced only in his mind but executed perfectly as his boss watched with a grin. Attempting to keep impressing his boss, he hoisted the two-hundred pounds of dead weight as best he could, having to manhandle the body to get a grip on it and exit the room, leaving his boss alone to do his work. He backed out the door, half dragging the corpse.

Once Nicky was out of sight, BogataOne, carefully stepped over the sticky puddle and righted the chair. Taking a seat, he rewound the tape of Jeannie Smith in her cubicle, watching her supposed protector being terminated. He howled as terror splashed across her helpless face; life being extinguished before her eyes. It was her fault. Just as everything had been her fault. Her perfect ideas, her wholesome image, her virtues. Besides, it seemed Gagne had developed a little crush on Jeannie and had attempted to place a call to the FBI, not knowing the call was intercepted. He had to go.

It had taken him years to hatch this plan, and she tried to undo everything because *she* was too honest to touch anything other than goodness. She'd been that way as far back as he could recall. Never cheating on an exam, never having to. Never breaking traffic laws, no speeding in her gorgeous sports car. Never causing public embarrassment to the senator until the trial. No headlines about drug-use, partying, or any indiscretions. Never being anything but the goody-two-shoes she was born to be.

He scowled as he thought of Jeannie Smith, formerly Rachel Rose. It was time for her undoing. Something she would do herself if his plan was executed perfectly. She should have laid low, stayed in Houston, Texas, but she couldn't leave well enough alone. He'd been willing to let her live, but then she went on a revenge quest, unable to give up trying to prove her father's guilt. Seeking out Java Connection with disregard for her own fate, her critical mistake. Once she walked into the trap, then it was easy. He pulled a few strings, setting temptations into motion that he knew she wouldn't pass up. Again, her fault. She'd sealed her own fate.

When the world becomes aware of her real demise, they will believe the media spin all over again, and she will be the imperfect one. They will scorn the dead daughter of Senator Rose.

He'd make sure of that.

He rewound the tape further, before the untimely death of Gagne, back to the footage of Senator Rose's playmate in D.C. Such an easy kill. Having been summoned by the senator to take care of his pregnant mistress had allowed the perfect opportunity to practice his new trade.

The senator assumed the girl was being sent off to a new life for an abortion and silence. Ecstasy surged through him, knowing the reaction when the pictures of the mutilated body appeared on the senator's desk a few years later, planted there so Rachel would find them. Considering the girl's dangerous profession of being a hooker. It could have been anyone who killed her. *Poor Natalie*, he laughed.

The tape continued its journey backwards, revealing more images, including those of Senator Rose, Roger, and Rachel. He enjoyed the next few hours, splicing and rejoining, creating his masterpiece. They would all be surprised when the final tape was revealed on national television. That would be the culmination of his unrecognized hard work. He would have everything then, including the nation's pity, and the senator would be out of his way.

Walking across the catwalk to the adjoining building, he returned to his own plush office, relaxing comfortably in his leather chair, clasping his hands behind his head, tipping back in his chair, and congratulating himself on creating the perfect plan to destroy the trio simultaneously.

Pushing his shoes off one at a time and propping his feet on the contemporary acrylic desk, he finally relaxed, the reflection of the multicolor lights soothing his mood. Watching the lava flow through the Java Connection sign further lulled him into believing his own thoughts of grandeur. He smiled contently. Impressed with his own cleverness.

Chapter 22
Do As You're Told

S enator Rose arrived back in Santa Monca around eleven p.m. His work in D.C. was complete, so he begged off the last days he was supposed to be there for meetings.

He'd managed to finagle his manipulations of the others for the unquestionable support of his end goal of streamlining the inspections under the auspice that doing so would make it easier to sniff out the drug runners if there were fewer ports to control and monitor. The truth was, the port inspector in his pocket only had control over six ports.

It appeared on the surface to be rational and logical; it was working beautifully. Senator Johnstone presented the brilliant plan when Jay graciously stepped down from the committee for the vote. All it took to buy his persuasion was a few measly greenbacks.

Taking in the streets as his driver wound his way through the hills to his home, he knew it was his town. California was a soothing sight after the gray skies of D.C. Even in the darkness, the sky appeared brighter, stars sparkling clearly instead of being lost in the haze of the cloudy November skies. Jay relaxed in the back of the limousine and poured himself a scotch, settling in to open the package he received from the private investigator.

He'd resisted the urge until now, not sure if he truly wanted the information inside. Once he knew for sure where his daughter was, then he would have to make certain decisions that were difficult for a father, even a betrayed father.

Expecting to find the current whereabouts of his daughter, he tore open the envelope. Reading the updated report, he was disappointed by the news. Rachel had only been tracked to two cities and disappeared after the second. Jay shoved the envelope back into his briefcase. Patience was not something he was blessed with.

As the soothing effects of the scotch worked his muscles into a calmer state, he closed his eyes and found himself revisiting the face of a beloved young daughter. A daughter he hoisted proudly onto his broad shoulders. A daughter he bought a pink rocking horse for and smiled at her giggles of joy. Cuddling in his arms every night when he sat working late into the evening, because she simply loved being near him.

When did it all change?

He knew the answer and reluctantly accepted the blame. The change was prompted by his metamorphosis, the catalyst that set the events in motion. It began with the last visit with his mother and father, a meeting that was imprinted on his mind. It was the day he officially took over the family business and was told in no uncertain terms that it was up to him to keep the legacy going.

His father had become even more cruel in his advanced age, drilling home his belief year after year that Jay was a disappointment and didn't have what it took to be a Rose. His father's death was a relief and a spark to catapult Jay's political ambitions. He felt no guilt in using it as fuel for his meteoric rise.

Knowing he could make the family influence more powerful than it had been under his ruthless father. Jay simplified the process. Instead of taking years to do favors, with a reciprocal deed in return, he secured his power with money.

Total control of the blue-blood money after his mother's death was a springboard to further what he'd started, using money to wine and dine the "right" connections in a world that could bring him more money than even the Rose family could imagine. He would out-earn his father, even if his father wasn't around to witness it.

And his mother, well, she was crueler than his father, making sure Jay understood that there was no room for failure, and he had better not disappoint her and ruin their legacy. There were plenty of family members who looked up to him. And he would be revered. He was, after all, the eldest living Rose with needy nephews and nieces seeking guidance, not that he'd communicated with them in years. Seemed bad blood made its way down the lineage instead of being buried with the death of his father and his uncles.

Jay slid his thoughts from the past to the present, watching the driver maneuver the long drive to the mansion, sunken in unusual darkness. Why the lights were not on probably had to do with his wife being drunk and asleep. Scott was most likely at the condo. He knew Linda wasn't waiting up for his late arrival from D.C., and he was glad about that.

His journey home came to an end, and he was content to step back into his plush surroundings. The driver pulled to the side entrance, a familiar routine, allowing Jay undetected entry so he could head toward his suite of rooms on the opposite end of Linda's without the risk of being intercepted and peppered with endless questions. Many years had passed since they shared a bed. It suited them both.

He tossed his overcoat on the chaise lounge as he entered his bedroom and sat to free his feet from the binding shoes.

"Well, so the prodigal son returns," a female voice taunted.

Jay jumped up from the chair, startled by the unexpected presence of another person in the room. He flicked on the light, surprised by the company who had come to call.

"What are you doing here?" he asked brusquely.

"I live here, remember?" Linda reclined across Jay's bed on the satin sheets, a glass of wine in her hand, obviously not the first of the evening. Clad in a flimsy negligee, it gaped open as she let her arm fall across her body.

"What are you doing in my room? I thought you despised this end of the house." He couldn't help but notice the cleavage staring back at him.

"Oh, snooping around to see what you've been up to," she slurred.

He stared at the woman he had been married to for thirty-six years, trying to remember what it was that had drawn them together in the first place.

"Come sit down here and let's have a little talk, or something," she said seductively as she patted the bed.

"Mrs. Rose, are you trying to seduce me?" He leered at his intoxicated wife.

"Oh, don't be ridiculous. My use for you is strictly business," she said pointedly.

Insulted by his wife's apparent lack of interest in him, he dropped his pants intentionally, stepped out of them, then joined her on the bed, moving around behind her, spooning her, and gripping her waist.

Linda tried to escape his grasp, spilling her wine onto the carpet. Her little joke now spinning out of control, having forgotten how strong he was.

Jay straddled his wife, pinning her arms, leaning down, placing his cheek next to hers as he kissed her gently on the neck. She thrashed her head from side to side, blonde hair flinging back and forth, but the harder she fought, the more aroused the senator became. He clasped her small wrists in one hand and held her face tight, forcing her to look into his eyes.

"You will cooperate," he ordered.

Linda knew there was no use in fighting him. Her husband always got what he wanted. Maybe Linda wanted the same thing, she told herself. Maybe she had come to his bedroom for this reason after all. He released the grasp on her wrists, and she slid her arms around his neck. He kissed her hard on the mouth; she returned the passion. They wrapped themselves around each other, a routine they'd developed throughout their dysfunctional marriage as he initiated and directed their movements. Submitting to a carnal need, both engulfed by the physical satisfaction each could provide; they continued their play well into the night. Linda finally objecting as the effects of the alcohol and pills wore away, and soreness took over.

Moving away from her husband, Linda went to the bathroom, bundled herself in her husband's designer robe she'd given him years ago when appearances still mattered, and faced him. "Is Rachel dead?" She asked without emotion.

Jay was taken aback by his wife's question. Up until now, she appeared to be consumed by grief and powering through it with alcohol as her crutch, not having spoken Rachel's name since the news of the crash except with slurred sobs.

"Of course, she's dead. You saw the news. The officials called and told you."

"I know all of that, but I don't feel like she's gone. I feel like she's here."

"Here?" The Senator was unsure what his wife meant. "Here, as on this earth? Or here, as in this house?"

"As in this house," she said, her voice breaking into a soft sob as she spoke.

"As far as I know, she is dead," he told her. He moved off the bed and pulled on his pajama pants, void of any empathy for his wife and needing a drink to continue the conversation.

"I don't believe you," she challenged him. "You're looking for her, aren't you? I found receipts from the private investigator."

"You found them? Where?" He knew he had not been that careless.

"In your office."

"What were you doing in my office? You know it's off limits to everyone when I'm gone," he said harshly, his face reddening as he squared off with Linda.

"Scott was in there working on some assignment. I went in to take him to lunch. I happened to see the receipts in his briefcase."

Idiot boy! "What did Scott tell you?"

"He said you were being cautious, that Rachel was dead." Her voice quaked as she admitted what Scott had told her. He'd also told her that his father thought Rachel was alive, but she knew better than to disclose too much.

"He shouldn't have told you about the investigation. It's a technicality since there was no body recovered. It's strictly for insurance purposes, and I do believe Rachel is dead, as Scott does," he lied.

"I don't believe you." She stood near him now, staring deeply into his eyes, searching for a glimmer of truth.

"I don't care," he said, returning the stare. He grabbed her face and pulled her close again, planting a rough kiss across her slightly swollen mouth.

She kissed him back, then pulled away swiftly.

"You owe me the truth," she insisted in a hushed whisper.

"I owe you nothing."

It was more than Linda's fragile mind could absorb. Instead, it cracked open along with her heart. Reflexively, she swung at him, wielding a full palmed slap across his smug face.

He returned the gesture.

She grabbed her cheek.

"We have one child left. Leave it alone, Linda," he warned.

"We?" she chided. "I have one child left."

"What is that supposed to mean?"

"Ask Scott. I'm sure he'll explain it to you!" She stormed out of the room, stopping at the doorway. "By the way, your affairs outside this marriage will stop. Do you understand?"

Jay grumbled a laugh at the command. "What would you know about affairs, madam?"

"You'll find out what I know about affairs. You'll find out soon," she hissed, then disappeared to her side of the mansion.

Jay stalked to the door, slamming it behind her. "I'll stop having affairs when hell freezes over," he announced to the empty room. Her words still ringing in his ears. He'd never understood the crazy woman anyway, pushing her demands out of his mind.

Chapter 23
How?

Roger heard the banging on the door. Staring annoyingly at it since he wasn't expecting anyone at this hour, he sighed, pushing himself from the chair he'd settled into. Reluctantly, he peeked through the viewer, not recognizing the shaking young woman on the other side. He opened the door anyway.

"Can I help you?" he asked.

"Can I come in please, Roger?"

Roger stared at the girl, trying to recall where they might have met. She knew his name, but he couldn't seem to draw her from his memory.

"Do I know you?" he questioned, fearing he might offend the distressed stranger, clearly needing to be saved.

"Yes, let me in and I'll explain." The shaking was growing worse. Rachel glanced down the hallway, her nerves jumping uncontrollably.

Roger opened the door wider, allowing entry, not feeling threatened by the obviously frightened woman, who calmed the minute she stepped into the room and the door shut behind her.

"Thank you so much. Don't you recognize me?" she asked. A heavy sigh released the deflation she felt from Roger not recognizing her. Maybe the agents had been right that she'd be unrecognizable. Who could blame him?

Roger stared at her harder, then turned on the light.

"No, turn it off," she snapped, slapping the switch down. "They might see me," she stammered, attempting to explain her reaction.

"Who might see you?" Roger was now concerned.

"The people who are after me, my father." Rachel stared at him, trying to connect.

He stepped back as confusion prickled its way through his mind. She sounded like Rachel, but that couldn't be. It was impossible. Rachel was dead.

Growing tired of waiting for Roger to recognize her, Rachel said, "It's me, Roger. Rachel." Stepping toward him and taking his hands in hers.

Roger pushed the inclination away to believe what she was saying, stepping back, trying to escape the clutches of the woman he was now certain was deranged. "Rachel's dead. If this is your idea of a joke? It's not funny. Who are you and why are you here?" His voice escalated as he examined the details of the woman's face.

"It's me, Rachel," she insisted.

"Rachel?" Roger was sizing her up. Everything was right about her features except the eyes and the hair. "Rachel had unforgettable eyes. Yours are brown. You can't be Rachel."

Rachel popped the contacts out and stood before the love of her life. "It's me, Roger." She had no energy for this back and forth.

Mesmerized by her hypnotic eyes, he knew it was Rachel. He moved toward her with caution, then reached up and touched her hair softly. She closed her eyes, pressing her cheek into his hand as she used to do. The touch of his fingers sent a shock through her body, a want she'd long forgotten with distance and time and anger and pain. She hardly recognized that feeling anymore, but now it surged through her vividly.

"My God, it is you. Where have you been all this time?" He pulled her into him, encasing her in his strong arms.

The tears came without warning, his touch evoking a cascade of years of pain and longing that came tumbling down harder than the waves pounding outside. He pulled her down with him onto the sofa, holding her and rocking her like a child as the flood of memories washed over them both. Grasping each other with desperation, Rachel's tears slowed and dried, her sobs silenced by her heart, now pounding against Roger's chest. His heart joining in tempo with hers.

"I thought you were dead," he said softly, continuing to stroke her short hair, placing a caring kiss on the top of her head.

She couldn't answer. Not wanting to speak or let thoughts invade her mind. Only wanting to feel his touch, his strength, to feel safe, as she had years ago. "It's a long story. I've been living in Houston most recently," she answered, knowing he deserved an explanation.

Roger propped himself up and moved her shoulders away from him so he could look into her eyes. "Are you okay? I like your hair." He half-smiled, though the answers weren't important to him now. Exhaustion sat across her face, coupled with a look that told him one thing: she needed him. "I'm so sorry, Rachel." Roger wanted to tell her that he hadn't been with that woman on purpose, that he couldn't even remember her, but he didn't want to ruin the moment, so he stopped his confession short. "I'm so sorry."

"It's okay. I'm sorry too. I'm sorry I had to let you believe I was dead. I saw you on television…" Rachel choked back soft sobs that threatened to erupt from her throat once more. "I saw you on television. Thank you for saying nice things about me." The emotion seeping out despite her best efforts.

"It's okay. I never stopped loving you, not for a single minute." He took her chin in his hand, lifting her face again to his, calming her instantly. Roger placed his mouth gingerly on hers, cautious of how she might receive his kiss after all this time. She accepted it warmly and returned the affection.

Rachel's mind ceased the internal battle it was waging as soon as his lips pressed against hers. Excitement inching over her skin, transforming into a tingle that danced slowly and lightly across her chest. Smiling inside as the tingling danced faster throughout her body, awakening sensations she'd forgotten existed.

Roger's head was spinning as he deepened the intensity of his kiss, which felt unreal and more like the dreams he'd had too many times over the past three years since they'd broken apart and only intensified when he learned of her death. As the realization grew that Rachel was alive and, in his arms, happy vibrations surged through him, a small groan of delight rolled from his throat. He scooped her up into his arms, not wanting to let her have control over her movement so that she couldn't change her mind and flee from him again.

Rachel wrapped her arms around his neck, their lips only parting for a well-needed breath. She let her head fall back as he carried her to his bedroom and laid her gently on the bed. She glanced around dreamily. Everything she saw was familiar and comfortable. Nothing had changed from the blissful nights spent in his arms so long ago. She pushed away all the doubt and the voices trying to caution her against the direction she was headed, ignoring what her head was bullying her to feel. Instead, feeling something strong and powerful again was her lifeblood now. It had been so terribly long since she felt safe and needed, and Roger was the only one who could give her this, now and possibly forever. Refusing to think about the future, or right or wrong, all she wanted was to focus on the moment and savor the embrace enveloping all her heartbreak and fear.

When Roger lay beside her, the heat from his body intensified her craving for him, prompting a silent internal scream of joyous pleasure. Not wanting to wait for what she knew he would provide. Needing it all now, all at once, again and again, but he moved slowly, building the anticipation that lit every nerve ending.

Roger pulled her tighter against his body, kissing her ear, savoring the moment as he became reacquainted with her curves and her skin and her taste. Tracing her lips with his finger, he slid it down her chin, across her neck, down to her breastbone.

She relished the pressure of his single finger as it drew over her skin. Closing her eyes, concentrating solely on the touch, absorbing the sensation at every point and blocking out the dangerous world circling around her, she melted into the moment. Roger moved his hand to her thigh, lightly skimming it down her pant leg and back up to her stomach. She waited for more, but he'd stopped touching her and had sat up. Rachel's eyes flew open.

"Don't stop," she heard herself say.

"Shhhh." He pulled his shirt over his head. Then gently took her hands, pulling her up to him. With careful fingers, he unbuttoned her blouse, letting it slip to the floor.

Jeannie watched his face, noticing details she'd forgotten, taking them in as if she'd never seen him. Now exposed, any self-conscious tendency she felt moments earlier fell away, replaced by excitement, his touch awakening memories tucked away for self-preservation, they crashed over her, warming her, and for the first time in three years—she felt free.

They helped each other discard their remaining clothes, cradling each other as their tongues explored the other's mouth, desire rising from the connection and years lost. Desperate need unfolded with the touch of their hands, intensifying within their bodies, and bursting through their hearts. The passion struck them hard and fast and recoiled again and again as they joined together as they knew they should have always been. As if they'd never been parted by life, by time, or even by death. They became one again, recovering their buried emotions and transforming them into what they had been before and rediscovering what had never left either of them.

Love.

When the intensity reached its peak and could grow no more, they released it to the other and then let it subside as gracefully as it had grown. They lay expended and satisfied, holding each other with no regret. Words weren't needed; they instinctively knew the thoughts the other held. Exhaustion and satisfaction drove the fear from Rachel's heart as she rested beside her love, as if years and anger never tested or separated them.

"I love you," she mumbled as Roger drifted to sleep.

He barely heard her, but the words awakened his heart. "I love you too," he whispered back, then pulled her into him again, fearful to let go, afraid it was all a mirage, and she would disappear when he woke.

~

Rachel slept for only a short while before the thoughts of Marshal Gagne rolled her out of her bliss and back to reality. She screamed herself awake.

Roger grasped her shoulders, comforting her as he spoke assuredly to her, "You're okay, Rachel. You're okay."

God, what did they do to you?

Roger was frightened by Rachel's nightmare. He wanted to keep her safe, but he had to know what she was afraid of, and at this moment he had no clue.

"Roger," she gasped as she realized her dream was not real, but she didn't cry again. Her resilience had been strengthened by the reemergence of herself and by Roger lying next to her.

"It was a dream, Rachel," Roger reassured her.

Rachel was on her feet now, dragging the sheet along with her and covering herself as she moved from the bed. "We have to talk, Roger. There's a site. It was Java Connection, but then it became a live feed." Rachel scrambled for her bag, pulling the training materials out and tossing them aside, searching for the earrings before recalling she'd flung them across the cubicle. She began rambling details and explanations rapidly, too rapidly for Roger to follow.

"Whoa, slow down. You aren't making sense," he told her. Roger took her hand to calm her.

"I've been in a witness protection program. My death was faked to try to protect me."

"I assumed you might be. Who is after you? Your dad?"

Roger had already guessed the government had a hand in this since she was here and alive. He only wished he had known eight months ago and not punished himself for her death. His shattered heart had barely kept pace through it all, believing he'd lost her forever.

"I'm not sure. They said there was a credible threat. I'm sorry. They wouldn't let me contact anybody. It was for your safety, too." She calmed herself and sat on the bed next to him, dragging the sheet back with her and wrapping it more securely. "Recently, though, I have been trying to trace Java Connection to my father. Well, it's a long story. The federal agent, Marshal Gagne, he was accompanying me on this trip." Rachel stopped speaking as she looked at Roger. His face apparently caught in disbelief at all she was unloading.

"What are you talking about? Where's the agent now if he's supposed to be protecting you?" Roger asked.

"They killed him," she told him with a heavy heart.

"When?" Roger was sure he already knew.

"Last night, right before I came here." Rachel tossed the sheet aside and began dressing, touching the coffee pin on the lapel of her jacket. The pin with the relay to the killer. Her head spun as she realized she'd unwittingly placed Roger in jeopardy.

"Oh, my gosh," she mouthed, removing the pin and holding her finger to her pursed lips. She placed the pin in Roger's hand, then leaned in to whisper in his ear. "It's a camera to *them*."

Roger examined the pin carefully. He set it on the desk and ran to the kitchen, returning with a small screwdriver. He separated the pin, looking at the clasp, the pin casing, and the jewels, slowly removing each from the other until the pin lay in many pieces. There were no electronics embedded.

Roger looked at Rachel. "There's nothing in here, Rachel."

Rachel had been watching closely as he dissected the pin and she, too, knew he was right.

"I don't understand," she started.

Roger finished dressing. "Tell me exactly what happened." He sat at the end of the bed, rubbing his hands through his tussled hair. Exhaustion beginning to ravage him.

"I went to this training program at Java Connection headquarters. They passed out links to our manager's portals for training. After the session, I went to the computer lab, as Marshal Gagne instructed me on Sunday. He told me an IT specialist would walk me through the computer so they could get access to the backend and see if they could find anything to connect my dad and the drugs. I didn't have access to the full corporate site yet, only my portal. I thought I was talking to the IT guy. He asked me to text the URL, and then he texted me a site to look at. When I looked at it…" Rachel looked away from Roger, swallowing hard, then told him, "They killed Marshal Gagne, and I saw it. It was on my phone." Rachel held her phone out to Roger.

Roger crossed the room and removed the phone from Rachel's hand. It was turned off. "Let's see if we can find it again," he told her.

They retreated to Roger's office, and he powered on his laptop. She opened the text message that was still there with the URL. When he typed it in the search bar, the site popped open. Rachel showed him exactly how she had entered the room of the murder, through the V on Java.

"It was right here. I don't see it now, though. It has to be here. I saw it. I'm telling the truth."

"Rachel, are you sure? There's nothing here but a landing page for Java Connection reviews. Besides, if it were truly live, it would be gone now. I don't think we can access the room you saw last night." Roger was growing a little irritated as he searched the page looking for a secret portal but finding nothing. "You know, you're really tired and I'm drained. This has been a jarring night. Why don't we get some sleep, and we'll try again when the sun comes up?"

Rachel looked at Roger, knowing he must be confused by her mere presence. "Okay, you're probably right," she agreed. She didn't know much about smartphones, computers, or websites, but she knew enough about Roger to know he didn't believe her.

They both went back to bed, but she turned away, hoping to clear her head. She'd burst through his door, fallen into his arms, and his bed despite her determination to extract him from her life and douse the last ounce of love from her heart. How could she have backslid, reverting to a life that ended up in tatters? It had to be the trauma of watching the murder; it broke her defenses. But how could Roger not believe her? He'd always thought she was the most honest person he'd ever met. How many times had she heard that out of his mouth over the years?

The murder happened. She saw it. But he was right except "tired" didn't begin to describe what she felt, the weariness taking control and sinking her further from consciousness. Perhaps her mind had played tricks on her.

Maybe she imagined it all. God, she hoped not.

Chapter 24

Insanity At Its Finest

Roger woke before Rachel. It was difficult to watch her sleep without examining every inch of her face. Trying to figure out where Rachel ended and the new person began, and how they morphed into the woman lying in his bed. Everything was so different from before, not only the hair color, but the once casual, confident person had been replaced by a suspicious, jumpy woman.

He noticed as she slept that tiny crinkles were beginning to appear at the edges of her eyes, making him smile, remembering his dreams of watching her grow old as they tackled future years side-by-side. He was sorry he'd missed the past several years, but so grateful that Rachel was alive and had come to him for help.

Dreams of this moment had skipped through his nights often since he'd lost her. It was difficult to believe that she was alive and here next to him. He wanted to touch her again, but he had to figure out what was real or imagined in Rachel's world. Had she truly suffered a break from reality, as the news reported repeatedly after her death?

He picked up her shoulder bag off the bedroom floor and moved to the living room, being careful not to wake her. He needed some time to do a little digging.

The contents of the bag seemed relatively unimportant, all the literature about Java Connection and her wallet. He scanned the driver's license and bank card, all with the name Jeannie Smith. At the bottom of the bag, he located a prescription bottle for someone named Susan Phillips. He unscrewed the top and poured the contents into his hands, not recognizing the pills, not that he would. Medication was rare in his world. Scouring the bottle again, he located the name of the doctor and the pharmacy. He dialed the doctor's number.

"Psychiatric Group," the woman said politely.

A psychiatrist?

"Hi, I'm looking for a Dr. Franklin. Is he in?"

"He is. One moment, he may be in session." Roger was placed on hold.

"This is Dr. Franklin," the voice was professional but hurried.

"Hi, my name is Roger Williams. I'm calling for a friend of mine, Susan Phillips." There was silence at the other end. Roger continued, "Her prescription has run out, and she needs a refill. I was wondering if you could call that in?" Roger was trying to be careful.

"Is Ms. Phillips there? I'm not sure who you're speaking about," the doctor questioned.

"She's asleep. She's having some issues with reality lately, and I'm a little concerned about her, Doctor. Can you tell me if I should be concerned?"

"I can't even tell you if she's my patient," the doctor said flatly.

"Well, I'm looking at the prescription bottle right here.

Your name is on it, so I know she is your patient or was."

"What kind of problems are you concerned about?" The doctor still didn't volunteer any information.

"She thinks people are following her and says she witnessed a death, but I can't find any evidence of that. She seems quite jumpy and a little paranoid."

The doctor stewed for a moment. "How long have you known Ms. Phillips?"

"I've known her for about eight years."

"Who is this again?"

"Roger. Roger Williams."

The doctor wrote the name quickly. "Give me a moment, please." He put Roger on hold as he retrieved the file from the locked cabinet in his office. He thumbed through the papers until he found his background notes. Roger Williams, former fiancé. He went back to the call.

"Roger, listen. I can't tell you anything about Susan Phillips or any diagnosis. What I can tell you is that, generally speaking, it's not unusual when individuals experience a great deal of stress to suffer a break from reality in some form as a means of coping. It can be as simple as flashbacks and nightmares, to full-blown anxiety attacks, and worse-case scenario, paranoid delusions. I can't tell you if Ms. Phillips is experiencing any of this, but it might be worthwhile to have her examined by a psychiatrist. The standard caution I would issue when an individual is in this state of mind as you are describing is they may not be the person you once knew. I wish I could tell you what you need to know, but there are confidentiality laws and all. Proceed cautiously."

Roger disconnected, taking in the words, trying to

understand exactly what the doctor meant. Was Rachel in danger or was Rachel dangerous? The next call Roger made was to the FBI field office in Santa Monica. He would get to the bottom of this.

"I need to speak with the agent who handled the investigation of Senator Rose several months ago," he said to the receptionist.

"One moment, please."

"This is Agent Tolliver," the voice said.

"This is Roger Williams. I need to talk to you about Senator Rose's case. Specifically, about Rachel Rose." Roger was trying to keep his voice hushed so Rachel didn't overhear the conversation.

"That case is over, Mr. Williams," the agent said dryly, fearing that his life was about to open up an old wound.

"I know it's over, but Rachel is here, in my apartment. She said the agent who was protecting her was murdered last night."

"What? What agent?" Sitting up straighter in his chair at Roger's revelation, he frantically logged into the daily action reports. This was news to him, and the last thing he needed was an agent dying on his watch. He dialed up Marshal Mayer's location tag.

"Marshal Gagne. The person assigned to her in Houston. He came with her to Santa Monica," Roger told him.

"Marshal Gagne?" Agent Tolliver accessed the marshal's office directory. No, Marshal Gagne was listed. Then he went to the file cabinet and dug out Rachel's file to confirm his memory with his notes. "Mr. Williams, I don't know what kind of joke this is, but there is no Marshal Gagne with the Marshal's office or the FBI, and as you well know, Rachel Rose is dead."

"She's not dead. She's here. I'm telling you; she's in my apartment." Roger's anger growing with the FBI's denial of her existence.

"Goodbye, Mr. Williams." Agent Tolliver slammed the phone down and rubbed his beard. Thoughts of pulling it out hair by hair flooded his body. He logged into the case file and made a note.

Roger paced the living room, organizing and reviewing all the facts once more. They had to deny her existence, keep pretending she was dead. But why deny Marshal Gagne's existence? Roger cracked the door to the bedroom and peeked in. Rachel was still sleeping. Quickly scribbling a note about picking up breakfast, he skipped telling her he'd be making an essential detour to the FBI office. He'd been there once before for a deposition for a case he'd worked, so he knew exactly where the field office was. They couldn't give him the brush-off in person, and maybe he could get some answers. He gathered Rachel's license and medication bottle and jammed them in his pocket, leaving her sleeping and safely locked in his apartment.

⌣

Dr. Franklin hung up the phone, tapping his pen against his desk in rapid succession. Grabbing his cell phone, he dialed the number reluctantly and waited to hear a voice he'd been avoiding for months.

"Yes, what is it?" the voice asked with irritation.

"It's Franklin. You need to know she's with a Roger Williams. He knows she's alive."

"Hmmm, that's perfect. Thank you for the update."

"I expect to be compensated," the doctor demanded before smashing the disconnect button.

Chapter 25
Found the Blonde

Rachel woke slowly, stretching and easing the events of the night from her joints. Her mind was slow to join her body in its waking, and she was grateful for that. Pushing real-world thoughts away was easier than thinking about what had transpired over the past twenty-four hours.

She'd stubbornly convinced herself before drifting off to sleep that she would prove to Roger that she was telling the truth. Now, all she wanted to think about was lying in his arms and returning to the life she once had. Reaching her hand across the bed, she inhaled a sharp breath when all she grasped was an empty sheet. Instantly comforting herself, remembering Roger was an early riser and was probably already sipping his second cup of coffee waiting for her to wake.

Tugging the comforter up around her shoulders, she snuggled deep into the mattress and drifted into a half-asleep dream state, casually listening for Roger in the shower or moving about in the kitchen. She heard nothing. Her eyes flew open as she sat up, looking around the room for anything amiss.

Maybe he had to go to work.

Forcing herself to calm, she tossed the comforter off, unable to remain oblivious to her dark reality. Eyeing the clock on the nightstand, it chimed eight. The Java Connection seminar would be starting about now. It's where she should be, but she didn't dare go back. She slipped one of Roger's T-shirts over her head, soaking in the sweet musky remnant of his cologne. Then pulled her trousers on, wishing she had her suitcase and clothes. She tiptoed into the living room; the air was still and quiet. The morning light was drifting in through the partially open shades, sparking a faded emotion to bubble to the surface.

Tranquility.

Something she'd missed deeply over the past three years. Thoughts of her and Roger reclining on opposite ends of the sofa, perusing the morning papers, legs entwined, sipping the coffee she would have carefully brewed to perfection. It had slipped away so easily, or maybe she'd tossed it away, but he'd left her no choice. Rachel felt the crease come across her brow as the memories reeled her in and then cast her back to her harsh reality.

A reality that was much too quiet. *Where was Roger?* Finally spotting the note on the dining table, she smiled as the warm feelings returned, anticipating his momentary arrival with food. The low growl in her stomach agreed.

Ignoring the intrusive memory of the disturbing images of Marshal Gagne was a struggle, and Rachel finally settled on the sofa and clicked the TV on to search the news for any report of the agent's death. Flipping channel after channel produced nothing. No news. No reports of suspicious deaths. Nothing. Maybe Marshal's office kept agent deaths confidential, she rationalized. Or maybe they hadn't found him. Maybe they never would if the cartel was responsible for taking him out. Rachel shuddered, then fixed her eyes on the front door, willing Roger to walk through it. He didn't.

Rachel gazed at her phone lying on the desk. Moving hesitantly from her spot of safety on the sofa, she picked it up and powered it on. As she examined the screen again, the hyperlinked V popped into view. *Why couldn't Roger and I find it earlier?* Maybe it had been the exhaustion.

Eagerly pressing on the V, double-clicking to make it come to life again, anxious to prove to herself that she had witnessed the murder, and it wasn't her imagination. The phone screen flickered, and piece by piece the grainy room appeared. The room was clear and had been scrubbed clean, absent any evidence of a murder. Rachel closed the site, then opened it again, hoping it would take her back to the scene of the murder, thinking maybe she'd be able to recover proof of the vicious act she'd seen. The screen flashed as it had before, but another room popped open. The image on the screen was too familiar for Rachel to stomach. She stared at the blonde woman filling the screen. Her past had come back to haunt her.

The last time she'd seen the woman, there'd been another face in the video too, but in that video, the woman's face was full of life and lust, one she would never forget. Not having managed to eradicate the memory of the face of the woman that destroyed her wedding and her life. Remembering the image of the woman straddled over Roger, naked and laughing. Followed by the busty blonde laying down beside him. His eyes were already closed. The woman cradled against him before they appeared to drift off to sleep.

That's when Rachel had run from the room, not bearing to watch any longer. Overcome with shock at the ultimate betrayal, she barely comprehended what was happening, and even though the video had no sound, she could imagine what was being said. Later, she was grateful she hadn't heard them together; it would never have left her soul if she had.

Now, as the video played out again in front of her, the pain in her chest surged, breaking her heart all over again as it had done three years ago when the cut was fresh. This time she didn't run from the room. Instead, she set her feet and made herself watch to the end.

She could see Roger wake and robotically climb off the bed, then disappear from the screen. It was a scene she didn't recall the first time she watched the video but now couldn't look away as the scenes advanced.

The blonde woke and moved to the edge of the bed, seductively posing for whomever was in the room. It had to be Roger. A man's hands appeared on the screen, pushing the woman back onto the bed, then pulling her hips to the edge. The hands reaching up to fondle the woman's large breasts, the top of the man's head barely visible in the clip. His hands stretched up further, tracing their way up her body, closing easily around her dainty neck. The hands tightening as the man moved his hips to connect with hers; the camera following the hands, the hips an afterthought, his face still hidden from view.

A burst of horror shot through Rachel when the woman's eyes flew open, the grip of the hands squeezing tighter. She flailed and tried to pry the fingers loose, but his hips pinned her as he thrust and choked until the flailing stopped. Her eyes open and fixed. The man's grip released the constriction on her throat, moving back to her breasts, where he grasped them tightly, bringing them full together, constricting them, then letting them fall away roughly. The screen went blank.

Rachel felt herself gasp for air in short, quick huffs of hyperventilation as she turned away from the phone. *Roger killed her?*

The question peppered her mind over and over again. Not only had he been unfaithful three years ago with this woman, but he killed her? How could he? He couldn't! But she saw it. Nothing made sense as her thoughts whirled.

But it would explain why he was silent during the confrontation about the affair. Why he never offered an explanation or defense for his actions. She hadn't known the entire story, and he couldn't chance her finding out. She should have forced the issue then, provoked him to tell the truth. To explain the woman in the video, the photos, and how the video ended up on a flash drive and delivered to her by courier.

Instead, not wanting to hear the truth, she'd fled, shutting him out of her world completely, refusing his calls, his visits, even his grandfather's attempts to speak with her. She'd cut off all communication, certain he was no good, and their life together was over. It was necessary to survive the pain he caused her and to keep breathing with a shattered heart.

At the time, people told her she wouldn't die of a broken heart, and she hadn't, but each minute of that first year without Roger had felt like a pain worse than death. And as inescapable and unfathomable as it all was, never in a million years would she have believed he could have committed murder. There were no photos of that in the package three years ago. This was a new revelation.

Rachel grabbed her things and scrambled to the door, freezing with her hand on the knob. *Where can I go?* There was nowhere safe. She couldn't go back to the hotel, and she couldn't wait for Roger to come home. He might kill her, too. She searched her brain frantically for the answer, slumping against the door and sliding to the floor.

The house phone rang, sending a shock through her, paralyzing her as she listened. Contemplating whether she should answer it or not, she chose not and let it go to voicemail so she could hear the message. Maybe it was Roger, but she wasn't certain she had the wherewithal to have a civil conversation with him at this moment. The recorder clicked on, answering the caller.

"Hey Roger, it's Chuck. Your cell went straight to voicemail, so I'm leaving this here for you. Stayed up all night researching the porn sites and guess what? I found her, buddy. The blonde who wrecked your life. I found her. Call me for the details. Boy, haven't lost this much sleep since we studied for the bar exam, up all night on this one. Tough job, but somebody had to do it. Right?"

Rachel recognized the room-filling laugh. The only Chuck she knew was an old friend of Roger's back in D.C. She'd met him several times during a brief stint of working for her father in Washington. Her affection ran deep for Chuck, who had a personality that was always elevated, punctuated by a contagious laugh. She'd never seen Chuck in a bad mood. Even when she knew he was angry.

Rachel scrambled to her feet to go listen to the message again. She dropped her belongings on the table and hit the replay message on the machine. *What blonde? THE* blonde? It had to be. Who else would Roger have entrusted Chuck to find?

Replaying the message a third time, it was evident that Roger hadn't killed anyone. Setting her jaw, she was determined to get to the truth this time and find out who was trying to destroy her life. No more running. She would stay and wait for Roger, after all. The litany of questions looping through her mind was growing exponentially, and he had better have the right answers.

Chapter 26
You Lost Her

Roger arrived at the local field office, not sure exactly what he was going to say or how he was going to persuade the agents to give him any information. The security guard at the door practically made him strip before allowing him entry and directing him to the reception area. He stared at the woman at the desk, sizing her up and formulating his game plan.

"I need to speak to Agent Tolliver," he tried to sound as if he knew what he wanted.

"Do you have an appointment?" the young, modestly pretty woman asked.

"No, but it is a matter of life and death," he said, trying to maximize his drama and relay his importance.

She looked at him carefully as she picked up the phone and pushed a button on her antiquated phone system containing dozens of small, square buttons.

"Agent Tolliver, there's a Roger here asking for you," she spoke into the receiver. "What is your name, please?"

"Roger Williams," he replied.

"Wiliams, Roger Williams," she relayed to the agent. Listening for a response, she replaced the receiver without another word, then pushed a clipboard with a lined page towards

Roger. The title across the top read "Visitors." He filled out the appropriate information, then slid it back across the counter to exchange it for a badge to clip on his shirt.

"Please have a seat and I'll let you know if Agent Tolliver can see you," she said, and motioned routinely to the sofa and chairs a few feet from her tall, protected desk.

Roger walked across the tile floor to the awaiting chairs, the echo of his steps filling the atrium. The receptionist was engaged in other phone calls, too busy to notice his noise. The armed guard near the front door eyed him warily. Roger looked around the sterile offices. The flooring was new, but the walls needed paint, the furnishings sorely outdated, making him consider that his tax dollars were not at work.

"Mr. Williams," she finally summoned, "Mr. Tolliver will see you now."

Roger stood, not knowing which way he should go, but before he could ask, an older woman materialized through a heavy steel door.

"Mr. Williams, follow me, please," she ordered. She turned and left him on his own to keep pace with her quick strides.

Roger hurried to keep up with the gray-haired woman as she wound her way through the maze of hallways before she stopped, hands clasped before her like a teacher about to scold a naughty student, lips pursed conservatively. Without speaking another word, she side-stepped away from the doorway and permitted his entry.

Behind the desk sat a man twenty years his senior, Roger recognized him from the media coverage of the trial. A square jaw partially covered by a peppered beard, a serious look, gray hair, balding slightly on top.

"Please have a seat, Mr. Williams. What's on your mind?" He was cordial, but obviously irritated by Roger's unannounced presence.

"I told you on the phone, Rachel is at my apartment. I know she is alive, so you can drop the charade. What I'm worried about is the agent she said was killed last night."

Agent Tolliver diverted his gaze from Roger and shuffled through a few papers. "Mr. Williams, may I call you Roger?"

"Certainly." Roger sat up a little straighter, hoping to emit some professionalism and be taken seriously by Agent Tolliver.

Agent Tolliver stared down at his hands clasped together, resting in front of him on the desk. "I know you once had a close relationship with Ms. Rose, but you have to come to terms with the fact that she is dead."

Roger was angered by the mere implication that he was somehow imagining Rachel or creating some fictional character. He stood, placing his hands firmly on the agent's desk. The agent was on his feet quickly.

"Please sit down, Mr. Williams, or this conversation is over."

Roger pushed his hands off the desk and took his seat again. "I'm sorry," he apologized, raising his hands in resignation, his frustration seeping through his words. "Look, I am an attorney. I understand the process and your obligations and duties. And I know Rachel. I know every inch of her and her body and her beautiful eyes. And believe me, the girl that slept in my bed last night was Rachel Rose, right down to the birthmark on the small of her back. She is not dead, and I know it." Roger moved to the edge of his chair, imposing his presence on Agent Tolliver. "Here, look at these." Roger pulled the driver's license and the medicine bottle from his pocket and turned them over to the agent.

Agent Tolliver reached across the desk and took the items from Roger's outstretched hand. He examined them carefully. "Excuse me for one moment, please." The agent quickly exited the room, shutting the door behind him.

Roger tried looking through the tall rectangular window next to the door, but Agent Tolliver caught his glance and moved out of sight. Roger leaned back in the stiff chair and waited.

Agent Tolliver hustled to the office at the end of the hallway, the corner office with a view of the ocean. It was an office he aspired to, and this case had been a stumbling block to taking residence there anytime soon. If he could resurrect the case, though he would be a hero, but if he lost a witness in protection, well, he might as well move to the other side of the building altogether to wait out the long days until retirement. He'd been hoping to finish what was left of his career going out on top, but that was looking doubtful with every step he took towards the boss's office.

"Agent Bellows, do you have a minute?" Agent Tolliver stuck his head in the door, ignoring the secretary trailing after him.

"What is it, Tolliver? I have a conference about that counterfeit ring in ten minutes," he barked.

"I think you'll want to see this," he told him, entering the room, pushing the door closed.

"What do you have?" He gathered his glasses from the desk and slipped them over his nose to assist his aging eyes.

"A Roger Williams is in my office. He says Rachel Rose is at his apartment. He brought these in as proof." Agent Tolliver explained.

"Hmmm," he scrutinized the medicine bottle and the driver's license. "This is the girl, isn't it?" He stared up at Tolliver.

"Yes, sir, it appears to be. The name on the bottle is the first alias we assigned her, and the picture is definitely her, but the second name is not familiar. I'm not sure who Jeannie Smith is."

Agent Bellows really didn't want to figure it out. In fact, he didn't want to solve any more mysteries or crimes. He wanted to go fishing and sit in the sunlight, heat penetrating his golf shirt as he waited for the big one to bite the line. To sit in a boat beside his grandson, who was a foot taller every time he saw him, which wasn't often enough. He didn't care about Senator Rose, the drug cartel, or even Rachel Rose. He wanted to retire, and he would happily hand over the keys to the next guy, who was foolish enough to think he really wanted them. Sitting back in his large, well-earned chair of authority, twisting back and forth, he considered the objects laid out before him.

"Well, it looks like your witness has slipped through the cracks. Have you checked with the watch lately? When was the last check in?" Agent Bellows pulled his glasses off his nose and rubbed his exhausted eyes.

"An hour ago. I checked right after Mr. Williams called. Everything checked out okay in Phoenix," Agent Tolliver informed his boss.

"Let's go to the war room," he ordered. He grabbed his glasses as he led the way out of his office and headed toward the hall. "Reschedule my conference," he barked to his secretary as he passed. She nodded and reached obediently for the phone.

The two men made their way to a secure door at the end of the long corridor, punching in a code to gain entry. The door buzzed, and Agent Bellows pulled it open.

The guard on the other side stood stationary. "Sir," he said respectfully. Agent Bellows nodded his acknowledgment toward the young trainee agent.

"Come on, Tolliver, let's make a call to Arizona." The men stopped at a computer terminal where a serious man sat, watching monitors and making notations. Agent Bellows advised him about the information he wanted, and the man began typing rapidly. When he stopped, a projector next to the terminal lit up, and an area map appeared on the screened wall. The map arranged and rearranged until it zoomed in on an individual house located in Arizona. The men watched as the cameras focused and refocused, making the images clear. There was no activity outside the house.

"Go inside," Agent Bellows ordered.

Within a second, the outside image of the house was replaced with an interior picture of the living room. A black and white bird's-eye view. The men watched and waited. A woman crossed the room and came into view. She wore dark, short, cropped hair and was trim, the same exact build as Rachel.

"There she is," Agent Bellows looked at Tolliver. Tolliver still seemed puzzled. "Go get your guy Tolliver, let's get to the bottom of this."

Agent Tolliver disappeared and returned to his office to collect the awaiting "former fiancé." Roger came to his feet when the agent appeared.

"Come with me, Mr. Williams," Tolliver directed,

holding the door open. Roger complied. Agent Tolliver led Roger back down the secure hallway to the war room. His entry should have accompanying paperwork, but Tolliver didn't question his boss.

"Hello, Mr. Williams." Agent Bellows extended his hand to greet Roger. "I'm Agent Bellows. I'm the head guy around here. I hear you have questions about Rachel Rose." Agent Bellows knew he shouldn't be allowing the entry or viewing by the civilian, or acknowledging that Rachel was not dead, but he also knew that he wanted Roger to shut up and there was the issue of a girl in his apartment claiming to be Rachel. If she weren't careful, she might get herself killed.

"I know Rachel is not dead, sir. She is at my apartment right now," Roger explained again.

"Please take a look Mr. Williams." He pointed to the screen. "This is Rachel Rose, and she is alive and well in a city far away from your apartment. She's in a protection program."

Roger stared at the screen. The woman in view was strikingly similar to Rachel, but Roger knew it wasn't her. "I'm sorry, sir, but that is not Rachel."

"Son," Agent Bellows put on his mature, learned approach, "I'm sorry, but some young woman is playing a hell of a trick on you."

Roger was growing impatient with being treated like a dawdling fool. "Look," he raised his voice, drawing a harsh glare from the young guard at the door. Taking heed of the well-armed man, he simmered before he spoke and lowered his voice. "I made love to this woman last night. I assure you, gentlemen, this woman on your screen is not Rachel Rose. The woman in my apartment is. I can promise you that this woman," Roger gestured wildly, "does not have the hourglass birthmark on her lower back or violet-rimmed eyes. And I saw both last night. And if it is, as you insist, that this other person is Rachel and the woman who is in my apartment is not, then I was engaged to some unknown person three years ago."

The agents looked at each other cautiously. Agent Bellows walked over to a red phone and made a call. Roger tried but couldn't overhear the conversation.

Bellows hung up the phone with emphasis. "Let's go back to my office," Bellows led the men back in silence.

Roger sat down in Agent Bellows' office, impressed by the plush surroundings, a sharp contrast to the meager lobby, rivaling that of the senior partners in his law firm; a place where he was sure he was missing in action. He wondered if his secretary had called looking for him or whether he was missing a court date. His own calendar escaping him at the moment. He quickly pulled his cell phone from his pocket, noting five pending voicemails, three from his office. He'd changed his number after Rachel's "death" to stop the media from contacting him, realizing now that Rachel had no way to reach him. She must be awake and wondering why it was taking close to two hours to get bagels.

"Do you mind if I make a call, gentlemen?" Roger asked.

"Be our guest." Agent Bellows gave permission.

Roger stepped into the hallway and dialed his apartment. The phone rang until it switched to the answering machine. "Hello, it's me. Pick up, please."

"Roger?" Rachel's voice came on the line. "Where are you?"

Roger could tell she was angry. Even after all these years,

he still recognized the voice of a scorned woman.

"I'm sorry. I had to take care of some business. Please wait there for me. I'll be home soon. Can I bring you anything?" He was trying to be thoughtful.

"No!" she said sharply. "Your friend Chuck called. About some blonde woman and pornography."

Roger's heart skipped a beat. His eyes glancing at the FBI agents staring at him. "Okay, I'll explain everything when I get home. Sit tight and don't answer the phone or the door. You got it?" Roger commanded.

"Don't worry, I'm not an idiot. How long before you come home?"

Roger loved the sound of her asking when he was coming home. He softened his tone. "I'll be there soon, sweetheart," he tried to resume the place he'd left three years earlier. "I'll call when I'm almost there."

"Okay, but hurry. I don't like being here by myself." As soon as Rachel spoke, she wanted to take it back. Suddenly unsure if she wanted Roger there with her or not. She hung up the phone, cutting the conversation short.

Roger ended the call and returned his phone to his pocket, stepping back inside the office and closing the door behind him. "I'm telling you the truth gentlemen, Rachel Rose is in my apartment, and she saw Marshal Gagne murdered."

The men exchanged looks again. "Mr. Williams, there is no Marshal Gagne."

"Are you sure? She talked about him a lot. He's been protecting her."

"I'm sorry, but there's no marshal by that name. I re-verified that within the hour." Agent Tolliver confirmed.

"Then who was murdered?" he asked.

The agents shook their heads. Before the conversation could continue, the phone rang.

"Yes," Agent Bellows spoke into the receiver, "I see." He grabbed a pen and began scribbling on the pad by the phone. "Really?" He wrote some more. Roger tried to read upside down what the agent was scratching across the page, but the distance across the desk was too far.

Agent Bellows hung up the phone, his face dropping into a frown as he sat back hard in his large chair. "It seems we owe you an apology, Mr. Williams. Apparently, our Rachel Rose is the imposter, not yours."

"You mean you've been providing protection to the wrong person? How can that be? Who has been taking care of the real Rachel?"

Neither of the men had any answers. Agent Tolliver felt his career careening out of control and a complication falling right in his lap again.

"They have taken the woman into custody and are interrogating her as we speak. I suspect we won't get any answers anytime soon." Agent Bellows said almost apologetically. He could feel the fishing pole in his hand. It would most likely be forced upon him sooner than he planned after this debacle. But maybe the universe was watching out for him and delivering him a gift. Agent Tolliver had been eyeing his desk for years. Maybe it was time to scratch his own name from the door and let Tolliver find out how thankless it all could be, if he didn't get canned too. "We would like to go pick up the real Rachel. We need information about this murder. First, I need to take your statement. We'll send an agent to watch your apartment in the meantime."

"Somehow, Agent Bellows, that doesn't give me much comfort." Roger said honestly.

"Agent Tolliver will take your statement."

"Roger, it might take a while. I also want you to look at some psychiatric records. There are some things you need to know about Rachel Rose," Agent Tolliver said.

Roger turned to the agent. "I know all I need to know about Rachel. I know I love her, and I'm not going to let anyone hurt her or use her."

Agent Tolliver led Roger away.

Chapter 27
As You Wish

Senator Rose couldn't shake the thought of the encounter with his wife from the night before. Some were pleasurable images. Others, rather disturbing. What had driven her to join him in his room? He was angry with Scott for encouraging his mother's curiosity about Rachel. His wayward son should have known better and should have quelled her questions immediately. Grabbing his phone, he pushed Scott's contact.

"Scott, this is your father," he said gruffly.

"Hey, Dad. How was Washington?" he replied cheerily, knowing what was coming from the tone of his dad's voice. "Business go all right?"

Going straight to the point and ignoring the question, he had no interest in engaging in D.C. chitchat, Jay grumbled, "I'm calling about a conversation you had with your mother. Do you want to tell me about that?"

Scott knew his mother wouldn't keep quiet. He'd tried to backtrack his words when they accidentally poured out of his mouth at lunch. He had a hard time not being truthful with her. She was the one person in the family who consistently provided him with support and unequivocal love. Not like his demeaning father or even his perfect sister.

"Dad, she asked the questions. I tried my best to assure her that Rachel was dead. She's hurting and wants to know the truth. Would it be so bad to tell her your suspicions?" he offered.

"Yes," the Senator screamed into the phone. "It would be absolutely horrible. She'd go blabbing it to all her gossiping bitches of friends, and before long, the media would be nosing around and camping out on the front lawn. This has to stay quiet. If anything happens to Rachel and the world were to find out, I want to be the least likely suspect. You got it? Or so help me, Scott, you will regret ever being born into this family."

Scott already regretted it. "I understand exactly what you want, Father."

The senator recognized Scott's tone but was confident he understood what needed to be done. "Tonight is the cancer benefit. You will attend in my place. Stop by my office first. There are some sizable donations that you need to handle personally and some VIPs you need to go out of your way to greet." The senator expected full cooperation from his son from this point forward.

"I'll be by around five. The benefit starts at six. You know that Mother is planning to go. She showed me the dress she bought for it," Scott informed his father. He hated ratting out his mother, but he knew if he didn't, he would catch hell again later from his father. His mother was easier to placate when she was angry than his father. Some days, he had to pick his battles strategically.

"She doesn't need to be there. I'll take care of your mother. You be here at five and take care of business tonight. And Scott, there better not be any slipups," he warned.

"Don't worry, Dad, I know exactly what I'm doing."

Jay hung up the phone and went straight to Linda's room, where she was soaking in a tub full of bubbles, a glass of wine perched on the tub step.

"Isn't it a little early for a drink?" the senator snubbed his wife.

Linda removed the cloth covering her bloodshot eyes and stared vacantly at her husband.

"You are not going to the cancer benefit tonight," he told her.

"I've already informed them that I'll be there. It would be rude not to show." She placed the cloth back over her eyes and leaned her head back.

"You will not leave this house. Is that understood?" he said again.

She didn't acknowledge him. He grabbed her arm, jerking her out of the tub, and with one fluid move, backhanded her across the face, splitting her lip and sending blood dripping into the soapy water.

"You're now not presentable to appear at the benefit. Don't leave this house." He'd control his wife as he'd always done. Her recent assertiveness was becoming too much for his taste. "I'll check on you later. Be in your room." He shoved her back into the water.

Linda settled back into the bubbles, fumbled to retrieve the submerged washcloth, then closed her eyes and covered them again. The blood ran down her chin, but she made no attempt to wipe it away. She reached blindly for her wine and took a sip.

The senator returned to his office, his use of her complete.

Scott appeared at the office door exactly at five. He had seen his mother minutes earlier. Trying to contain his rage as he watched her fumble a lame explanation about having a headache and not feeling well enough to attend, he hugged her and promised to make her excuses. The odor of alcohol told Scott all he needed to know, that and the swelling and fresh cut on her lip. Certain about how it made its way there. He hadn't bothered asking a useless question about its origin. Per usual, she would have lied. His blood boiled, knowing who had put the bruise there.

Scott steeled himself as he entered his father's office. "I'm here, Dad. What do you need me to do tonight?"

The senator looked at his son with regret that they weren't more alike. They could make an indomitable team if life had flowed differently. But Scott was a follower, not a leader like Jay, or even like Rachel had been. He wanted to connect with him, but time had stolen those opportunities, and they could only function now with the strained relationship that was set in stone.

"Mr. Ramirez will be at the benefit tonight. He wants to make a sizable donation. You will accept it personally. Here is the thank-you card you are to deliver to him. Make sure he gets this card. Also, there will be a woman, dark hair, beautiful lady, her name is Ramona. Please make sure you introduce her to Senator Waters. I invited him personally. He's a do-gooder, and his eyes were popping at my mention of rubbing shoulders with celebrities and politicos, but his causes are pure. Introduce him, and Ramona will do the rest. Leave the benefit and meet me at the condo at exactly nine-thirty. We will make the exchange there."

Scott took in all the details. He knew Ramona well, a

high-priced hooker that his father had employed many times over the years. *Senator Waters won't know what hit him.* As for Mr. Ramirez, Scott knew the transaction should be easy and profitable for both him and his father.

"I'll see you then, Dad," he said as he left to do his father's bidding.

Jay looked at his watch and went to check on his wife. He wanted to make sure she didn't slip out of the house tonight. If he had to inflict another bruise to do the trick, then he would.

Chapter 28

Bambi

Rachel was growing more impatient by the minute. Resorting to raiding the kitchen one more time out of sheer boredom, but she had no appetite now that her adrenaline had taken over. She tried to watch TV, but the racing thoughts made it impossible to follow the storylines.

Snooping around the apartment from end-to-end, she searched closets and dresser drawers for any evidence of an old or new girlfriend, and to her relief, found none.

She opened Roger's Rolodex and looked at the phone numbers of his friends he always jotted on the little cards. Who actually used a Rolodex anymore? She flipped to her name card with her old phone number scribbled on it, topped with little pink hearts encasing her number. She'd teased Roger about the Rolodex and doodled hearts on her card, telling him to never forget how much she loved him when he looked at her name and number. The card was pristine and as stiff as it was three years prior when she walked out. Her heart lurched.

Where is Roger?

She paced relentlessly, periodically darting to the window, concealing herself behind the drapes. Nothing. Rachel checked the time on her phone. Nearly five-thirty.

He should have been here by now.

Fear and frustration seized her simultaneously with the idea of Roger lying dead somewhere and being irritated that he hadn't yet arrived. She wasn't convinced that the pin she and Roger had dismantled earlier didn't have a camera in it.

What if they know where she is? Her insides began to quiver. Bending over, tucking her head between her knees, fighting to slow her breathing, she forced herself to reclaim serene thoughts. She had to stay in control if she wanted to get out of this alive. She also had to do something other than sit and wait for someone to walk through the door and gun her down.

Grabbing her phone, she brought it to life, then flicked the power button on Roger's computer. She slid drawer after drawer open, looking for a cable to attach her phone and mirror the phone screen on the monitor for a closer look at the web link. Something she'd done years ago for happier purposes. Hoping he still had the app to do it.

Once the computer whirred to life, she found the cable, connected her phone, then found the app, watching as the link loomed large on the computer monitor. Frantically clicking on the images, searching for the secret entry, stalled the monitor, which couldn't keep up with her hectic click pace, causing the screen to freeze. Rachel screamed in frustration as she impatiently squeezed the side button to turn her phone off, disconnected it from the monitor, then powered it back on and re-plugged.

The phone loaded more slowly than usual, threatening to refuse to operate and simply crash. Grinding her teeth and feeling the pressure rise in her head, she started the process all over again, turning it off for the second time before resuming the sequence and reconnecting. Finally, the phone stabilized, and the home screen icons popped to life, one-by-one.

Returning to the browser, she slowed her clicking, hoping the page was still remembered in the search history. It wasn't. Opening her texts, she found the site, heaving a deep sigh of relief. Searching for the right spot to click on, it once again evaded her. Wanting to scream and throw her phone across the room, she closed her eyes and steadied herself.

Roger's landline rang again, sending her heart into her throat. She followed Roger's instructions and ignored the phone, listening as the machine clicked to life. "Hey buddy, Chuck again. Thought you would have called back by now. You were so insistent yesterday. Hope everything's all right. Listen, I'm going to bed, got an early day tomorrow and, well, hell, I was up half the night looking at smut." Chuck laughed, "Go to www.whitehouseinterns.com. You'll find your girl under the name of Bambi. Call me, bye."

Rachel listened to the message, her curiosity rising. She abandoned trying to locate the access point on her phone and disconnected. She clicked the browser and typed the website provided by Chuck and waited. Gigantic breast images popped onto the screen, startling and disgusting Rachel as she looked away. She didn't understand the attraction to such an unreal image.

Using her disgust as fuel, she navigated her way around the website, seeing more than she cared to of strange women, looking for the familiar face of the blonde. Rachel checked the time: seven-thirty. She tapped her foot. *Where the hell is he?* Refocusing, she continued with the hunt, clicking on micro pictures, forcing them to expand and expose themselves to her.

So many women and so many icons. She tapped an icon of the Whitehouse. The blonde she had become familiar with came to life. Her hair streamed across her face seductively. Her pose, more than revealing. Rachel cringed.

At the bottom left was a phone symbol with the words, "I'm Bambi, call me for a good time," slithering across the page under her name. Rachel clicked on the phone icon. A payment agreement appeared and asked for a credit card. Knowing she couldn't use hers; Rachel ran to the bedroom where Roger once kept an emergency card in the dresser. She searched manically until she found the card tucked under a pair of socks. She hustled back to the computer, peeking out the peephole of the door as she passed. The hallway was eerily empty. A chill shuddered through her.

Rachel typed in the credit card information, and an instant message box popped up. The livestream of naked Bambi emerged.

"Hello, I'm Bambi. What's your name, lover?"

Rachel could hear Bambi's voice now and could see her on the screen, full screen at that. She minimized it, forcing her stomach to stop rolling. Rachel wasn't sure she knew how to play this game and was even more unsure if she wanted to, but she had to know the truth. "I'm Romeo," she typed.

"Welcome to my room, Romeo." The camera in Bambi's room focused squarely on her, showing her entire body. Bambi sat on the bed, legs crossed. "What's your preference tonight, sweetie?"

Rachel had no idea what she meant. Her head spun for a response. *Might as well get to the point.* "Do you know Roger Williams?" she pecked out on the keyboard.

"You know, sweetie, you should be able to talk to me if you have a microphone on your computer. You don't have to type all of this, and it'll free up your hands, baby. You may need them later. Click on the little button on the right side of your message box." Bambi giggled.

The last thing Rachel wanted to do was talk to Bambi live. She didn't want her to know she was a female. She cleared her throat, clicked on the microphone, and made her best attempt at a masculine voice. "I was curious if you knew a Roger Williams."

"Why do you ask?" Bambi was careful.

Rachel thought fast. "He said I should check you out and ask for the same thing he got."

Bambi cocked her head and stared at the camera. "Are you sure you're old enough to be on this website?" she asked. "You sound a little young."

Great, Rachel thought, I sound like a pre-pubescent boy. She tried to lower her voice. "I'm sure. I have a touch of a cold." She rolled her eyes at her own explanation.

"Roger Williams," Bambi began thinking, "Can't remember exactly. Tell me what you like, lover boy, and I'll figure it out." Bambi didn't mind the time being wasted. At $8.99 a minute, she could engage in conversational banter all night.

"Do you do murders?" Rachel asked bluntly.

Bambi uncrossed her legs but didn't answer.

"I don't mean, do you kill people." Rachel backpedaled. "I mean, do you do fake death scenes? Like you have sex and then you are murdered? Do you do that?" Rachel tripped over her own tongue, stammering like a teenager looking at his first naked woman.

"Honey," Bambi relaxed again, "I get requests for everything. But I don't get that request often. Yeah, I've done that. Is that what turns you on, sweetie?" Bambi made herself comfortable and spread her legs wider, playing with her own breasts as she did.

Looking at the ceiling, Rachel pushed on. "Can you show me the murder scene?" Rachel felt her stomach lurch.

"You relax, doll. I'll get you going," Bambi purred.

Rachel watched as Bambi stepped forward, making an adjustment on something out of the vision of the screen, then lay back, performing erotic maneuvers that Rachel didn't know were possible. Concluding her performance with the exact death scene that Rachel had witnessed earlier that morning, foreign hands choking the life out of her body. Rachel watched in horror. It seemed so real, but she knew it couldn't be.

"Are you okay?" Rachel finally whispered to the lifeless body on the bed.

Bambi sat up. "Of course, sugar. I hope that moved you darling, come back and see me real soon." Bambi blew a kiss to the screen and was gone.

Rachel logged off the website. Doing a quick calculation of the charge that was going to appear on Roger's card, most likely close to four hundred dollars. Breaking down the details of Bambi's acting scene, she tried to understand how it was orchestrated, scolding herself for thinking Roger could ever kill anyone. The chaos known as her life had turned everyone into a villain, even with no proof. Roger didn't deserve that. He'd never been violent, was a pacifist when you examined him, except in the courtroom. Then he was a fighter, but words were his weapon, not his fists. She rubbed her hands over her face, berating herself again for doubting him.

Checking the time, it was eight fifty-five and still no Roger. The anger propelling her through this day now morphed into worry. Reconnecting her phone to the computer, she attempted to pull up the images again. As it connected, a new location popped up on the site and a new room.

Nothing in her life up to this point could have prepared her for what she saw on the screen. It was Roger, tied and bound to a dining room chair, like Marshal Gagne had been. Rachel's heart shattered, followed by a quiver in the back of her neck threatening to take hold. There was one notable difference between this scene and that of Marshal Gagne. This room was exquisitely decorated and looked familiar. Rachel stared at the surroundings, her eyes tearing up as she watched Roger struggle. He wasn't gagged, like Marshal Gagne had been. Instead, he was talking freely to someone in the room.

Shoes of the other person became visible on the screen, then the legs covered by dark suit pants, then the man himself. Rachel clasped her hand over her mouth to prevent the scream in the back of her throat from escaping. Hot tears rolled down her cheeks, not wanting to acknowledge the image she saw. Her father was the man facing Roger. He stood above the seated Roger, towering over him. Rachel searched the room, then it hit her. She knew the room they were in; it was her condo.

No wonder he hadn't come home. He couldn't.

Rachel jumped up, knocking the chair to the ground, and flew out of the apartment without thinking. It was all her fault. Bringing danger to Roger's door with her stubbornness. Why hadn't she left it all alone and lived the new life she'd been granted? The only comfort she could muster was that she was responsible for getting Roger into this mess and she would get him out.

An unfamiliar fury ran through her. It was time to finish this twisted game.

Chapter 29

Scott - A Good Cause

The cancer benefit was being held at the secluded beachfront hotel, The Pink Marina. It was the hotel of the rich and famous. A huge fountain sat majestically smack in the center of the circle driveway leading to the grand entrance, where pink water soared high into the air through the gold fountain spouts, falling gracefully in arcs to the middle of the carefully crafted stone circle below. Gold inlaid bricks lined the walkway to the massive marble canopied entry, where a pink carpet was perfectly rolled out, guiding the way to the twelve-foot-tall, beveled-glass front doors. Doormen clad in pink uniforms, with gold buttons and hot-pink fringe adorning the epaulet shoulder jackets, stood stoically, guiding guests into the massive fundraiser. Professional expressions plastered across their faces, bowing at commands, never breaking character as the VIPs stepped on the plush pink carpet when exiting their limousines and privately driven executive cars.

Bellhops hustled to carry packages and luggage, never seeming to stand idle. Certainly never chatting or ogling the celebrities. It was the norm, and the norm meant large tips and job security, and dreams of a condo on the beach one day. So, all employees took their positions to heart and made sure to keep their jobs at The Pink Palace.

The ballroom was the perfect location for the cancer fundraiser. The cost of the decorations alone could have funded an entire year of research. Spend money to make money was the way of the California money men whose wives planned the fundraisers, and they did know how to raise money. The wives were experts at throwing parties. With nothing else to occupy their time, their husbands turned them loose for the planning of such grand events. They were happy for months and out of the way so their influential husbands could concentrate on operating their profitable businesses.

Scott was familiar with most of the kept wives hosting the benefit. They all enjoyed flirting with him, hoping for a connection to his powerful father through a hot, strong young man. Which wasn't the worst thing their husbands had them do. A few had entertained Scott privately for late lunches and reminded him of those times by gracing him with dangerously intimate hugs. Scott relished the attention he received from these women. It was something he desperately craved, and he drank it up.

He had learned how to shake the appropriate hands, including the fake-nailed hand of the infamous Ramona. The newest madam in town. A high-dollar organization that hadn't been exposed for prosecution due to some influential customers who had strong motives to protect her. It would, however, serve her right, considering she was the one who ratted out her predecessor in order to set up her own operation. It was not public knowledge, but the right people did know the truth, they chose to keep it to themselves, to retain the personal benefits it afforded them. There were many dysfunctional celebrities needing to get some confidential loving from somewhere.

As ordered, Scott made the rounds, encouraging donations, dropping names and amounts of those who had already made impressive contributions. Fueling competition and envy, the next check larger to outdo someone and show off obscene wealth.

The band played swing music, urging guests to get on the dance floor and cut loose, as much as some of the plastic women and men could. Scott watched it all as he worked the room. The champagne flowed while the caviar disappeared. When the meal was served and devoured, the real-life impact of the event's purpose took center stage. One by one, stories from the young, the old, the middle-aged, were spilled through tears and smiles, all invoking hope for life, for cures, for donations. Checkbooks plunked down on linen covered round tables, and pens frantically wrote large numbers.

Scott raised his chin, feeling his successful persona taking hold of him. Knowing his worth and affirming his father was right to send him to such events. Despite his father's doubt about Scott's academic ability, his social skills were ironclad, at least in this crowd they were.

"Senator Waters?" Scott located the man he was supposed to make contact with. It wasn't difficult. All he had to do was scan the room for the biggest stuffed shirt, standing awkwardly in the swarm of people. "I'm Scott, Senator Rose's son. He asked me to extend a welcome to you and his apologies that he couldn't be here to greet you himself." Scott didn't wait for the senator to extend his hand, instead grabbing the man's arm and melding their hands together.

"It's a pleasure to meet you, Mr. Rose," the senator was

gracious.

"Please call me Scott. Mr. Rose is my father, and I don't want to be mistaken for him." He flashed a toothy grin.

"Scott, it is."

The men laughed, though Scott was serious.

"I hear your wife was instrumental in launching the breast cancer walks and organizing a community support system in your state of Texas. That's quite an undertaking for the second largest state in the nation." Scott had done his research on almost all the influential players that were attending the benefit. Connecting personally was a lure to snag more donations. The more that was donated, the less his father monitored his whereabouts.

"Yes, she is quite a woman. Her sister suffered from breast cancer and actually died shortly after being diagnosed. My wife took it hard, and it became a personal cause for her to bring awareness and education to the community, which eventually became a statewide platform." The senator spoke proudly of his wife.

Scott didn't envy Ramona's job tonight. This would be a tough one. He almost felt sorry for the unsuspecting wife back home on the range. Almost, but not quite. Ramona had already worked on her plan of entry. Now it was time for the handoff.

"Really? That is so tragic," Scott empathized. "I spoke to a woman over there," Scott said, turning to point in Ramona's direction and waving, signaling her to join the men. Scott continued, "The raven-haired beauty by the buffet table was explaining to me that she is a breast cancer survivor." Scott leaned in close to the senator to impress the confidential nature of what he was about to unload. "She underwent a double mastectomy a couple of years ago. I think the reconstructive surgery was quite a success. Don't you?"

Scott timed it perfectly. Ramona was by his side when the last word fell out of his mouth. Senator Waters was clearly offended by Scott's lack of candor and turned sympathetically to Ramona.

"Hello," the senator greeted Ramona, shaking her hand.

"Oh, Ramona." Scott sounded surprised at her presence. "I was telling the senator about your interest in furthering the fight against breast cancer. You'll enjoy the senator. He's a world of information. You two should really sit down and discuss this cause. I think the two of you can help each other immensely."

Scott knew the senator would fall into the noble position to rescue the poor, stricken Ramona. Who accepted the role easily, even bringing a crimson flush to her cheeks, being appropriately demure. Senator Waters predictably came to her rescue. Little did the naïve senator know he would be the one who needed rescuing in a few hours.

Scott was nearly finished with his father's dirty work. The last assignment to complete the night was Mr. Ramirez. "Hello, Mr. Ramirez," he said. "Thank you for attending the benefit. It's certainly philanthropic of you." Scott and Mr. Ramirez were well acquainted with one another.

"Good evening, Scott. I have a considerable donation to make to cancer research."

Scott smiled suitably. "That's wonderful. I'm sure many people will thank you for your generosity." Scott checked his watch, nearly nine p.m., time for him to leave.

Mr. Ramirez handed Scott an envelope; he slipped it into the inner pocket of his jacket. He completed the handoff by sliding the thank-you card into Mr. Ramirez's open hand. "Please, a personal thanks from my father, the Senator."

The gentlemen exchanged pleasantries with the few remaining guests, then Scott made his exit, waving to the stragglers as he left. It was time to meet his father at the condominium. Nine-thirty was his deadline. And this was the one meeting he didn't want to be late for.

Chapter 30
Welcome Home

Rachel impatiently pushed the down button repeatedly on the elevator, then smashed the interior close arrow button the minute she stepped inside. Unfortunately, she hadn't heard the ringing of Roger's landline in his apartment in her hurry to leave, hoping not to encounter anyone in her escape.

There was a second-floor exit she could take to the stairwell and leave out the back of the building, through the small courtyard. She'd never seen anyone use it in the past, which gave her comfort that she'd have protection from watchful eyes that might be searching for her.

The condo was several blocks past the bridge on the inlet side. She picked up the pace. If her father had Roger, then he knew where she was, too. Why hadn't he taken her? Why did he snatch Roger? Rachel wondered how long Roger had been captive, maybe all day.

God, please don't hurt him. It felt like years since she'd said a sincere prayer, but now she couldn't stop praying. No longer concerned for her own safety, her prayers were all for Roger. Every day and night since the trial started, she'd been solely focused on keeping herself alive. Now the day to look death in the face had arrived, but she wasn't scared anymore. Facing her father was an event she was looking forward to.

The words she planned on unloading on him were sitting on the tip of her tongue, ready and waiting to be unleashed. Craving the same look on his face the last time she stood up to him and forced his hand, she was primed to see that pained expression again. He might kill her, but at least she wouldn't show any fear. It had dissipated, pushed away by the rage consuming her with each step she took, bringing her closer to the condo, and to Roger.

Catching her breath as her adrenaline surged and her pace increased was becoming more taxing the further she went. Realizing her condo was a longer distance on foot than she remembered, and then recalled that she never walked between the two locations she'd always driven, she had to get help. She flagged a taxi and dug out what money she had in her pocket. Barreling out of Roger's apartment, she'd carelessly forgotten her bag. Ten dollars wouldn't get her far, instructing the driver to take her as far as it would get her. He shot a disgusted look in the rearview mirror. She smirked back.

The driver crossed the bridge and drove a couple of blocks, then abruptly stopped as the meter clicked onto ten dollars. Rachel surveyed the neighborhood. It hadn't been that long since she resided here, but it all looked foreign now.

Tossing the money in the driver's direction, she climbed out and slammed the door behind her. The night was cool, the ocean air settling over the area as it sometimes did when the cloud cover was dense. Moving to the sidewalk, her determined trek to the condo perched on the rocky shore of the beach continued. Four long blocks away. With her head down to brace herself against the ocean wind, she wrapped her arms around herself as the bitter air cut through her, chilling her to the bone.

Roger pulled into the parking garage of his apartment building, knowing how late he was, much later than the time he left on the answering machine in the message for Rachel. He wondered why she didn't answer when she heard his voice. The FBI folder lay on the seat. He opened it and scanned the psychiatrist's report one more time before he went upstairs.

"After multiple sessions with Ms. Rose over the past several months, it is my conclusion that she may be delusional. Her obsession with her father controls her every thought and decision. She truly believes that her father is somehow connected to the Colombian cartel, but even she admits that no uncontroverted link or proof could be uncovered. Because I believe Ms. Rose is sincere in her conviction, I can only conclude that from the lack of evidence supporting her thoughts that she has created this fantasy. It is possible that the breakup with her fiancé prompted an escape from reality. She is tearful and trembles at the mere discussion of Roger Williams. Her emotional state is tenuous at best, and she should be monitored closely."

Roger couldn't help reading the report over and over again. Had he really caused Rachel to sink into some kind of delusional, imaginary world? Had she constructed all of this cloak and dagger in an attempt to somehow reconnect with him? Roger didn't want to believe the psychiatrist, but how could he dispute the words of a medical doctor trained to uncover these dysfunctions?

Roger wouldn't doubt that Rachel could have suffered a

breakdown of some sort, but he couldn't fathom that he was the cause. She appeared so strong when she told him the wedding was off. As he replayed the scenario that he endured three years ago, he decided she had been too calm. Roger pushed his fingers through his hair for the tenth time in the past hour, hoping to drive away the stress that had expanded throughout each hour of this confusing day. He would ask her, talk to her, comfort her. They could talk it through and, hopefully, it would help her get past this mental crisis the doctor had described in the report.

The doctor's notes, coupled with Agent Tolliver's words that continued to ring in his ears, sent an ache creeping across his furrowed brow. The FBI hadn't believed she was in any danger when they put her in protective custody, but they couldn't be sure. They suspected that the woman posing as Rachel was hired by Rachel to take her place so she could slip away and back to Roger without the FBI monitoring her.

It had taken all day for the imposture to reveal that she'd been hired to pose as Rachel, but wouldn't give up anything else, like who hired her. Their theory made the most sense, the FBI agent explained to Roger, her moving cities suddenly, the job with Java Connection, the trip back to California, and showing up at Roger's condo. Rachel could have orchestrated it all. The FBI assured Roger it would take only a few hours to trace the bank records, but by the time Roger insisted on leaving, they knew nothing more.

Roger had asked them about Marshal Gagne and the murder, all a figment of her imagination, they claimed. She probably invented it to gain sympathy from Roger. It all laid out logically, especially since she was the only one who saw the things she described. Roger asked about Houston. They knew nothing about it, though they did confirm the employment of Jeannie Smith at Java Connection in the Westside Houston mall, but the marshal's office confirmed they hadn't placed her there.

Roger wanted to scream. The love of his life had returned to him alive but marred by life and trapped in her own fantasy world. He rubbed his forehead thoughtfully as he climbed out of the sports car he'd paid too much for, another attempt at soothing his broken heart after the breakup. He'd opted for financial destitution, and she opted for a leave of her senses.

Roger glanced at the lighted windows above him. There was no use hurrying to the apartment. There was no real danger. But even considering everything he had learned over the past few hours, he still wanted to hold Rachel in his arms.

"Rachel," he hollered as he entered the condo. Met with silence, no answer or movement, Roger went straight to the bedroom. The bed was still a mess from the night before, his clothes strewn from the dresser drawers. Leaving a bed unmade and the room a wreck was unusual for the neat freak he used to know. A sick ache accompanied by the feeling of dread sank like a rock in his gut.

"Rachel, where are you?"

When he came to the overturned chair at the computer, his heart hitched. He gazed at the computer screen, paralyzed by the image he saw. It was himself and Senator Rose. Senator Rose was about to shoot him. Roger stared at the picture, trying to get the image to penetrate his mind. Searching for a clue as to what was going on. He recognized the room; it was in Rachel's condo. Roger leaned on the desk to look closer, knocking the mouse to the floor. The picture vanished.

Roger grabbed Rachel's phone, which was still connected

to his monitor, disconnected it, and put it in his pocket. Taking the card from his pocket, he pulled out his cellphone and frantically pushed the numbers to reach Agent Tolliver.

"She's not crazy," he said the minute he heard the agent's voice. He pulled his topcoat back on.

"Who is this?"

"Rachel Rose. She's not crazy like you think."

"Is this Roger?"

"Yes, and I have the proof. She's gone. I don't know if they got her or she left in a hurry, but there appears to have been a struggle." Roger was speaking rapidly as he paced back and forth.

"Slow down, Roger. Tell me exactly what happened."

"I came in and she was gone. There was an overturned chair and a picture on the computer. A picture of my murder about to be committed." He took his coat back off, unsure of what he should do. "Someone is trying to make her think she's crazy. Which she's not, but she's in danger."

"Okay, stay put, Roger. I will be there in fifteen minutes. Don't touch anything or move anything. Just wait."

Roger hung up the phone and noticed the red flashing message light on the answering machine. He touched the button, replaying the messages, fast-forwarding through his own until he heard Chuck's message, grabbing a pen to jot down the website so he could check it out later. It was critical he didn't disturb the computer, hoping the FBI could find the room again.

Agent Tolliver arrived in fifteen minutes as he said, he and his crew picking apart every inch of the apartment. Roger sat on the sofa, cradling his head in his hands, trying to fit all the pieces together.

"I don't think it was a struggle. I think she left in a hurry," the agent finally told Roger.

"I think she went after them." Roger responded.

"Maybe, or maybe she went back to Houston."

"What about the girl in Phoenix? Did you find out anything more?"

"She's not talking. Said it was a job. She's a fledgling actress and thought it could help her. The financials have been traced back to a California corporation based here in Santa Monica. The agents are running the address and the P.O. Box now. Let's look at that site."

The men took Rachel's phone, examined it carefully and brought the site into view, but they couldn't retrieve the picture Roger had described earlier.

"I think the best thing to do is wait for her to come back. Call us when she gets here. We need to talk to her. I'm going to contact the psychiatrist and see what he recommends. Until we figure this out, I'll do a drive-by of the senator's house and take all the precautions we can. That should make you feel more comfortable. Don't worry, we'll find her."

Roger shuffled his feet, looking down and falsely nodding in agreement with the agent. He withheld knowing the location where the video was staged, certain Rachel was on her way to the condo, believing Roger was in trouble.

"You'll call us if she comes back?" Agent Tolliver questioned.

"Sure, sure." Roger avoided eye contact, hurriedly showing the agent to the door, noting the agent camped out in the hallway. Pressing the door closed, he sighed. Time was not on his side, but he had to wait long enough for the agents to finish their work and the ones that remained behind on the watch to get bored. Then he would find her himself.

Chapter 31
Hello Father

Scott arrived at the condominium right on schedule, the time rolling past nine-twenty, ten minutes before his father would arrive. A man who was always punctual, almost to a fault, and didn't excuse tardiness in anyone, especially Scott.

Checking the room, making sure it was in order and ready for his father's company, he took a seat on the sofa, patiently waiting, staring at the door. As expected, his dad walked through it at exactly nine-thirty, as Scott knew he would.

"Hello, father. Join me for a drink?" Scott extended his arm, holding a scotch already prepared the exact way his father liked.

Jay crossed the room, removing the drink from Scott's hand. "What's wrong, Scott?" Jay knew the use of the term "Father" meant Scott had a problem of some sort.

"Nothing, nothing at all." Scott checked his watch.

"Why's it so dark in here?" Jay asked.

"I like it dark." Scott reached over and twisted the knob on the table lamp next to him, bringing it to life. "That better?"

Jay shrugged, choosing to ignore his son's mood. "Did you take care of things at the benefit?"

"You mean that's all you want to know? You don't want

to hear about people with cancer, their suffering, their plight? Aren't you the least bit interested in the research being conducted and the amount of money needed to keep that going? Don't you even want to know how much money we've raised to help cancer research?" Scott was sarcastic and hostile.

"No! I want to know how much money I made. That's all." The senator placed his full glass on the table and stood in front of Scott.

Scott reached inside his jacket and pulled out the envelope, already having removed the extra cash Mr. Ramirez placed there for him, and handed it to his father.

Jay pulled it open, took out the folded papers and unwrapped them, revealing a stack of money. He smiled and folded it again, placing it into his own pocket, patting it to ensure it was secure. "Now, that wasn't so hard, was it?" Jay straightened, making himself stand taller.

Scott smiled and stood up to face his father. "Why don't you have a seat, Dad," Scott suggested.

"I need to get back to your mother," he said, brushing off his son.

"I want you to sit for a moment. I have something for you."

Jay sighed, then begrudgingly indulged his son, removed his coat, and sat in the easy chair. It was the single item he'd selected for Rachel when they bought her the condo. He'd battled with Linda, who didn't believe it suited the mood of the room, but he bought it anyway. "What is it, Scott?"

"I'll be right back." Scott disappeared up the staircase.

Rachel saw a few lights on upstairs in the condominium, the downstairs barely lit, as she crept into the common area. She peered in the window and could see her father sitting in a chair in the den. Crouching below the windows, she snuck around the side of the unit, headed to the kitchen door in the backyard. It was surprising the family still owned her condo; she assumed they would have sold it by now.

She climbed over the short white fence and sidled along the stucco wall to the kitchen entrance. Standing on the step and reaching her hand up to the top of the door, she slid it across the shingles until she found the cold metal stuck tightly under the second overlay. Peeling it up a tad; the key fell to the ground, making a loud clink as it hit the concrete. Rachel ducked at the sound, which was probably louder in her ears and inaudible on the other side of the door. Quickly groping along the ground, finding the key, gripping it tightly, she carefully slipped it into the lock. Easing it to the right, she rotated the metal, releasing the deadbolt with precision and stealth.

Rachel coaxed the door open, clenching her teeth when it squeaked, pulling it wide enough to slip inside. Nobody had oiled the hinges like she used to do. She squinted and closed it gingerly behind her. Holding her breath, listening for voices, she tried to assess what the situation was in the living room where Roger was most likely being held. There was only silence.

Her eyes darted toward the hallway, then to the dining room, which sat across from the path of the entryway into the den. She spotted her father in the chair by the window, not seeing Roger from her vantage point.

Tiptoeing into the dining room, hiding in shadows as she moved through the dark hallway, the pounding of footsteps on the stairway echoed overhead. Someone else was in the house.

Crouching below the stairs, tight against the bookcases, hidden from sight of whomever was descending the stairs, positioning herself in the ultimate spot to be a voyeur. She watched with wide eyes as her brother stepped off the landing. Was he helping her father now? It would make sense, remembering his reluctance to testify against their dad.

Scott was in on it?

"So, what did you want to show me, Scott?" Jay asked.

"I'll show you in a moment. Be patient. Isn't that what you've always drilled into my head? Patience?"

"I'm out of patience. I've got to go." Jay stood, making a move to gather his topcoat he'd dropped on the sofa.

"You'll wait," Scott pushed his father down onto the sofa.

Watching her brother's aggression against her father unnerved Rachel. There had never been a day in their lives when Scott stood up to their father, ever. Shock ran through her, trying to unravel the situation and make sense of the alarming interaction between the two. Studying her father's expression, a look she'd never seen sat across his face. All that she had planned in her mind to unleash on her father threatened to spill from her mouth, but she hadn't found Roger. She had to keep it together; she lectured herself.

"What are you doing, Scott?" Jay was back on his feet. The two men squared off.

"We're going to have a brief family reunion, Dad. You won't want to miss it." Scott smiled and turned his head in Rachel's direction.

Rachel thought about trying to inch her way out of the

kitchen door, certain she wasn't visible from where Scott stood. However, seized by the thought of living her life as she had been for the past several months, the waiting, the fear, the not knowing who to trust, it had to end. And it had to end now. She stepped out into the light, where both men could clearly see her.

Chapter 32
The Prodigal Daughter

Jay gasped when his daughter's face came into view. But the anger at the sight of her didn't hit him like he had imagined it would. Instead, all he felt was confusion about her presence, and by Scott obviously keeping a secret about her whereabouts.

Jay looked at Scott, waiting for an explanation. Rachel stood motionless, trying to assess what was unfolding.

"Come over here, Rachel." Scott finally spoke, "Come join the party. I have cameras outside the condo, dear sister." He waved his phone at her, revealing the monitoring app, then slid it into his back pocket.

Jay remained silent and on his feet.

Rachel stepped cautiously toward the men, looking across the room wondering where Roger was, stopping momentarily at the step-down into the den.

"Sit down, dad!" Scott ordered harshly.

"Don't tell me what to do, Scott," Jay snapped back.

"I said, sit down." Scott reached behind his back, then raised his right arm. In his hand, he held a Glock.

Rachel's breath caught in her chest, watching her brother aim the gun barrel straight at her father. The senator relented, raising both hands slightly in front of him as he sat, taking a spot on the sofa. Rachel took one step backwards.

"You don't move," he ordered. Turning the gun towards her, motioning with it, commanding her to move to the spot next to her father.

Warily, she walked behind the sofa where her father sat, standing only inches away from him. She hadn't been this close to him in a long time. His familiar cologne urging guilt for not wanting to embrace him. She stopped to his left.

"No, no," Scott whined, "over there, get over there." He raised his impatient voice. Rachel moved farther to the right, to the other side of her father, stopping when she reached the media cabinets.

"Now stand there and don't move," he said emphatically.

"What's this all about, Scott? What's going on?" she asked calmly.

"This is my show now, Rachel. I'm running things, so don't try to take over. You've always taken over. This is my show." He leveled the gun at her again, his voice stressed.

She stepped back as far as she could, bumping into the cabinet.

"Scott," Jay said smoothly, "let's talk about whatever is going on." He had negotiated with many men, fueled by flaring tempers and unclear thinking. It was his specialty, and he knew he was good at it, but this was the most important negotiation he'd ever faced. The negotiation for his life and Rachel's. As much as he had nursed his hatred for what Rachel had done, the love he tried to stifle bubbled over as he contemplated losing her for real.

"So, now you want to talk?" Scott questioned. "Why? Feeling a bit derelict of your parental duties? A bit negligent of your children?" Scott laughed, a crazy, irrational babbling of a laugh, not his usual infectious noise.

"We should be celebrating. Your sister is alive after all. I thought...," Jay closed his mouth when Scott interrupted him mid-sentence.

"Don't think, Father. Do as I say and shut up. You don't care if Rachel is dead or alive. And another thing, Father, if I want your asinine opinion, I'll ask for it." He trained the gun on the senator's head, raising his other hand to steady the heavy metal, taking aim at his father.

"Okay, Scott, I'll be quiet. You're running the show," Jay said compliantly, giving Scott the attention he craved.

Scott smiled with an evilness Rachel had never known her brother to possess. Her eyes scanned back and forth between the men. This was leading nowhere good, trying to think quickly to devise something to diffuse it.

"Scott," Rachel spoke softly, "you don't have to even my score with him. I can take care of him on my own. I'm okay." Rachel assumed that Scott had come over to her side against her father.

Scott laughed again. "You think this is about you? You always think everything is about you. Well, guess what, sister dear, it's not about you. It's about me. Don't you see? It is your fault that he never loved me, never appreciated me, never cared. He was so consumed with his 'perfect daughter,' his 'angel girl,' his 'bright one,' he didn't have the time of day for me, the 'stupid one.' Even when I remained loyal and you didn't, he was still obsessed with you." Scott spoke loudly and irrationally.

"That's not true, Scott," his father threw out. "I love you equally. But you're my son, and it's different between men and their sons."

Scott roared with laughter.

Rachel and Jay looked at each other, unprepared for what was happening and not understanding Scott's reaction.

"Your son? Is that what I am, your son? Here's some news for you, Dad. I'm not your son." A devious grin revealed itself as he absorbed the look on his father's face when he delivered the news.

"What are you talking about, Scott? You are my son, whether you like it or not," he replied.

"No, you see, you're not the only one who went outside the sanctity of your marriage for some carnal pleasure. Mom is human, you know, with needs like yours."

Jay's skin burned hot, and his chest tightened. He knew his blood pressure was rising as his son taunted him. "Really? So, whose son are you then, Scott?"

Scott looked at Rachel, then at his Father, "I'm the son of Julio Leguardo." He smiled, letting it sink into his father's mind. Jay closed his eyes momentarily.

"Who's Julio Leguardo?" Rachel asked, unaware of the significance. Neither man answered her. They were locked in silent, deadly glares. "Who is Julio Leguardo?" Rachel demanded.

Jay broke his lock on his son and looked at his daughter. "Julio is the head of the Colombian cartel."

He wanted to deny the revelation in his mind as an absurdity, but as he did the math, he knew it could be true. He and Linda had been introduced to the mobster in Europe at a party ages ago, searching his memory for the exact year, knowing the timetable fit perfectly. He should have suspected then, but he hadn't cared and was happy to have Linda occupied and not having to entertain her. She acted so happy with her alone time at the hotel. Looking back now and assessing it in retrospect, Linda had been giddy, assuring him she was fine and could take care of herself. He guessed she really had. Jay fought to assemble his thoughts and deal with his son.

"What now, Scott? What do you want, and what is this all about? So, you're not my son. I see that's a relief to you. Maybe you would be happier if you go join your father in Colombia?"

Scott grinned. "I don't have to go all the way to Colombia. You see, my real father believes in me and trusts me. In fact, he trusts me so much that he's given me the great pleasure of running his business. What you don't know, Jay, is I'm BogataOne. In fact, your little friend, Mr. Ramirez, works for me and delivered a little holiday bonus from my real father. All I have to do is one little magic trick. Well, technically two, make you both disappear." He delivered the news with a smile, taking great pleasure in watching the face of the stunned senator.

"You? You're not BogataOne."

"Whatever you say...BostonPops."

Upon hearing the screen name, Jay knew it was true, which meant he'd been secretly working with Scott all these years. The thought circled in on him. It couldn't be possible. The shock of the news reeled through him.

"Who is BogataOne? Who is BostonPops?" Rachel was confused by the exchange. She'd missed something important.

"Don't worry about it, Rachel. It really doesn't concern you," Jay dismissed her, hoping to protect his daughter from knowing too much.

"Oh, let's tell her. She worked so diligently, trying to discover the truth for so many months. She even implored me for my help. Ironically, I was the one who kept her from uncovering you." He directed his hostility at his dad. "You wanted to know the connection between daddy dearest, and the cartel, right, Rachel?"

"Right," she said, glaring at Scott.

"Well, that connection is me. I'm the one who's been making his money laundering possible. I'm the one who allows him access to the cartel for the import of the drugs. It's me. All me." Scott was proud of himself.

"You? You were the link?" Rachel questioned.

"I was more than the link. I was the one who masterminded all of this. You both underestimated me all these years. It was easy because neither of you ever thought I was capable. Now, what do you say? Are you impressed?" Scott screamed.

Rachel stared at the person she believed was her brother, not recognizing any part of him. She didn't know what to say, so she said nothing. Instead, she was thinking about how to get out from behind the gun.

"Here." Scott pulled the envelopes from his pocket. "I have presents for you both."

He tossed the envelopes to each of them. Rachel bent to get hers off the floor, taking another look around the room.

Where was Roger being held? Could he be hurt or dead?

Jay caught the envelope Scott threw his way, watching Scott carefully before he pulled the flap open. Inside were the pictures of the dead girl, Natalie. A picture of himself shooting Roger. And a picture of Rachel shooting him.

Rachel peeled the flap back, bracing herself for what was inside. There were several photos, one of her sitting in her SUV in Houston. The next was a photo of Marshal Gagne, dead in a pool of blood.

"Marshal Gagne," Rachel gasped. "You killed an agent?" She looked at Scott in disbelief.

"You are so naïve, Rachel; he wasn't an agent. He worked for me. An expendable nobody, kind of like the two of you. In fact, as far as the world knows, you're already dead. Nobody has missed you yet, not even your mother." He wanted to hurt her now.

Moving the photo aside, behind it sat a photo of herself shooting her father, and Roger dead on the floor behind him. None of it was real, but someone looking at these photos would believe it was. The last image was the missing photo of Natalie. She closed her eyes, not wanting to see the brutality, wondering if it was even real.

"What about these pictures, Scott? Some of these clearly aren't real. Which ones are? What about Natalie?" Jay growled.

"Well, Dad, that one is real. We couldn't have another heir to our family fortune out there, and she wouldn't agree to the abortion you so conveniently arranged. What can I say? I took care of it for you. Like I always do, and like you wanted."

Jay shook his head. "That's not what I meant when I told you to take care of her. I wanted her to have an abortion. I wanted you to find her a decent place to live down south, give her a chance at a new life, that's all. Not kill her."

"Ohhh, I'm sorry. Did you love her?" Scott mimicked his father. "Too bad. She's better off dead. You'd have disappointed her, too."

"So, you're the one who had the photos this entire time?" Jay half-heartedly asked, not sure the answer mattered anymore.

Natalie was dead. He finally knew the truth. The pain of it wrecked him, but he stood stoically, wiping any emotion from his face.

"Yes, it was me. I was the one who made sure Rachel found the photos. I needed her to believe you were evil enough to kill someone. Her virtuous soul would cave with the knowledge. I wanted her to fear you so she would cooperate with my plans. But somehow she found out about the drugs and went to the authorities. For some reason, she didn't tell the FBI about the dead girl. Why not?" He turned to Rachel.

"Because the photos disappeared. I thought Dad had them." Rachel tried to force the anger from her voice, but it was no use.

"Oh, that's right, you didn't have any proof because I had it. After all, it was my creative abilities that were captured in the pictures." Scott was babbling incoherently.

"Is that what you're planning, Scott? To kill us both?" Rachel clenched her fist, crushing the photos in her hand. There was no shaking in her bones. It had evaporated, replaced by determination.

Jay stared at Scott. "I don't understand, Scott, you can't get away with this. The police will know these are fake, that Rachel didn't kill me or Roger. Roger's not even here. Look, we don't even have the same clothes on." Jay tossed the pictures on the coffee table in front of him as if Scott were indeed an idiot.

Rachel could have strangled her father for his continued pretentious attitude.

Scott moved toward the bookcase and picked up a black bag sitting behind it, opened it and removed clothing from it. "I've thought of that, Daddio. Here!" He tossed the clothes at

Rachel. "Change your clothes." He pulled out a shirt for his father and threw it at him. "You know, senator, have you noticed that you always wear the same color pants?"

"You won't get away with this." Jay's anger increased to match Scott's.

"Change!" Scott ordered.

Rachel pulled her jacket off. "If you don't mind." Turning her back to the men, she removed her blouse and put on the one Scott had provided. Looking at the media cabinet, she remembered the hidden operational panel she'd installed for the lights, the stereo, and the television. She thought it was extravagant at the time but praised its usefulness now.

Taking her time to change, she placed her hand on the panel door to steady herself as she slid her pants over her feet. She pushed slowly, and with a little effort, popped the door slightly. Once the new pants were on, she pretended to have trouble with the zipper and pried the door open enough to look over the buttons. She stepped into her shoes and slipped her jacket back on, turning around with her arms up as she pretended to adjust the collar, hiding the small open panel behind her.

"There, happy now?" she turned and asked Scott.

Jay finished tucking in his shirt.

"Why did you lure me here? You could have simply killed me in Houston. Obviously, the marshals weren't watching me closely if you found me."

"Dear sister, darling, the marshals were watching you, but they thought you were in Phoenix. I was the one who moved you from Phoenix to Houston. I was the one who provided your new identity, your house, your name. I took care of everything. I knew you wouldn't let it go. You would have to come after Dad at some point in time. I didn't know you would make it so easy. The part I hadn't figured out, you took care of. I didn't know how to get the link to you, but when you decided to come to Java Connection for the training, it fell into place. You see, Michael Long, the trainer, is a friend of mine who has no life and lives vicariously through me. I happened to drop by his apartment the other night when he was preparing the new trainee packets, and the brilliant idea hit me. That's when you got the promotion to manager and the chance to come home."

Rachel looked at Scott, her voice steady as she spoke, formulating her own plan, one to get herself and her father out of this alive. "So now what?"

Scott walked towards her, kicking her discarded clothes away as he approached her. She backed up against the panel.

"Now, Rachel darling, you are going to shoot Daddy." Scott grabbed her by the arm, pulling her in front of him, wrapping his arms around her, holding her hands to the gun.

"No, I won't. I'm not a murderer like you. I won't shoot my own father, no matter what he's done," she protested angrily, fighting Scott's grip on her. Scott held her tight.

Jay stood up from the sofa, noticing the open panel. He faced his son squarely to provide some distraction. "Don't hide behind a woman. Be a man for once in your life. You always hid behind your mother, now your sister. If you have a problem with me, then solve it." He knew the scolding was sealing his fate, but he had to give Rachel an opportunity to get out alive.

Scott shoved Rachel back to the wall, incredulous that his father still showed him no respect. He was the one in control.

The events happened too quickly for Rachel to react. She watched in horror as Scott leveled the gun, took aim, and shot her dad without a blink of an eye. Smirking as he watched the man who raised him grasp his side, trying to cover the hole in front and the larger exit wound, to stop the bleeding and keep his insides from oozing out. Rachel watched helplessly.

Jay felt hot pain shoot through his side and spread sharply up his back. Blood soaked through his fingers as he held his side as tightly as he could, sliding slowly down onto the couch. Words wouldn't form as he fought for his life. He focused on Rachel, flashes of her as a sweet child. The only person whom he had truly loved in his life. Confirmed by the surge of such pleasant emotions racing through his mind and heart. The comforting memories flooded in until she screamed, and he remembered where he was and what was happening.

Helplessly watching her father fight to maintain his focus, Rachel shouted, "Dad! Good God, Scott, what have you done?"

"I love you, Rachel," he barely whispered.

Scott shot him again. He teetered off the sofa, crashing onto the floor, lying motionless on his back. His hands melted away from his side, dropping to the floor, his white shirt flooded with crimson, his open eyes fixed on the ceiling.

Rachel turned slightly toward the panel, reached in and slid the volume buttons as high as they would go, then smashed the power on. The lights flashed on all at once. The stereo blared the last playlist Scott had listened to, a heavy metal rock song, while the fireplace popped to life, followed by the blinds raising simultaneously. A serious reporter screamed a breaking story at full volume.

Rachel dove at her brother, catching him off guard as he reacted to the alarming sounds and lights. He stumbled and fell onto the coffee table, striking his head and sending the gun spiraling under the bookcase. Rachel jumped over him and raced out of the house toward the ocean, hot tears blurring her vision as fear propelled her to find safety.

Chapter 33
The Last Shot

Running blindly, Rachel fled out the back fence and onto the beach, knowing the terrain by heart, having spent many nights alone sitting on the rocks, staring at the ocean, and contemplating her life in the desperately painful years after the breakup. Pouring through thoughts of her blessings and other times of her curses and heartbreak, the trial, and the decision to give up her identity.

But tonight, in the darkness, she wouldn't enjoy the quiet and solitude of the private beach. Tonight, she headed for the rocky caves and the cliffs, fleeing for her life. It could offer a brief respite until she could think, figure out a plan, then go call for help and hopefully get out of this alive. She was certain it was too late to help her father.

Scott rubbed his forehead, his senses spinning wildly. He would have a nasty bruise to explain, but he would have to worry about that later. Rachel was ruining his plans, and he wasn't going to let that happen. He smashed the media controls off, silencing the blaring noise. Gazing around the room, he half-heartedly searched for the gun, but it was nowhere in sight. He stumbled upstairs, trying to regain his focus, to retrieve his other gun from the bureau. This one was registered to him. The other one wasn't.

It was registered to Jeannie Smith to ensure Rachel would be blamed for killing their father. The psychiatrist he'd been paying handsomely would certify that Jeannie…or Rachel…or whatever alias they chose to call her was delusional and homicidal.

Regaining his determination to have his plan succeed, he ran down the stairs and out the open back door. He stumbled through the darkness, his feet sinking in the heavy, drenched sand. The moon was hidden behind the clouds, shielding the cove in darkness. He cursed his sister and the moon.

Watching Scott emerge from the yard onto the beach, Rachel sprinted straight for the jagged rocks, the only path up and out of the beach area. Feeling the high-tide lapping at her ankles as she made her way to the rocks, the freezing water anchored and slowed her movement. To keep them from freezing, she lifted her feet quickly in mini steps, propelling her through the rising water until she reached the sharp black lava hills on the other side of the shallow inlet. Placing each foot firmly before moving was the only way to climb higher toward the more stable area above her. It was one thing to climb in the sunlight of the day, but one wrong move in the dark could have her tumbling into sharp pieces below.

Her thighs burned as she took high steps, scaling quickly as possible until she reached a plateau where she could crouch behind the coarse rocks. The view between the two jutted pieces of rock allowed her to hide and watch Scott approaching from the condo. She waited, her heart pounding from the exertion and fear, straining her eyes in the darkness.

She heard him before she saw him. He was walking toward her, calling out merrily. "Rachel, where are you? Come out and play with your little brother. Alle alle oxen free. Where are you? You, bitch!" he yelled.

Scott's the crazy one, she thought furiously, shifting her feet, sending little pebbles down the face of the rock she was leaning against. She held her breath as they fell. Fortunately, Scott was still maniacally calling out for her and didn't hear the sound.

Moving up the cliff face farther toward the grassy ledge several feet up, she'd positioned herself above him. But she could tell he was getting closer from the increasing volume of his voice. There were only seconds that she could remain still, or he'd find her for sure. Looking up, if she could get to the next ledge, she could make her way across the hillside, back to the street, to the condo, and find her dad's phone and call 911.

Groping at the ground, she fought to pull herself up across the rocks. If she slipped, there was a rocky landing below her and a painful, bloody death.

With one last push off the rough rocks, swinging her leg up onto the ground above her, she'd almost climbed to safety. Unable to fully gain her balance, she used her fear to propel her upward, pulling her torso as high as she could, ignoring the burning in her arms, scooting her hip over enough to get the leverage to maneuver her other leg onto the grassy ledge.

Her breath was coming in large pants now, which she was trying to muffle as she lay flat, hoping to locate Scott. He'd stopped shouting and was absorbed into the blackness of the beach below her. Frozen to her spot, she listened hard for any discernable sound he made before she dared move.

The water was sloshing rhythmically against the rocks as the waves caressed the shoreline. The sound was one that brought harmony to her life in days past. Now, she wanted it silenced. She searched for shadows through the darkness, looking for any movement. The clouds opened up a small circle of light; the moonbeams breaking through for an instant, hitting the beach below her. She saw Scott at the bottom of the rocky cliff, standing, ready to climb, his face skewed by his mood. The moon disappeared quickly, washing the inky night over them again.

This was her opportunity to make her break. She rolled away from the edge of the ledge and stood up, sprinting across the grass, toward the street and to the condo, fairly confident Scott hadn't seen her. She had to know if her father was dead. If he wasn't, maybe she could save him.

Rachel barreled through the front door, running straight to the den. Kneeling frantically next to her father's body, checking his wrist for a pulse, it was weak but there. She looked maniacally for the gun, knowing it slid toward the bookcase. Hoping Scott hadn't picked it up.

Lying as flat as possible, extending her hand under the shelves, she located the cold metal. The opening under the case wasn't wide enough to get her full arm under, so she inched it with her fingers to the side of the bookcase until she could push it far enough and slide it out. With the gun gripped tightly, she moved back to check on her father. His pulse was gone now. He was dead.

Rachel closed her father's eyes and said a prayer for his soul. She heard the front door open and heavy steps on the tile. Standing quickly, moving to the shadows against the wall, she raised the gun, pointing it in the direction of the person entering the condo. Her heart seized in her chest, recognizing the creak of the floor as light steps creeped closer.

He saw the gun staring him in the face as he came around

the corner. He threw his forearm over his face in a panicked reaction. "Don't shoot, don't shoot. It's me, Roger," he called out.

Rachel was already pulling the heavy trigger, the words signaling her brain to shoot and stop simultaneously. She released the lever and lowered the gun.

"Roger, my God. I almost shot you," she stuttered.

"What happened, Rachel?" he said, looking at the senator and back at Rachel, not sure whether to approach or not, trying to keep the situation under control. "Let me go see if he's alive."

"He's not," she whispered.

"Why did you shoot him?" he asked, moving guardedly towards her.

"I didn't shoot him." She looked at him, that old sense of betrayal nudging at her. "Scott shot him."

"Scott?" Roger bent down and touched the senator's lifeless body, feeling his neck. He stepped over him to reach Rachel, keeping an eye on the gun she was still holding. Carefully, he pried her fingers from a death grip on the gun handle and eased it into his pocket. He wrapped his arms around her.

"Are you all right?"

Her hands covered her eyes as she tried to make sense of what had transpired, not accepting any comfort from Roger. "We have to get out of here. He'll be back." She pulled away from Roger. He stepped toward her, pulling her back to him.

"Who? Who will be back?" He looked into her eyes and saw desperation.

"Scott, he'll be back."

Hearing the fear in her voice, Roger took her hand to leave the condo, but it was too late.

"So, the lovebirds are back together." Scott stood leaning against the wall, blocking the exit out the front door.

Roger looked toward the open kitchen door. They could make a dash for it, he calculated, believing it was a sound plan, until the faint light coming through the window bounced off the metal of the gun in Scott's hand.

"Don't think about it, lover boy." Scott moved closer to the couple, blocking their exit. "Get over by the wall, both of you. I hadn't planned on it this way, but I'll improvise. Rachel was actually supposed to shoot her hero when he came to rescue his maiden in distress, but of course, she doesn't have the guts. Please sit down, everyone. Let's have a little chat so we can make sure this ends as I've planned." Scott motioned towards the sofa with the gun.

"Why are you doing this, Scott?" Roger asked, pushing Rachel securely behind him, not moving as ordered.

"Oh Roger, it's far too complicated and I don't want to go through it again. Suffice it to say that I had some valid reasons." Scott stared blankly at them both, his head cocked sideways.

"So, Roger, let's talk about your former girlfriend. You know, the one that you rolled around with in bed a few years ago. The one you killed." Scott looked at Rachel, hoping to draw a reaction of anger and hatred.

Roger kept Rachel out of sight, hidden protectively behind him. "What are you talking about, Scott?" Roger asked.

"Oh, come on Rachel, come out from behind your ex-fiancé and let's explore Roger's problems here."

Rachel pushed Roger's hand down and stood beside him, in Scott's full view.

Scott sat down on the stair step. "Please, sit down. This might take a while."

Rachel and Roger did as Scott wanted and sat on the floor to keep as much distance between them and him, their backs against the wall, waiting for Scott's next move.

"Why don't you tell me about the girl, Scott? I have a feeling you know her much better than I do," Roger said, stalling to distract him and prolong the sadistic plan.

Scott looked smug, then grinned sheepishly at Roger. "I guess I do know her pretty well."

"I know Roger didn't kill her, Scott. I found her on the internet, alive and well. Your dirty trick didn't work," Rachel informed him.

"Kill her?" Roger looked at Rachel with confusion.

Scott drew his mouth tight. He hated his smartass sister. "So, he didn't kill her. It doesn't change the fact that he fucked her, does it? He had a great time with her, too. You should have seen them go at it. Boy, it was a thrill watching them. He was drunk out of his mind, but he was still able to do the deed." Scott laughed.

"So, it was you? You're the one who sent that girl to me. You set me up?" Roger couldn't hide his surprise.

"Yeah, old stupid Scott. I did it all by my feeble little self. Although you're the one who did the dirty deed with her, I didn't have to help you with that. What an animal you were!" Scott beamed.

"Why? What did I ever do to you?"

"What did you do? What you did was take Rachel's attention away from our father and my plans. You were a distraction, and she was going to marry you and leave. I needed her to get what I wanted." Scott stood up and paced in front of the couple.

"What did you need, Scott?" Rachel asked, trying to coax him to a calmer state of mind.

"I needed the Rose legacy. I needed to be what you were to him. I needed you to help me with him, to convince him to let me in. I needed you to get him to the Whitehouse then to help me follow in his shadow, to take my rightful place. A place where I'd be respected and not looked at like I was a failure. But you, you were going to mess it all up. And then you had to destroy our father, my legacy, my chance." He stood, moving toward the body on the floor, pointing the gun at the dead senator.

"You aren't even his son, remember? You're the son of some drug lord, Julio, or somebody," she reminded him.

Roger scrunched his face, staring at Rachel.

Scott giggled. "That was such bullshit. Did you really believe I was the son of a Colombia mafia boss? I guess I'm a better actor than I thought. Maybe I missed my calling. I should have gone into acting." Scott was absorbed in his own self-congratulating and didn't notice the men approaching him from behind.

Roger and Rachel saw them. Roger exhaled; relief washed over him when Agent Tolliver's face came into view. Roger pulled Rachel up to stand and face Scott, hoping to distract him. She kept talking as they stood so the men could get into position. "Then why tell Dad you weren't his son? What was the purpose of that? Just cruelty?"

"You don't know? It wasn't for me, you dumb bitch. It was for her, for Mom. Once when she was drunk, she told me about having a crush on Julio thirty years ago, about the time I was conceived evidently, and how she wished she could feel that way again. And so I figured he would believe it. My gosh, Rachel, you know how he treated her. The affairs, the torment. He crushed her like anyone who dared get in his way. I wanted him to die knowing that she wasn't weak like he thought. I wanted him to know that," he shouted at them both.

His pacing stopped. With wild eyes, he ran his hand through his hair three times in succession. Rachel knew it was a habit from childhood, right before he would throw himself on the floor in a full tantrum. Instead, he smiled and exhaled, then raised the gun, pointing it toward them. "Now, you're going to die with him, as I planned."

Multiple shots cracked the air simultaneously. Rachel felt the heat of the bullet rip through her shoulder, the pain permeating her body in a single flash. She collapsed against Roger from the impact. As she fell into his arms, she could see Scott lying face down in a puddle of blood. It was the same blood she'd seen when Marshal Gagne died. She watched it ebb out larger and larger, spreading quickly across the tile floor. She knew it was real.

Roger held her tightly, and she was grateful, as her knees melted away underneath her. Roger guided her to the ground. Calmness ebbed through her. The pain was hardly noticeable any longer; it was the first calmness and peace she'd felt in months.

Chaos broke out around her as the room filled with men in FBI jackets. All coming in and out of focus, voices fading, too muted to understand. Staring at golden-brown eyes brought a piece of a childhood melody to her mind. She closed her eyes and rested as it played repeatedly, soft and low, spreading a numbing warmth throughout her body.

Chapter 34
Fight—Don't Give Up

Roger held Rachel against him, trying to locate where the blood was coming from. Pressing hard with one hand over the front of her shoulder and the other on her back, but the blood was still coming fast.

"Stay with me, Rachel," Roger repeated, not knowing whether she could hear him or not. Her eyes remained closed. "Come on, baby, I love you. Stay with me."

The ambulance sirens screamed outside, the rotating lights circling through the den, seemingly multiplying, reflecting off the tall glass windows. Paramedics scrambled to bring the stretcher through the doorway. Taking Rachel from Roger, they worked quickly to stop the bleeding. Inserting an IV in record time and strapping the oxygen mask on Rachel's face; grasping her by the head and feet, plopping her onto the gurney and whisking her away to the hospital where the emergency crew was assembled and waiting for the 32-year-old female gunshot victim, whose pulse was thready and dropping rapidly.

"I'm going with you." Roger followed them to the ambulance.

"Follow behind," one of them ordered, slamming the doors shut.

Roger bolted toward his car parked down the street.

"Hop in," Agent Tolliver pulled his patrol car beside him, reaching across, pushing the passenger car door open. Roger climbed in, noticing the trembling of his hand as he slammed the door.

"Go, go." Roger's voice sounded foreign in his own ears.

Agent Tolliver pushed a button on the console control panel, bringing the lights and sirens to life. They raced after the ambulance.

Roger dialed his phone frantically. "Linda," Roger spoke in tight words, "this is Roger. Roger Williams."

Linda was shocked to hear from Roger. It had been so many years. She panicked immediately, knowing there was something terribly wrong for him to be calling her and at the late hour.

"What is it Roger? What's wrong?"

"I know this is going to sound crazy, Linda, but it's Rachel. Please hurry and get to Memorial Hospital right away. She's been shot."

Linda's shock cut through her drunkenness and sobered her. "Rachel?"

"Please get to the hospital. I'll explain it all when you get there." He ended the call with no more explanations.

Roger and Agent Tolliver arrived at the hospital before the ambulance, the agent having broken a few traffic laws on the way. Roger jumped out of the car, rushing into the emergency entrance, running to alert anyone he could find to Rachel's condition.

"We know Mr. Williams. We're waiting for her now." A sympathetic nurse led him to a chair. "Please stay here and let us do our job. The ambulance will be here any second. We've been getting reports from them during the transport."

Roger clasped his hands behind his bowed head, assuring the nurse he was fine. The seconds passing slowly as he stood by the entrance as they wheeled Rachel through the automatic doors. She was unconscious but alive; the doctors took over CPR from the paramedics.

Roger watched helplessly as the motion of the doctors and nurses kicked up to warp speed. Instructions, shouts for equipment, orders flying without question as she was rushed away to surgery.

He'd already experienced losing her, the grief, the pain he thought would never leave him, contorting his view of the world. Now, the loss was doubly heart-wrenching. He couldn't survive it again.

Roger was led to the surgery waiting area to wait with uncertainty while they worked on repairing the damage the bullet had done and tried to save Rachel.

"While it first looked like a clean shot through the shoulder, the angle took it through her back. It's going to be touch and go," the nurse told him as she left him alone in the empty room.

Linda ran in, dressed in sweats and no makeup, a rare occasion for her. She grabbed Roger. "What happened? I thought Rachel was dead, but she's not? They told me downstairs that she's still alive. I don't understand." Linda was near hysterics.

Roger held her until she calmed down, then he told her everything he knew. She didn't cry when he told her that Jay was dead, but collapsed into uncontrollable sobs when he talked of

Scott.

"Please come get me, Roger, when you know anything," Linda managed to say between broken breaths, inconsolable, as the nurse led her away to a private room.

Roger nodded before resuming pacing as he waited for an update about Rachel.

Several hours passed before the doctor emerged from the locked metal doors. Pulling off his mask, blood on his scrubs, the doctor faced Roger. "Roger Williams?"

"That's me." He stood up. He was the only one left in the waiting room in the wee hours of the morning.

The doctor approached; his face revealing exhaustion. "She's out of surgery and in the recovery room. We'll watch her in the ICU the rest of the night, or morning, I guess," the doctor checked his watch, adding, "and make sure her vitals are going to hold. If she makes it through the next twenty-four to forty-eight hours, then she'll be through the worst of it." The doctor placed his hands on his hips, his exhaustion apparent.

"She's alive though?" Roger smiled a little.

"She's alive and a pretty tough young lady, but that bullet did a lot of damage internally. It'll be up to a higher power now. I've done all that I can."

"Thank you, doctor. Thank you." Roger shook his hand ferociously.

"Careful there, I'm a surgeon," the doctor half-joked.

"When can I see her?" Roger released the doctor's hand.

"You need to give her some time. The nurses will come get you when she's awake." The doctor turned, leaving Roger standing in the hallway with tears of gratitude welling.

Roger found Linda lying down on a sofa in a small empty

office. "Linda, she's alive. It's serious, but she's alive."

Linda embraced Roger and began crying again. Roger cried too, releasing hardened emotions he'd stitched himself together with for far too long.

Chapter 35

Put Back Together

Rachel finally regained consciousness late in the afternoon. When she woke, she saw two familiar people asleep on either side of the bed.

"Hey, why are you guys so tired?" she said, her voice hoarse and shallow. She attempted to smile, but the pain brought her back to the here and now.

Roger lifted his head. "Hey sleepyhead, how are you?" He smiled, stroking her short hair. Rachel turned her head to confirm that the person asleep on the other side of the bed was her mom. "Hey Mom," she said weakly.

"Hi sweetheart," Linda said quietly, "my sweet girl. I'm so sorry." She collapsed in tears again.

Rachel patted her hand. "It's okay, Mom. It wasn't your fault." She saw no reason to place any guilt on her mother. It was time to end the pressure of crumbled expectations, hurt, and anger in the Rose family. She'd been given a second chance at life and couldn't stand anymore separation or grudges. She'd decided that the moment her eyes finally opened and she realized she was alive.

Linda bent over and kissed her daughter on the forehead. "Well, I think I'll go home and freshen up a little. I need to tell

Mable the news. I ran out of there last night like a crazy woman and I haven't let her know where I am. She's probably called out the National Guard by now. I can't believe how lucky I am to have you back." She gripped her daughter's hand and squeezed.

"I'm sorry, Mom, about Dad and Scott. I'm really sorry." Rachel felt her tears, but she didn't try to control them other than keeping the pain at bay when her chest moved too deeply. She knew she needed to cry. It had been a long time since she'd allowed herself to dump her emotions out, and it was time to enjoy it.

"They created the world they wanted. Don't blame yourself. I should have taken you kids out of that world a long time ago. But you made the right choices regardless, and you know Rachel, Scott could have too." Linda knew it was too easy to blame Jay for all the problems. It was a joint failure to provide what was necessary for a stable home, but they did all that they knew to do. They could have done a lot better, but it was too late now.

"I'll have to do better from now on, sweetheart. I promise I'll be a better grandmother than a mother." She winked at Rachel.

Rachel giggled as much as the pain would allow. They both turned and leveled a look at Roger.

"That's all right by me. But I think we are missing a step here," he cut in.

"What step?" Rachel was a little drowsy from the pain medication.

"You have to marry me first," Roger said, taking Rachel's hand in his.

"I can do that, Mr. Williams. I can do that," she said

happily before closing her eyes, feeling a peaceful sleep taking her under, the first in a long time.

Roger leaned over and kissed her on the head.

Linda squeezed Roger's hand before leaving. There were wedding plans to make right after she planned two funerals; one for a boy that broke her heart and the other for the man that broke her. But she was going to try to be stronger, telling herself she had no choice, but that wasn't true. She did have a choice. She could fall apart and seek comfort, as she had for years, in a bottle of wine. Or she could take control of her life. It was decided. She would choose to be strong.

Agent Tolliver walked into Rachel's room, having waited a couple of days to let her recover. He needed to talk to her to wrap his report before he could put this case behind him for good. When he spoke, she remembered him from the trial and placing her in the protection program, hazily recalling him from the shooting scene.

"So, do you still think I'm crazy?" she asked when he walked through the door.

"I'm sorry, Ms. Rose. I only made that judgment based on the psychiatrist's recommendation. I apologize that I didn't get to know you better, and I certainly didn't know your brother had paid off the doctor. The doc, if you can call him that, has been arrested, by the way," he stammered.

She pushed the button on the remote, bringing the bed up to a seat like recline. She was scheduled for discharge later in the afternoon, even though she should stay longer, according to the doctors. A home nurse had been hired, something her mother had insisted upon.

The funerals were set for the next day, and she was determined to be there, for her mom and for herself. It was time to get the closure she'd so desperately searched for over the past year. The media frenzy had taken hold, and she knew her mom would need backup, though Roger seemed to have it under control thus far.

"It's okay, Agent Tolliver, I understand, I guess." She remained aloof.

"I came to give you an update on the investigation. That URL you had was the break we needed. We were able to locate the hidden entries and, through those, we traced it back to the cartel's operating systems." The agent checked his notes. "It seems a Michael Long was helping your brother with his computer skills. Mr. Long thought it was an innocent game. He claims he didn't know what Scott was up to. Apparently, your brother wasn't exactly the computer genius he thought he was. Seems he had a lot of help from Michael."

"That makes more sense. Scott was never the studious type. But I could have missed that too. I never knew he was the murdering type, either." Rachel looked away momentarily at the thought of her brother and to stop the burn of tears threatening to spill.

"With the locations and dates of the drug deliveries, our agents were able to snag the drugs as they came into the port. It was quite a bust. We rounded up a lot of guys who won't be seeing the streets anytime soon. Unfortunately, some are also Colombian citizens. Most likely, they will be deported after conviction. It'll be up to the Colombian government as to their fate, which I'm not optimistic they'll actually receive any punishment."

He looked at his notes again, avoiding making eye contact with Rachel. "Your father was the one allowing the shipments into the states without inspection, but then, you already knew that, I suppose. I came to say, Rachel, that you were right all along. I'm sorry I doubted you." He looked her straight in the eye as he apologized.

Rachel closed her eyes, considering the agent's words. There was some relief in knowing she was right, but not as much as she'd imagined there would be. Mostly, sadness overshadowed the menagerie of emotions she was tiptoeing through. Mind-tripping back to the days when the pink rocking horse was the most important thing in her life. It was all upside down now. But it didn't really matter because even if she had to start all over again, even if she had to change her beliefs about her family, she was still here, and more importantly, she was here as Rachel, not Jeannie or Susan or any other person the government wanted her to pretend to be. She had her life back, and it was hers to live, and that's what she was going to do.

"Tell me, Agent Tolliver," Rachel said, looking at him squarely, "what happened to Marshal Mayer?"

Agent Tolliver looked at the ground apologetically. "Quite frankly, we're still trying to figure that out. I'll have to get back to you on that one. Marshal Mayer was in San Diego, where he's based. Witnesses are monitored remotely. We don't position agents to keep tabs on protectees. We have surveillance, as you know, but unless there's a threat, we don't review the tapes. There was no reason for him to review the surveillance, as there were no credible threats."

"So, what about the other two threats, the ones that

prompted my prior relocations?"

"Those were real, but from the preliminary information, it looks like they were orchestrated by Scott. Not your father or the cartel. There are still some details we are trying to pull together. And we are trying to sort out how we lost you."

"Don't bother. I'm found now, and that's all that matters. And quite honestly Agent Tolliver, if I never have to see your face again, it will be fine with me. No offense."

They both laughed. He patted her arm and started to leave but turned around to tell her, "To cover all bases, here's my card." He laid his card on the table and left.

Chapter 36
Final Goodbye

The media frenzy was a chaotic mess of scrambling to get the true story, which was never achieved. It was a disaster, worse than when the esteemed Senator Rose went on trial. But a double funeral was perfect gossip to make the reporters slap-happy.

Rachel stepped out of the limousine, flanked by her mother and Roger. Thankfully, Roger had arranged to have police security as the media converged on the funeral home. She ignored the flurry the best she could between shouts of insensitive comments and curious fact seeking. Clinging to her focused solitude in order to say her goodbyes and give her forgiveness to the two men whom she once loved most in the world.

As her mother stood stoically beside her, there was a flicker of strength and resolve that Rachel had never noticed before. Certain it must have been embedded all along. Only recently appreciating what it must have taken for her mom to navigate a marriage under the spotlight of the media and the public scrutiny, and to watch her father morph into a man far removed from the one she fell in love with. She squeezed her mother's hand as the minister said a final prayer for the lost souls.

Her mother raised her chin, returning a slim smile of courage and acknowledgment of the pain they were both managing.

As they walked back to the limo, Roger told her, "I've let Senator Johnstone know we are declining a public memorial."

"Thank you, Roger. I'm sure Jay would have wanted one, but I don't see what is to be gained at this point. And frankly, I'm tired, and Rachel needs time to recover." Linda leaned on him as they crossed the grassy field to the awaiting car. He'd been a rock for what remained of the family.

Rachel held tightly to Roger's hand, emotionally conflicted between wanting to forget and wanting to remember so many memories. It felt wrong leaving her father and brother behind in plots side-by-side that would soon be overgrown with grass. Both buried by greed. She would give anything to reverse time and have them back, to ask them if it was all worth it.

"Watch your step," Roger told her as he helped her into the limo.

She breathed a sigh of relief once back in the car, watching the camera crews pack up. Another sigh of relief when they pulled into the drive of the family home, and there were no reporters loitering outside the gates. Cars of friends would soon pack the edges of the long drive.

Exhaustion weighed down on Rachel as she and her mother shook hands, listened to stories, and tried their best to keep tears at bay. After the house cleared of close friends and the food from people expressing their condolences was packed into the freezer, Rachel collapsed on the sofa in the den, watching the fire hop and sparkle in the hearth. Hoping to release the tightness stretched across her back and stave off the pain seeping through her shoulder, she removed her sling and straightened her arm briefly. Her relaxation was cut short by a call from Agent Tolliver.

"This is Rachel." Surprised to hear from the agent.

"I'm sorry to interrupt you at night, especially this night, but I wanted to update you before I go on vacation for the holidays," he said.

"Update me on what?" she asked.

"I've been working diligently to try to determine if those photos were really of a young lady named Natalie. So far, we've not identified any deceased Jane Does that fit Natalie's description. I can't say with certainty whether those photos were real or AI-generated, like the others Scott created. We do know there is or was a Natalie that your father was associated with, but beyond that, the trail runs cold. I wish I could provide something more definite."

"That's okay, Agent Tolliver. I appreciate your efforts," she thanked him graciously.

It gnawed at Rachel, wondering if the girl was dead or alive and living in a quaint house with a child that might be her half-sibling. Finally, convincing herself that it was probably better not knowing, and to let the truth die with her father and brother. Perhaps naively believing it was that simple, but if there was one thing she knew for certain, life would play out as it should and her control of that had finite limits.

She placed her arm back in the sling. Tomorrow the holidays would be in full swing, Thanksgiving, Christmas, and then they would sachet into a new year. Today had been a time for mourning. Tomorrow would be a time for moving forward. Rachel watched the fire dance, then went to find Mabel.

Chapter 37

Pack it Away

Rachel and Roger moved through the holidays with a heavy weight in their hearts. As the New Year rolled in, they sat on the couch in Roger's condo, watching the New York ball drop, excited to welcome in fresh beginnings. Life had settled into a lazy rhythm that suited them both.

"How are you feeling? Is the physical therapy working?" Roger asked as he slowly rubbed Rachel's shoulder.

"It's getting better. The PT says I'll make a full recovery in time."

Roger hugged her tightly. "Chuck reached out today; he had some news. He said there will be no hearings about your father's conduct, so the media should be moving on to their next scandal soon. The internal investigation by the Senate committee determined that the only questionable bill your father was involved with was the export/import security bill."

"Well, I guess that's good." Rachel closed her eyes and snuggled against Roger.

"All the other senators have been cleared. And there's no evidence they were aware of what was going on. According to Chuck, it's good law in spite of how your father planned on using it. Senator Billings is retiring at the end of his term, supposedly to spend time with his family."

"I saw Senator Johnstone interviewed. He made some nice remarks about Dad. He claimed he was unaware of any intended misappropriation, and no inspections were compromised."

"It's hard to know what to believe. It's a strange world up on Capitol Hill sometimes."

"Agent Tolliver called today to wish us a Happy New Year and to let me know that the FBI is releasing its formal report of the incident next week."

"Oh really? Are they admitting they lost you?" Roger smirked.

"No, officially, they will be praising me for working with them undercover and being instrumental in bringing down one of the most notorious drug rings, reaffirming that I am not now and never had been delusional. And admitting that I was in the witness protection program and under their watch the entire time. The report won't indicate anything about my being misplaced or shot." Rachel announced.

"I'm ready for this to be over." Roger admitted.

"Me too." Rachel stared at the twinkling lights on the Christmas tree, forcing away thoughts of holidays from the past. This Christmas had flown by in a blur of heartache punctuated by little steps they all made to try to regain a new normal. At least she'd not spent it alone. It was hard to reconcile her anger and grief, but slowly each day, she felt a little more progress in trying to understand and, more importantly, trying to forgive.

"It will all be over soon. Right after we go to D.C. next week to clean out your dad's office and apartment. Now that the investigation is wrapped up, we'll be able to move forward with our life and our wedding."

Rachel sat up and turned to Roger. "I'm ready to be married."

Roger kissed her, squeezing her against him, never wanting to let her go, still battling the nagging feeling she would slip through his fingers again.

He hadn't told her yet to keep from ruining the holidays, but there was one piece of unfinished business he had to clear up before he could move forward. He had to know the truth about the blonde. And if Chuck came through, as Roger believed he would, when they went to D.C., he would finally get that closure one way or another.

"I heard the breaking news tonight is supposed to be about some celebrity breakup, so maybe life will get back to normal soon." Roger chuckled.

"Perfect!" Rachel giggled, pulling her feet onto the sofa, a smooth warmth edging through her. "Thanks for going with me to D.C. to take care of Dad's things," she added.

"Of course. I'd never let you do that alone." He kissed her cheek and wrapped the throw around them as the last seconds of the year ticked away.

A sense of peace washed over Rachel while trying to avoid thinking about the task she had to undertake next week. It was a move she never imagined, and the end of her father's legacy, a heartbreaking end to an era. She was grateful she wouldn't have to face it on her own. But she did have to face it, and she would.

"I had no idea how difficult this was going to be." Rachel wiped away the last tear of the day as she stood in her dad's D.C. apartment, taping and labeling the final box with a marker. Most of the items they'd thrown away or donated, but there were a few mementos, some antique furniture, and photos she knew her mom would cherish.

"I'm sorry, sweetheart." Roger pulled her close. His phone dinged. Checking his text, he told her, "Chuck's in the lobby. He said the movers are here to get the boxes to ship home. I owe him for all his help. I'm going to go down and make sure everything is arranged and ask him to be my best man." Roger grinned proudly.

"He's a great friend," Rachel smiled, a light glimmer of amusement spiraling through her, knowing how happy Roger was.

"When you're ready, come down. Take your time and say your goodbyes. We'll be in the lobby waiting." Roger kissed her again before leaving her to make her peace.

"Okay, thanks, honey." She smiled as she watched Roger walk to the elevator.

Rachel picked up a photo of her grand-ma-maaa Rose, that she found stuffed in the back of her dad's credenza. She wiped the dust from the silver frame and ran her finger over her grandmother's face before she conversed with the past. "Grand-ma-maaa Rose. The Roses of Boooston. The matriarch of the Rose family, with our embedded wealth and command of politics. A true royal family, if such a thing existed in America. Our property and influence once spread across Boston, to the beaches of Martha's Vineyard, down to Washington D.C., and expanded across the nation to the coast of California, where what's left of the family is living quietly now," she told the photo.

She placed the picture in a small box of photos that she'd be taking home with her, adding a last sentiment as she spoke again to the ghost of a dead woman, "Goodbye, Grand-ma-maa Rose. In case you don't remember, I'm Rachel Rose, and I'm tough. I'm also a strong and independent woman and not a disappointment, and I didn't have to break the rules to succeed, because while accumulating all the money in the world may be your measure, it's not mine. It may be awhile until we meet again. You see, I've got a full life of happiness to live and a joyful family to build."

There was no sharp reply from beyond the grave from her grandmother scolding her or encouraging her to walk over the people she loved to achieve success, as measured by others. There was only a still, comforting silence as a flood of light shot through the windows when the January clouds broke. And with her phenomenal packing skills, Rachel taped the box tightly and scribbled across the box a single word: *family*. Then tucked it in her bag and headed to the elevator to find her love and Chuck.

As Rachel stepped out of the elevator, she was greeted by an upbeat baritone voice.

"Hello." Chuck scooped Rachel up in a bear hug and spun her around. "I had to come see the tough undercover FBI informant who took a bullet. At least that's the word on the street."

"You're hilarious," Rachel laughed as he set her down, then watched him shift to Roger. Pretending to bear hug him, too.

"We can't thank you enough, Chuck, for all you've done." Roger beamed.

Chuck grinned. "You know I'd do anything for you,

buddy. But there's one more thing we need to discuss. I looked and looked for this girl. I had to go to some seedy places, but I finally found her. She told me some things that were quite interesting, and I think you two should pay her a visit," Chuck told them.

Roger had divulged to Rachel on the flight to D.C. his need to find Bambi. Rachel was skeptical and had no desire to find the woman Roger slept with. She wanted to forget it all. Roger believed Rachel when she said it was in the past and she could forget it and move forward, but he couldn't.

"Please, Rachel, I need to know what happened that night. It's really important to me to hear the truth. If you don't want to go, you can wait at the hotel. I'll take Chuck with me."

Chuck winked at Rachel and told her, "You should go, darlin, trust ole Chucky. I know what I'm doing. I'm not here to destroy the two of you, but if you get married not knowing the truth, I guarantee it will come back to haunt you."

She knew Chuck was right. They should know the truth so they could talk about it and work through it and never let it rear its ugly head in the future.

"Okay, okay, I'll go. Both of you quit pestering me. I'll go." Rachel gave in.

"Okay, get out of here. I'll go direct the movers. And I'll see you kids soon at a wedding." Chuck's deep, soothing laugh echoed through the foyer.

"Yes, and as my best man," Roger added with an unrelenting smile.

"Wouldn't have it any other way, buddy." Chuck preened like a peacock before grabbing Roger's hand and pulling him in for a hug.

Rachel thought she witnessed tears in both his and Roger's eyes, but they both brushed them away quickly. After another bear hug from Chuck, Rachel and Roger exited The Watergate, climbed in the rental car and began the drive toward the Virginia line and hopefully to the end of a dark chapter.

Rachel lost herself in the beauty of the area. The magnificent trees, the time-warped architecture, the river trickling behind the road, darting in and out of view. It was no wonder so many people flocked to the region. The city held a rich historical power that sent an excitable buzz through her, one she hadn't recognized in a long time.

"I think I'm going to look for a job at the university when we get back home. I always loved history. It's my passion, and I should do it," she announced to Roger, not really seeking any approval, only wanting to share her thoughts.

"That's a great idea. You'll be a wonderful professor. I'd definitely enroll in your class." He glanced over and looked admiringly at her.

A grin burst wide across her face. They held hands until they arrived at the broken-down apartment complex tucked inside the Virginia line. Roger checked the address.

"Looks like this is it," he said with a tight breath. "Are you sure you're okay with this?"

Rachel thought for a moment. "Do I have a choice?" She smirked and squeezed his hand. "Actually, I want to know. I already believe you had sex with her, so I guess the worse she can do is confirm that. Then, can we not think about it or talk about it anymore?" she pleaded.

"Yes, absolutely. Do you understand why I need to know? I can't remember any of it and it's driving me crazy,"

Roger explained for the one-millionth time.

"I know. Let's go," she said, placing her hand on the door handle.

"Wait." Roger took her chin in his hand and kissed her deeply, his love transferring from his body to hers. She accepted the gift and returned it to him. They exited the car and walked to apartment #104.

Roger knocked on the door. A blonde, pony-tailed woman clad in a light pink sweatsuit answered. "Hello, I'm Roger, and this is Rachel."

"I thought that was probably you. Chuck told me I could expect you."

Rachel glanced at Roger, tightening her grip on his hand.

"Please come in. Evidently you have some questions for me," the blonde said, pulling the door wide open.

"Thank you, uhhh, Bambi," Roger said.

"It's really Cheryl. Please, I rather you call me Cheryl. Bambi's my working name, and I'm not working right now."

Rachel looked around the sparse apartment. The most elaborate decorations were those on the bed. The camera on the tripod was connected to the computer. Rachel's stomach sank as she thought of the last time she saw Bambi. The rest of the apartment was furnished with worn and obviously used furniture. Bambi led them to the kitchen area, where a tiny round table and two metal folding chairs sat. Roger offered one chair to Rachel. She accepted.

"I'm sorry about the space, but it's all I can afford. I've put most of my money into my computer and my equipment for my business." She pointed towards the bed. Rachel declined to look. Roger followed her finger with his eyes, taking in the setup.

"It's fine," Roger said apologetically. "We don't mean to intrude."

"Please have a seat." Cheryl pulled out a chair and pushed it closer to Rachel so Roger could sit. She sensed Rachel was not thrilled to be here. "So, I hear you two need some information about a job I did a long time ago." Cheryl lit a cigarette. "Do you mind?" she asked after the fact.

"It's your apartment," Roger answered for both of them. Rachel raised her shoulders in a half-shrug.

"Anyway," she started, but Rachel cut her short.

"Excuse me, Cheryl, but can I ask you a question?"

"Sure, shoot."

"Do you recognize my fiancé?" She put her hand on Roger's leg.

"Oh yeah, honey, I remember him. A looker like that. How could I forget? As I was about to explain, you see, this weird guy from out west found me on the Internet. Somehow, he tracked me down in the D.C. area. The next thing I know, the guy is at my door, throwing a lot of money in my direction. You see, I wasn't exactly doing the same kind of business as I am now. Back then, it was more customer-related." She looked at the couple and knew in the recesses of her brain that they didn't understand.

"Anyway, he gave me an airline ticket and told me that he wanted to hire me to break up his sister and her abusive boyfriend. He told me the guy beat the crap out of her all the time, but she wouldn't leave him unless she caught the dude in bed with some blonde. Me being the blonde, of course, you being the abuser." She pointed a well-manicured fingernail at Roger and took a long drag on her cigarette before continuing. "I guess

I thought I was performing some sort of civic duty, so I went with the guy to California. Man, California is sure beautiful and warm too, not like this freaking, winter-weather-from-hell place." Cheryl stared out the window, looking at the clouds rolling in, making it another gray day.

"Could you finish, please?" Roger urged.

"Sure, honey." She used the remark naturally. Rachel let it roll off her. "That's when I met you."

She really does remember him, Rachel thought.

"You were so sweet. I didn't get how you were an abusive asshole and all of that. Especially since you were drooling all over yourself waiting for your wife-to-be to come along. You didn't notice me in the least. That's when I slipped you a mickey. You began to feel a little nauseous. I helped you outside to where the guy was waiting in the car. You were pretty out of it. It was really difficult getting you in and out of the car and into the hotel. We told everyone you were drunk," she explained, as if that was a legitimate reason to be unconscious.

She tapped the ashes from her cigarette onto a metal tray with the Capitol etched on it. "The guy had everything set up. I undressed you." Rachel turned her head, not sure if she wanted to hear anymore. "I got undressed and, well, that whack-o guy videoed you and I supposedly having sex."

Rachel snapped her head back towards Cheryl. "Did you say, supposedly?"

"Yeah, that's right. You don't think he could have sex when he was knocked out on a mickey. I'm telling you, the guy was toast. He couldn't have gotten it up for all the tea in China. It was all some sort of AI, artificial intelligence, compilation. I don't pretend to understand, but it's what they call a deepfake, evidently."

Rachel burst out laughing. The statement by the hooker, or porn actor, or whatever she was, striking her as hilarious. The entire scenario of their sitting here in a seedy little apartment in the middle of the ghetto overtook her senses. Roger wasn't sure he saw the same humor in the situation, but his relief at finally knowing the truth and the fact that Rachel was in hysterics brought him to his knees with laughter as well.

Cheryl wasn't as amused, but she smiled, knowing they were both happy and that Roger wasn't an abusive jerk after all. When everyone had emitted their last giggle, Rachel and Roger stood up. "We've taken too much of your time. Thank you for letting us come here and telling us all of this. We really appreciate it." Roger shook her hand.

Cheryl extended her hand to Rachel, woman to woman, to make peace and convey an unsaid apology. Rachel accepted it. "You know, he was so excited to go pick out china patterns. It was the darndest thing I ever saw. He loves you intensely, you know."

"I do know. Thank you, Cheryl, and good luck." Rachel gave her a small hug, staring at the woman's face. Without makeup, there was a natural beauty buried under a slight sadness, one that matched the solitude of the life she had chosen to live.

Rachel and Roger practically sprinted to the car, both smiling uncontrollably. They kissed on the freeway and all the way back to the hotel. When they arrived, they went straight up to their room. Chuck was gone, but he had thoughtfully left a small gift. A bottle of champagne chilled and ready for a celebration.

Roger popped the cork, sending the bubbly spraying

through the air, then filled the glasses to the brim. "Here's to new beginnings."

"Here, here!" Rachel clanked her drink against her soon-to-be husband's glass. They took simultaneous sips of the champagne to seal the toast.

"And here's to love that lasts forever." Roger added. Their glasses met once again as they entwined their arms and drank one more sip to signal their new beginning. With the glasses aside, they intertwined their bodies and celebrated their new life together.

Epilogue

The summer wedding was a great distraction from all the media stories that would pop up from time to time along with the questions from the gossipy women at the country club, which took longer to die down. All swearing they knew Rachel wasn't dead or crazy. None of them having believed any of it at all, they professed.

Roger didn't get off the hook so easily, with a few women asking Rachel if she was sure she was doing the right thing. Rachel thanked them gracefully and promised that she knew exactly what she was doing.

When Rachel finally walked down the aisle, the memories of her father and her brother were tucked away in the appropriate place they needed to remain. She didn't mourn when her father wasn't there to escort her into her new life with her old love. Instead, she felt blessed that Roger's grandfather had shed a tear when she asked him to accompany her, and he did, in his wheelchair, with a smile of pride beaming across his face.

"I always believed you two would find your way back to each other," he told her the night before the wedding.

"Even though I was dead?" she teased.

"I never believed that either. It was too convenient. And you hate Vegas. Why would you have been flying there?"

Rachel laughed. "Thank you for believing in Roger when

nobody else did, even me," she told him, hugging his neck for a long time.

"I know that boy, and I knew he wouldn't do that to you. He's always loved you," he told her, squeezing her hands tightly when she released her embrace.

Roger's father even kissed Rachel on the head as he welcomed her into the family, relentlessly trying to convince her to change her registration to Republican. "I'll think about it," she finally told him.

The wedding reception was held at the Rose mansion, in the expansive and meticulously tended gardens. Mabel insisted on catering the entire event as a wedding present to the couple. It was spectacular.

"You may need to start a catering business, Mabel," Rachel told her at the end of the evening. Mabel laughed and bustled off into the kitchen.

The day after the festivities, Roger carried Rachel over the threshold of their new home. Stepping foot into her old condo was not an option for either of them. She sold it quickly once she'd recovered from the gunshot. His condo would be sold soon, wanting to free themselves of old memories and make new ones in the house they'd just purchased.

Rachel looked around, seeing a fresh and joyful start for their lives as she clung to Roger's neck before he set her down inside the door of their new home. Feeling comfortable and alive, she kissed him, and they danced without music by the fireplace.

The house didn't have fancy gadgets and electronics like the condo. There was no beachfront view, or high ceilings, and no famous architectural design, or Jacuzzi tub, nor did it have access to a pool and tennis courts. It didn't have the luxuries money could buy, but what it did have was the one thing that money couldn't buy, that others were desperately searching for, climbing over the little guy for, stabbing each other in the back for, black-mailing, cheating, and scheming for…it had something more valuable than luxury…it had love.

Honest and pure love.

Rachel started her associate professor job at the university and immersed herself in American history. Enjoying the wide-eyed freshmen that still believed the world was basically orderly and honest. It was refreshing to watch.

Roger split amicably from the family firm to venture out on his own for a while. He'd promised his father he'd be back. Launching his solo practice as his grandfather had done when he graduated from law school. Roger only wanted one boss for a while, and that was Rachel. His office wasn't the finest, but he had a head start with his connections and his attitude. Life was good, and he was eager to start over.

Linda was thrilled with the changes in her life. She stopped drinking and decided it was time to begin a new chapter as well. As a senator's wife for most of her adult life; she'd lost herself in the melee, but as time passed, she began to remember that she too had a right to be happy. She launched her own interior decorating business, taking classes at night to gain new knowledge to highlight her natural flair. Her first clients were her daughter and son-in-law for their new house. A house they were quickly making a home. It was small. Linda described it as a cozy bungalow, but it was perfect for a couple starting a marriage and planning a family.

"In a few years," she told them, "when you have a lot of kids, you'll buy a larger place and I'll decorate it for you."

Rachel was glad, she didn't have the patience or the taste to choose fabric samples or paint or furnishings. Linda tried her best to pull Rachel along and involve her in the decorating decisions for the bungalow. It was a fun experience for mother and daughter, and Rachel made sure her mother knew how much she appreciated her talent. Linda beamed with pride at her own accomplishments.

Rachel was proud of her mom for forging on, despite the path she'd been down. Choosing to reach for more. Maybe they weren't so different after all.

Roger and Rachel knew that they weren't always going to be happy with each other every minute of every day. They knew there were going to be days when they fought like cats and dogs and couldn't even agree on what to watch on television or where to eat. They knew that some days they wouldn't want to see each other's face at all. But in the end, the good days and the good times would outweigh the bad. They would also agree not to hurt each other, but to love each other and be friends, and never let the climb for success outshine the love they had for each other. That's what they promised each other in their wedding vows, and that's what they planned to do. Together…forever.

The End

About The Author
Leslie Asbill Prichard

Leslie is a Texas native but has resided in New Mexico for nearly thirty years. Leslie has four adult children and five adorable grandchildren. Leslie enjoys gardening, tennis, traveling, and writing, of course. Leslie hopes you enjoy reading her stories as much as she loves writing them.

Leslie is the author of adult fiction and children's picture storybooks. *Finding Elvis* was her debut adult fiction novel and is an entertaining time travel romance. Her children's books include *Brat the Pirate*, the first-place winner of the Southwest Writer's annual picture storybook award, and *But Where is God?*

For more information about Leslie's books and to receive information on future releases, sign up for her mailing list through her website at www.onenoseybroad.com. Follow her on Facebook and TikTok @onenoseybroad.com.

9 798988 948063